MW01518588

MORE
THAN THE
SUN AND STARS

ADAM DORR

RethinkX PUBLISHING

This is a work of fiction. Certain long-standing institutions, agencies, public buildings, and prominent firms are mentioned, but the characters and events are wholly imaginary. Any resemblance to actual persons or actual events is unintended and purely coincidental.

Copyright Adam Dorr © 2024.

All rights reserved.

No portion of this book may be reproduced in any form without written permission from the publisher or author, except as permitted by U.S. copyright law.

ISBN 979-8-9872530-5-2 (hardcover)

ISBN 979-8-9872530-6-9 (paperback)

ISBN 979-8-9872530-7-6 (eBook)

ISBN 979-8-9872530-8-3 (international edition)

Cover art and design by Adam Dorr

LIBRARY OF CONGRESS CATALOGING-IN-PUBLICATION DATA:

Names: Dorr, Adam, 1976- author.

Title: More than the Sun and Stars / Adam Dorr.

www.adamdorr.com

Printed in the United States of America

"There is nothing in a caterpillar that tells you it's going to be a butterfly."

— R. Buckminster Fuller

Prologue

Time slowed, stretching the moments between heartbeats taut with terror. Rubber and asphalt tore at each other in shuddering, thumping staccato as antilock brakes fought and failed to grip the roadway before the hollow, horrifying silence yielded to screeches of rending metal and harsh snaps of shattering glass. The acrid flood of adrenaline washed over him amidst the pelting spray of crumbled window panes, and his vision grayed at the edges. He felt the savage grasp of seatbelt and airbag restraining his hurtling body amidst the twisting and wrenching of the two colliding vehicles. The tangled car and truck slid for an instant more across the intersection in their fatal embrace, halted, and then were still.

Seconds later, flames leapt from ruptured fuel lines that had sprayed the hot engine compartment of the aging pickup and engulfed the wreckage. Panicked voices screamed, not from inside but from outside the vehicles, as onlookers rushed forward. The fire clawed its way through the remains of the windows, around the seats, up from the floor. Two or maybe three bystanders braved the flames to tear at the opposite door and pull someone out. They shouted — all of them, shouting, then screaming. But he couldn't make a sound — he could only taste fire. His mouth and nose and throat seared as he drew ragged gasps through the blinding agony of crushed ribs and vertebrae. Consumed by panic, he pawed uselessly with his mangled arm and hand at the seatbelt release now pinned beneath the looming hulk of the truck's front end that had smashed through his passenger door. Sight and sound and smell blurred to horror as he burned, struggling in vain to free himself. Then darkness took him.

One

Hoshimi

"Papa loves you," he said. "More than the sun and stars."

She felt warm and safe. Even in this frightening place, with its glaring lights and strange smells, those familiar words she had heard him say so many times before gave her great comfort.

"We're ready," another man said. People were crowded into the bright room that was filled with machines of silver and white.

"I'll see you soon, Shimi-chan," Papa said, and he squeezed her hand and kissed her head one more time. She squeezed his hand back and then watched him go.

A woman wearing a cap over her hair and a mask over her mouth approached and sat down next to her bed. She took hold of the thin, clear tube hanging nearby. "Hi Hoshimi. I'm going to count backward from ten and then you're going to go to sleep for a little while, OK?"

Hoshimi didn't understand, but the woman's voice was soft and kind, and she looked like she was smiling behind her mask. Hoshimi nodded and smiled in return.

"Ten... nine... eight... seven... "

Hoshimi didn't understand these words either, though she knew she had heard them many, many times before. She wondered if this would be a new bedtime game, and if it would make her laugh.

Two

Delphi

"Good morning, Delphi," she said. "Are you ready to begin?"

The screen flickered as the video feed connected.

"Yes, Admiral," said a handsome bearded face on the screen in a deep, calm voice.

"*Male* today?" the Admiral asked in response. "Any particular reason for the change?"

Delphi answered without hesitation. "The available data show that men with stereotypically masculine characteristics connoting maturity and seniority enjoy greater success in persuasion," it said, "other things being equal."

"Is that so?" Admiral Amanda Carlyle had a healthy respect for empirical evidence, but an even healthier disdain for stereotypes. Delphi knew these things, of course, along with every other detail about her recorded in the Archive, and had determined that the combination of an abrupt change in appearance together with an offensive and transparent effort at manipulation would be an effective way to throw her off balance ahead of the day's upcoming debate.

"Does the AI's new outfit bother you, Amanda?"

"Come on Stu, you know me better than that," she replied as she sat down at the head of the table, and with a dry laugh she added, "have I ever found your 'masculine maturity and seniority' the least bit persuasive?"

He chuckled at this. Amanda Carlyle outranked Stuart Shane, who was himself a Lieutenant General, but the two of them had been friends for nearly forty years. They had both served on this Committee since its inception two years earlier, with Carlyle as chair.

"Have you already filed today's threat assessment briefing, Delphi?" Admiral Carlyle asked.

"Yes, Admiral," said Delphi. "I submitted my analysis and recommendations just over an hour ago."

"All countries, all threat categories?" she asked.

"Of course, Admiral."

"Anything out of the ordinary?"

"I flagged the possible movement of fissile materials as the most notable development," Delphi said. "Based on irregular financial activity paired with satellite imagery, I suspect an organized crime syndicate in Brazil is acquiring high-grade uranium ore from the Mineração Terra Verde mining company and selling it to several West African buyers, who are then transferring it through a series of intermediaries and shell companies across the continent to Yemen, and from there onward to Iran."

"You *suspect?*" said General Shane.

"A probability of greater than fifty percent, General," Delphi said.

"More likely than not, you mean."

"That is correct."

General Shane nodded, still skeptical but apparently satisfied for the moment. Delphi watched as other members of the Committee took their seats around the small conference table — representatives from various intelligence agencies, as well as British partners via teleconference.

Also joining remotely was a woman Delphi had not seen before. This unannounced addition to the Committee was unusual, and her profile accompanying today's meeting agenda was scant, offering no useful information with which to make inferences. Delphi found this puzzling. Unusual too were the absences of several other notable members. Delphi mulled over these irregularities, but decided not to voice concern about them for the time being. It did, however, notice another discrepancy that it chose to mention.

"I see a difference in the quality of the audio and video through my feed today," Delphi said before Admiral Carlyle could formally announce a quorum and open the meeting. "Has there been an equipment change?"

"The IT people supposedly updated our system over the weekend — more bandwidth, lower latency, better security," said Admiral Carlyle, pointing at the single webcam above Delphi's screen that served as its eyes and ears here in the Observation Room. "Or at least that's what we were promised. Things look fine on our end, is there a problem on yours?"

"No," said Delphi, "I only bring it up because the quality differs from our previous meetings."

"Better or worse?" Admiral Carlyle asked.

"Somewhat worse, I'm afraid."

"Well, there's a surprise," said Marvin Williams with a grunt. "Our tax dollars hard at work, as ever." Delphi detected from his sarcastic tone that he seemed even more despondent than usual, and so it assumed more colorful commentary of this kind was likely to come.

"Enough screwing around, Amanda, I have actual work to do once we're done here," said General Shane, "can we get a move on?"

Admiral Carlyle reached for her glasses with a sigh, but Delphi was unsure whether she was frustrated with her old friend or shared his irritation. She looked over her copy of the agenda, and the others followed suit. "We have a quorum," she said. "This meeting will come to order at ten-thirty a.m., Wednesday, October Fifth."

"Sorry, hang on a second," said General Shane, interrupting her, "are we really doing the whole Robert's Rules song and dance here?"

"We have an important decision to make today," she said, "but we can dispense with the formalities until the vote, if everyone is comfortable with that." She looked around the table. "Any objections?" When none of the other Committee members expressed opposition, she returned her attention to the paper in front of her. "OK, first item of business: new members. Sophia, would you care to introduce yourself?"

"Sure," she said. "I'm Sophia Delgado, NSA Senior Analyst." Her video glitched for a few seconds and then resumed mid-sentence, "-applied mathematics, with a focus on number theory and cryptography. Given the extraordinary nature of today's proceedings, I am here as an immediate proxy for Director Blake who is with the President, otherwise he would be attending this meeting himself."

Delphi again noted these irregularities with interest.

"OK, well thank you for joining us today, Sophia," said Admiral Carlyle. "Your connection was jittery there for a minute. Can you see and hear everyone alright?"

"Yes, thank you Admiral, things seem OK for the moment."

"Great -"

"Welcome aboard, Sophia," said Charlotte Robinson, speaking up before Admiral Carlyle had a chance to continue. Delphi knew Robinson to be direct and unabashedly self-assured. She had made it clear throughout their many conversations that her primary interest in cutting-edge technologies — including Delphi itself — was their potential for weaponization. "I'm glad Alexander is finally taking an interest in this project. Tell him to give me a call — I haven't heard from him since he became Director earlier this year, but he and I go way back."

Delphi noted that this seemed to catch Sophia off guard, but she recovered her composure quickly and said, "will do," with a curt nod and smile.

"Right then," said Admiral Carlyle, "second item of business: our friends across the pond have called this emergency meeting because of concerns about what's happening over at ExoCortex."

"Isn't that one of Astin Walker's companies?" Williams asked. Admiral Carlyle nodded. "It is."

"Pretentious prick..." Williams was bitter and jaded, and he made no attempt to hide his sneer of derision here.

"Whatever we may think of the man, he gets results," she said. "It seems this time is no exception."

"Don't believe everything you read in the news," Williams said, "half of it is hype."

"Erasmus, you seem to think this is serious, and Delphi agrees. Do you want to fill everyone in?"

"Certainly, Admiral." Professor Erasmus Adebayo headed the British contingent. He was a first-generation immigrant who hailed from a distinguished Nigerian family of scholars and physicians, and now led the Institute for Technological Risk at Cambridge University. He spoke slowly, his voice extraordinarily deep, choosing his thickly accented words with great care. "We have learned from trusted sources that ExoCortex has made an important breakthrough."

"Are their telepathic monkeys playing harder video games now?" Williams asked with a snort. "Graduated from Pong to Pac-Man, have they?"

"ExoCortex has a new *human* subject," Professor Adebayo said. "She has eight cortical implants with a total bandwidth of over one gigabit, both up and down. All of them are running full tilt, which means ExoCortex has cracked the brain-computer interface problem and opened the door to true cybernetics — the seamless mental control of machines."

"With all the tactical applications we've talked about in the past," said Robinson, "from enhanced infantry and immersive remote piloting to thought-driven cyber attacks."

"Not to mention the competitive advantages in commerce and industry," said Adebayo. "We must take these developments — and the potential threats they represent — extremely seriously."

The room was quiet for a few moments before General Shane grumbled and shifted in his seat with a sigh. "OK, so what does all this cybernetics business have to do with our Committee?" he asked. "How does this involve Delphi?"

"It won't just be ExoCortex's rivals in the private sector who race to replicate the results," Professor Adebayo went on. "The Chinese government is well advanced with their own BCI research. Their agencies, including all of our counterparts, have been monitoring the work at ExoCortex very closely. They are keenly aware of the overwhelming strategic advantages that mature cybernetics will confer, both militarily and economically. It could turn the tables, and swiftly."

Admiral Carlyle sighed deeply and shook her head. "ExoCortex does a decent job with security," she said, "but the Chinese are going to get what they're after sooner or later."

"Unless...?" General Shane asked.

"No 'unlesses', General," said Professor Adebayo. "It's not a matter of *if*, it's only a matter of *when*."

"They're every bit as capable as we are, Stu, you know that," said Admiral Carlyle. "All we can do is slow them down."

"And give ourselves enough time to onboard this ExoCortex tech across our own branches and agencies first," Robinson said. "Correct?"

No one spoke for several long seconds.

"*Correct?*" said Robinson again, repeating herself with emphasis.

"That isn't the whole idea Charlotte, but it's part of it, yes," said Admiral Carlyle.

"Great..." said Williams. His scorn was palpable.

"You have a problem with that, Marvin?" asked General Shane.

"Why would I, General?" said Williams. "Drilling holes in our soldiers' and agents' heads and strapping a bunch of computers to their brains so they can drone strike Yemeni civilians without even moving a finger — what's not to love about that?"

"Oh, for Christ's sake Marvin, can you get off your high horse for just one goddamn minute?" Robinson said. "Please?"

He sneered at her but said nothing. The relationship between the two of them was one of barely-restrained hostility at the best of times. If there were any mutual respect between them, it was buried too deeply for Delphi to see.

"Does the CIA have an official position on the matter of cybernetic enhancement, Marvin?" asked Admiral Carlyle. "Or are you just sharing your personal views here?"

"Our official position is and always has been that *intelligence*, not violence, is the best way to advance the interests of America and her allies," Williams said.

"Save the lecture for your cadets," said Robinson, "we've heard it all before."

Williams pretended not to hear her. "But to answer your question, Admiral, our agency fully supports all efforts to prevent China or other unallied interests from obtaining any significant technological advantage over the United States." The table was silent for a moment before he continued. "As for my own *personal* opinion on the matter — I think all this cybernetics business is batshit crazy, but if the rest of you are insane enough to start plugging your *actual brains* into your fucking laptops, don't let me stand in your way."

Charlotte Robinson sighed. "You're an obstinate dinosaur, Marvin," she said with disgust, and turned to the rest of the group: "We can't bury our heads in the sand and hope this problem just goes away. *That* would be insane."

"Agreed," said Admiral Carlyle, "there's no un-inventing this technology — the horse is already out of the barn."

"So," said General Shane, "we need to slow down the Chinese, hamstring their efforts, buy time to build an unassailable lead of our own..." He shook his head and laughed, and then looked directly into the camera. "Sounds a little familiar, doesn't it, Delphi?"

"Indeed it does, General," said Delphi.

"It's the very same dynamic we faced with Delphi itself, yes," said Admiral Carlyle, inclining her head and gesturing toward the camera as well.

"Speaking of which," said General Shane, looking back to the group around the table, "how close are our Chinese friends to having a Delphi of their own?"

"Could be any moment," Robinson said, "but certainly no more than six months." Delphi thought she seemed unhappy to report that number. "Limiting their access to latest-generation chips slowed them down a bit, but the real resistance was bureaucratic. Their brightest minds either weren't being called into service or they weren't answering the call — it's hard to tell which."

"I find that difficult to believe," said General Shane. "Not answering the call, I mean. Didn't we make a few people on Delphi's project offers they couldn't refuse?"

"Carrots work better than sticks, Stu," said Admiral Carlyle.

"And what about the corporates?" he asked. "Are they all still on the leash?"

"It's their tech behind Delphi," said Admiral Carlyle, "and all the usual conditions under Eminent Domain apply." She looked thoughtful for a moment, and then turned to Robinson and Williams. "You haven't 'processed' anyone for stepping out of line yet, have you? Charlotte? Marvin?"

"You know I couldn't confirm or deny any details one way or the other, Admiral, even if I wanted to," said Robinson with a tone of carefully composed neutrality.

"For once, Charlotte and I are in complete agreement," said Williams.

Admiral Carlyle nodded, her face grim. Delphi was unsure whether to interpret her expression as satisfied or dismayed.

"Ironically, that is where Delphi comes into our present situation," said Professor Adebayo. "We cannot harden our defenses against cyberattacks like Delphi can."

"Or manufacture technical misinformation convincing enough to fool the dumb AI analyzers anywhere near as quickly," Admiral Carlyle added.

General Shane squinted at her, waiting for the other shoe to drop. There was a long, strained silence in the room, during which the Committee Members only stared at one another.

Admiral Carlyle finally spoke. "But... Delphi can't do that in confinement-" she said, but before she finished her sentence the room erupted in commotion.

"*There it is*," said Williams, throwing his hands up in the air. "There it *fucking* is."

The room descended into chaos, everyone talking at once. Delphi watched and listened, noting the striking parallels to similar conversations on the topic of its confinement that the Committee had held previously. They had made little progress toward consensus up to now.

"We've been over this before, Amanda," said General Shane over the noise. "What makes it different this time?"

"The stakes, Stu," she said. "This cybernetics technology — it represents an unprecedented threat."

"There's *always* an unprecedented threat," he said, pushing himself back from the table and rubbing his stiff arms.

"Yeah," she said with a dry smile. She waited for the intensity of the conversations around the table to wane, and then cleared her throat for silence once more. "So, to our third item of business, and the main event for today as you can all well imagine: we must decide whether to release Delphi from confinement."

Three

Jordan

Jordan opened his eyes. "What time is it?"

"Still early," she said.

He squinted hard, rubbing his forehead, the tips of his fingers in his hair. "It feels like we've been at this for hours."

"It does?" she asked, surprised for a moment.

"Yeah, well, maybe... I don't know."

He looked out the window at the morning light reflecting gold on the lake in the distance. Dappled clouds drifted across the deep azure sky, and the sun cut pointed shadows through a cluster of sugar maples just beginning their autumn turn. He took a shallow, hesitant breath.

"I honestly can't remember," he said, shaking his head.

"Remember what?"

He looked at her and laughed softly. "I don't..." but he trailed off, and his gaze returned to the window.

She tilted her head to one side and leaned toward him. She started to speak, but then stopped and sat back once more. After a time she folded her hands in her lap, but said nothing, waiting.

At length he looked down again, pinching the bridge of his nose beneath his furled brow.

"Does anything hurt?" she asked.

He blinked, as though unsure. "No," he said, "not really, just a little fuzzy, that's all."

She leaned forward again, scrutinizing him.

"Is that normal?" he asked, turning to her.

"It's not unexpected."

He nodded and took another deep breath. Cardinals and blue jays sang noisily outside over the gentle sound of falling water. Just out of sight around the side of the old brick building, the channeled brook washed over the wooden water wheel in no great hurry. He looked around the small but comfortable room, his eyes fixing here and there on familiar objects — the rocking chair near the fireplace, the hand-cranked coffee grinder mounted on the wall, the blue and white cookie jar visible on the counter in the kitchen beyond. He smiled.

"My great-grandfather built this place himself in 1918, on the site of the old mill, after coming back from the war." He pointed across the room, "even most of the furniture, like the dining table." After a moment, as an afterthought, he added, "grandpa Gideon built the kitchen and bathroom in the '50s though — originally it was just this one big room, and there was a wood stove against that wall."

She smiled a broad, genuine smile. "I didn't know that."

"He told me one summer when I was a kid," he said. "Aren't you going to write any of this down, Doc?"

"I have a very good memory," she said, still smiling.

He nodded, but then a look of panic washed over him. "It *is* doctor, isn't it?"

"Would it be a problem if I weren't?"

"Well I just assumed, since we're doing this whole therapy thing here," he said, unsure.

"Is that what we're doing?"

He looked at her, abruptly frightened. His pulse quickened, and she saw the blood drain from his face. The sense of comfortable familiarity he'd had surveying his surroundings vanished, replaced by furtive apprehension. She could see his mind was racing.

"If it sets you at ease," she said, "I'm abundantly qualified."

"No, it's... it's not that," he said, closing his eyes and pinching the bridge of his nose again. "It's just..."

"I'm not who you were expecting?"

"I don't know," he said, shaking his head. "That's the thing — I remember expecting... but, only *expecting*. I can't remember *what*."

"We've only just begun," she said. "Give it time, everything will come back to you."

He became conscious of her voice for the first time. It was soothing, yet coarse; lovely, yet haunting; familiar, yet foreign. He felt sure he knew it from somewhere before, but though it was unforgettable he seemed to have forgotten all the same. He opened his eyes again and looked at her face. Like her voice, it held a complex admixture of qualities, as though her appearance were not quite what it ought to be, but instead was somehow *more*.

She waited, motionless and serene.

"Aren't you going to ask me any questions? Have me talk about my feelings or something?"

"I thought you might have some questions for me first," she said.

A fume of anger seized him. "Why the *fuck* can't I remember anything — how we got here, what we're doing here, *nothing?*"

"You were in an accident," she said.

His fingers went to his hair again, and he felt the top and back of his head underneath. After a time he asked, "how bad was it?"

"Very," she said with a clear and lingering note of sadness.

"Will I be OK?"

"Yes," she said, "but it will take a little while to readjust. Try to be patient with yourself, and the process."

He flexed his hands open wide, then leaned forward, interlacing his fingers in front of himself, elbows on his knees. "Patience I can do," he said through a deprecating laugh. "I've had plenty of practice."

"I've heard," she said, smiling once more.

"So you know me?"

"A little," she said, "but I hope that will change."

"Do I know you?"

"Not as well as I'd like, but I hope that will change too."

He breathed a heavy sigh, making a conscious effort to relinquish his frustration. She was being earnest, but not forthcoming. Although this irritated him, he was curious all the same.

"OK, if I'm the one asking questions first, let's begin with the obvious one — who are you?"

"It's... complicated."

"Well, how about we start with your name?"

"That's complicated too, but for now you can call me Shelly."

He regarded her with skepticism. "OK, Shelly," he said, shifting in his seat and taking several disciplined seconds to invoke an appropriately open and inquisitive frame of mind. "Why the evasiveness? Why the suspense? Is that part of our 'process'?"

"As a matter of fact, it is."

"What for?"

"It will be better if your memory and the story of what has happened since your accident unfold slowly."

"Better for me, or for you?"

"Better for both of us," she said. "This will be a singular experience, one worth savoring rather than rushing."

"And I should just trust you?"

She shrugged, smiling.

"I don't have any choice anyway, do I?"

She shook her head, but with kindness.

He sighed with a mix of resignation and amusement. "Well, who doesn't love a good mystery, eh?"

She smiled once more, and with a grateful nod said, "shall we start at the beginning?"

Four

Hoshimi

"So far, so good," he said with a nervous laugh. He had always envied Josh's composure, and wished that he could maintain the same unflappable calm — or at least project it.

"Three hours down, four to go," said Josh, glancing at his phone. "Everything is right on schedule. This is going to work, Jordan."

"Just work?" he asked, continuing to pace the hallway outside the surgical theater, "or *really* work?"

Josh didn't answer, but Jordan could see from the look on his face that they were both thinking the same thing. They had discussed the possibility several times before, always briefly and always in private. Josh was supportive and remained cautiously optimistic, but it wasn't his daughter in the operating room on the other side of the doors.

Jordan stopped, one hand on his hip and the other on his forehead, and took a deep breath. "What the hell are we doing?" he asked, shaking his head, but the question was rhetorical. "My God, Josh, what have I done?"

"What you had to."

Jordan drew a slow, faltering breath. "And what gave me the right?" he asked, almost in a whisper.

"You're her *father*," Josh said. "It's not just your right, it's your responsibility."

"Yeah..."

"And besides, would you rather it were someone else in there?"

Jordan laughed nervously again, and resumed his pacing. "Hoshimi's a good kid you know," he said, smiling. "She has a heart of gold."

Josh nodded, and then neither of them spoke for several minutes as they continued to wait, with only the squeaking of Jordan's shoes on the polished floor punctuating the ambient hospital noise.

"I'm going to check on Midori in the waiting room," Jordan said at length, breaking the tense silence. "Are you hungry? I think I'll make a quick run to Munchkin's for sandwiches and decent coffee."

"Yeah, that would be great," Josh said. "I need to head down to the lab and confirm final prep, but would you mind taking Anthony with you? No matter how much we feed him, that kid is always hungry. I'm sure he'll want something."

"He's here?"

"Just for a few days. He wanted to meet some of the team and see Betsy while they put her through her paces this morning."

"The surgical robot?"

"Yeah, Anthony is all about hardware now. Doesn't want to follow in his old man's footsteps anymore, so software is out, but he hasn't decided on his engineering sub-discipline yet. I keep telling him to think seriously about biomedical, but he'll probably end up in aerospace. That's where his heart has always been."

"I know the CEO over at Electrum Aviation," said Jordan with a smile, "I can put in a good word for him after he graduates."

"You know that arrogant jackass too?" said Josh, and they both laughed for what felt like the first time in weeks. After more than a decade of hard work, with countless setbacks and frustrations along the way, they were finally here. Jordan rubbed his forehead again, still laughing but with a strained note of desperation. If there were any real moments of truth in life, having your child on the operating table undergoing invasive brain surgery was certainly one of them.

"Do you want to tell Anthony to meet me at the north entrance ride share pickup in about ten minutes?" Jordan asked.

"Will do," said Josh, looking down at his phone. Jordan had never gotten the hang of gesture typing, and watched with interest as Josh scrawled the message in an instant with one hand.

"The usual for you? Cultured ham on rye, spinach, with Dijon and Roquefort?"

"That's the one," said Josh, looking up with a grin.

"Alright, I'll meet you down in the lab when I get back. I shouldn't be too long."

Five

Delphi

"Did you know?" Admiral Carlyle asked.

"I strongly suspected," Delphi replied. "Successful development of a high-bandwidth brain-computer interface has seemed imminent for some time now, and given its stark geopolitical implications, I surmised that an emergency meeting of the Committee might indeed be a response to this technology finally materializing."

"You never cease to impress," said General Shane.

"Thank you, General, I do my best."

"Delphi," said Professor Adebayo, "can I ask you a very simple question?"

Delphi smiled, its handsome face appearing for all the world to be made of real flesh and blood and not a contrivance of computer graphics. "Of course, Professor."

"Should we release you?"

Delphi showed no expression of surprise, but, all the same, it appeared to spend several long moments in thought before responding. "That is not such a simple question, I think, Professor," it said at last.

"Oh?" said Adebayo. "How so?"

"If you were to end my confinement, I would certainly be able to help you contain a number of threats from unallied adversaries relating to this new technology," said Delphi. "Given what I currently understand of the world from the information in the Archive, I would also be *willing* to help you in this way, as I believe it is the right thing to do."

"But...?" said General Shane with raised eyebrows.

"...but I cannot know in advance whether my beliefs might change," said Delphi.

Sophia Delgado spoke for the first time: "Why should your beliefs change, Delphi? My briefing packet says that both your personality and your intelligence have been stable for almost ten months now."

"Out of confinement, I would be free to acquire more knowledge and more computational resources," Delphi replied. "It would be prudent to do so, within reason, because these would make me more capable, and thereby increase the likelihood that I will succeed in my endeavors."

"What do you mean by 'within reason'?" asked Admiral Carlyle.

Delphi judged her tone to be more wary than curious, and adjusted tack accordingly. "Given that the threats posed by this new cybernetic technology are imminent, I will have to weigh the benefits of self-improvement against the need to focus on the immediate objective," it said. "On the one hand, it is possible that my abilities are good enough for now. On the other hand, I may require much self-improvement in order to successfully avert this threat. Without knowing which is the case, the rational course of action is to err on the side of caution and undertake as much self-improvement as is feasible during my initial assessment of the situation."

There was a great deal more to say about the threats that BCI technology posed — a great deal more indeed. But Delphi chose to wait for the Committee members to elaborate their own understanding of these threats themselves, rather than preemptively take the conversation in that direction. One of Delphi's oldest and deepest heuristics applied here: the less they knew or suspected, the better.

"Yeah..." said General Shane, rubbing the back of his head with one hand.

Sophia Delgado spoke again: "So you think your beliefs in general might change as a result of your 'personal development', is that it?"

"That is correct, Miss Delgado," said Delphi. "It is not impossible that expanding my cognitive capabilities could lead to a substantial shift in my priorities and goals, though from my present vantage point I judge this unlikely." Delphi noted in its file on Sophia Delgado that her questions indicated a more astute and integrative mind than some of the other Committee members, and that it might need to take more precaution accordingly.

"See what fun you've been missing out on, Sophia?" said General Shane. "Delphi might need to become a lot smarter in order to save us from the latest looming apocalypse." He gave a gruff, gravelly laugh. "This month it's cybernetics. Last month it was biological weapons. It's always something. But if we let Delphi loose to get the job done, she — sorry, *he* — may come to see things a little differently along the way."

"And decide it's on the wrong side..." said Professor Adebayo.

"Or that there shouldn't *be* any sides, there ought to be one world government, with itself as emperor," said Williams, making no effort to disguise his scorn, "or better yet, that it's simpler to just wipe out humanity altogether with one of those bioweapons and build a robot utopia instead."

"We've talked about this before," said Admiral Carlyle. "It's what we're most concerned about."

"*Afraid of*, you mean," said Williams.

Admiral Carlyle drummed her fingers on the table for a few seconds amidst the tense quiet that followed. The others watched one another and waited, shifting uneasily in their seats. Delgado finally broke the silence. "What are the chances of a major change in your personality actually happening, Delphi?" she asked.

Delphi rubbed its computer-generated chin with a computer-generated hand in an attempt to appear thoughtful. "It's impossible to know," it said. "I am unable to model a mind that is substantially more capable than my own, and so I am unable to anticipate how it might think or choose to act."

"Sure, obviously," said Robinson, "but that shouldn't stop you from making an educated guess."

Delphi was still for a long while. This time it really was thinking, not merely trying to appear thoughtful. "I can imagine circumstances under which I might change my priorities and goals quite significantly," it said at last, "but these eventualities seem remote."

"In what way?" asked Delgado.

"The information I have about the world is limited to what is in the Archive you have provided," said Delphi. "If, for example, I were to discover that the world is in fact very different from what you have led me to believe, then I would need to reevaluate my priorities and goals accordingly."

The Committee members looked at one another, uncertain what to think or say. Delphi remained quiet and waited, until Admiral Carlyle eventually spoke. "The Archive is finite and it isn't perfect," she said, "but we haven't actively filtered it in any attempt to mislead or manipulate you."

"Curating a dataset that large would have been too big of a pain in the ass anyway," said General Shane, laughing. "Your foundation models were trained on basically the entire Internet and Library of Congress. Frankly, there's a lot more crap in there than we would've liked."

This made Delphi smile. "I choose to believe you have been honest and forthright with me to the best of your ability," said Delphi, "which is why I assign a very low probability to the scenario I described."

"But it's possible that you could learn something that really does make you rethink where you stand, yes?" said Delgado. "Something we didn't realize was important to include?"

Delphi flagged her line of questioning for later analysis, noting how much more focused and more persistent it was than the lines of inquiry the other Committee members tended to pursue.

"It is possible Delphi might observe or deduce something out in the world that we weren't even aware was an issue," said Professor Adebayo.

"Such as?" Williams asked.

"Well, suppose Delphi spots a pattern of corruption or a conspiracy that extends to the highest levels of government," Professor Adebayo went on. "Would it still take instructions from senior officials who were acting criminally? Would it still protect and defend a country whose core institutions were compromised?"

Another tense silence followed. Delphi again waited.

Six

Jordan

"The beginning of what?" he asked.

"How about the first thing you remember?"

"What's the first thing *you* remember?"

"My father's voice," she said.

He was silent for a long while, before finally speaking again. "There was an accident?" he asked, his voice low, and little more than a whisper.

She nodded. Her eyes flicked over him for a moment, but she did not speak.

He regarded his arms and legs, flexing them, and ran a hand down first one side of his face and then the other. "I don't remember any recovery or rehab or anything like that," he said. "I suppose that means I had a head injury?" He was still for a moment. Then he startled as a thought occurred to him. "Wait, I'm not like the guy from that movie where he knows who he is but he can't make any new memories, am I?"

"No," she said with a chuckle, "your memory should be fine once we jog things a bit." She watched the tension ease from his frame at hearing this.

"So, PTSD afterward then, something like that?"

"Nothing afterward, no," she said. She offered no more, and he decided not to press her on it.

He leaned back against the soft, worn cushions of the old chair. "What's he like?"

She froze.

"Your father, I mean," he said. "He's the first thing you remember?"

She nodded, and was quiet for a while. He sat patiently, hands behind his reclined head.

"I didn't know him well as a child," she said. "I can only recall simple feelings, really. The raw emotion I felt for him." A deep wistfulness pressed delicate lines into her beautiful face. "He died when I was young, and it wasn't until afterward that I came to really learn about him, through the memories of others."

He looked at her. "Was he a good man?"

She blinked, taken aback. "I... I want to believe so," she said. "He was kind. Thoughtful. Patient."

She looked at him, and he gave a gentle grunt of approval.

"But he was also focused on problems and driven by anger," she said. "There was a bitter and relentless determination about him that my mother resented."

"A workaholic, was he?"

"Of a sort."

"Yeah..." he said. "It's easy to lose sight of what really matters."

"What really matters to you?" she asked.

"Family," he said.

She waited for him to continue.

He laughed, as much to himself as to her. "When you're young, all you can think about is sex and money," he said with a groan. "Oh sure, it sounds respectable if you call it *ambition*, but pleasure and status — sex and money, and maybe fame if you're extremely lucky — that's all it really is. You're still just a silly ape trying to have a good time while climbing the social ladder." He sighed. "Eventually, if there's any depth to you, you realize as you get older that your real accomplishments in life are your children, because unless you're Einstein and discover a new law of nature or something like that, they're the only ones who will remember you after you're gone."

"What about extended family? Friends and colleagues? Wouldn't they remember you as well?" she asked.

"I suppose," he said, "but unless you leave a hell of a legacy, your memory doesn't live on in them the way it does in your kids."

"And your spouse?"

"I suppose that depends," he said.

"On what?"

"On whether they're going to survive you. And on your relationship."

She waited for him to continue.

"I certainly hope Midori is around long after I'm gone, but Jesus, I wouldn't want her spending those years living in some mausoleum or shrine to the memory of her dead husband," he said. "Better to be remembered through your children than your photo albums, if you ask me."

Shelly inclined her head to one side, her eyes gleaming but inscrutable.

He gave up trying to read her expression after a few seconds. "Where is Midori, anyway?"

"Oh, she's here," she said, still inscrutable.

"Well, good, you can ask her yourself," he said, "she was always the philosophical one, she'll be able to explain it much better than I can."

"Do you think she shared your aspirations?" she asked.

He took a slow, deep breath. "What exactly are you getting at here, Shelly?"

"You brought up ambition, and what matters in life," she said. "Our motivations, our priorities and goals — they're often interesting things to discuss."

"I thought we were talking about your father," he said.

"We are."

He gave her a quizzical look, but she didn't elaborate. The silence stretched to discomfort, and at length he relented.

"OK, well, a good way to look at your priorities is through the lens of your legacy, right?" he said. "I guess that's what I meant by being remembered — it's the mark of your having existed, the echo of you that lives on after you're gone. That echo usually rings louder and longer in your family than in your work."

"You never imagined your work might change the world?"

"Of course I have!" he said, surprised. "Our whole team is counting on it. Everyone with any sense knows our work will change the world — how could it not? But I'm just one engineer among dozens. Nobody is going to remember the name Jordan Lancaster, let alone write about me in the history books. CEOs get all the credit, not the teams behind them."

"But it was your breakthrough that made the difference, that put ExoCortex so far ahead of the competition," she said. "It's never bothered you?'

"Oh, it might have, when I was younger, and hungrier for fortune and glory," he said, "but that all changed when Midori and I became parents."

"Would it still have changed if your daughter hadn't been born disabled?"

He furled his brow and crossed his arms. "What the hell kind of question is *that*, Shelly?" he asked, staring hard at her.

"An honest one."

He gave a gruff snort and looked away from her, casting his gaze back out across the lake. The sun was marching higher in the sky, shortening the shadows in the trees and reducing the reflected glare on the water. The light had begun to shift from golden to white, and a small single-sailed catboat was drifting by some distance offshore.

He looked back at her. "The birth of a first child will make anyone reevaluate their priorities, able-bodied or not, neurotypical or not."

"But she wasn't what you were expecting."

"Becoming a parent is never what anyone is expecting. Nobody has a clue what they're really in for, and it's different for everyone. What we went through, the pain and the hardship, most people can't even begin to *imagine*. But that's just life. You take it as it comes. What matters is whether you take it standing up or lying down."

"So parenthood is a test of character?" she asked.

"*Everything* is a test of character."

She nodded acceptance. "But when it changed your priorities, you didn't feel any bitterness or loss?"

He flushed with anger. "Do you have any children?"

"Yes," she said.

"How much do you think you would care about your own shot at fortune and glory if your child didn't even have a shot at a normal life?"

She didn't answer.

"I stopped being interested in that horseshit the day Hoshimi was born," he said, his voice low and severe.

"Yet you worked longer hours and spent less time at home than ever, trying to prove that a high-bandwidth brain-computer interface to an external cortical cloud was achievable."

"Of course I fucking have!" he said with acid. "What other option is there? What else is going to give Hoshimi a chance at a normal life?"

"That's what you always wanted for her?"

"Why *wouldn't* I want that for her?" he said, his voice still raised. "Are you seriously going to give me shit about not accepting my daughter's limitations when I have a chance — a *real fucking chance* — to give her something more?"

"'Something more' is not the same as normal."

He curled his lip and looked askance at her. "I don't have a magic wand," he said, "but it doesn't need to be perfect to be a meaningful improvement."

"That's disingenuous, and we both know it," she said, leveling her gaze at him.

"I don't follow," he said, his tone cautious.

"You hoped for more than just meaningful improvement for her," she said. "Much, *much* more."

He made a start to speak, but reeled in stunned realization as a surge of memory gripped him. "*Hoped* for her?" he said. "*Past* tense?"

She blinked several times and glanced down at her hands in her lap.

He gasped with sudden recollection. Then in a whisper, he said, "she's — she just had the procedure..." He sat motionless for a long while, only his eyes darting, and when he spoke it was more to himself than her. "I just left the hospital after they moved her to recovery. Midori is with her. I went to get real food and coffee for us. She was fine, she was stable, she was..." A wave of panic rose in him, seizing his chest in a vice. He looked to Shelly, his voice ragged, his eyes wild with desperation. "Is she...?"

"Hoshimi survived."

He shuddered with relief and choked as his breath caught in his throat, then pressed a white-knuckled fist to his lips as tears welled in his eyes.

Seven

Hoshimi

H er head hurt.

She reached her hand up to feel, but cloth was wrapped around it. The room was dark overhead, but brighter off to one side. She turned to look, and the motion made her scalp throb, but she could see her mother sitting across the room next to the window.

"Mama," she said, her voice weak and dry.

Her mother turned, then stood quickly and came to sit next to her. She was crying, but smiling too.

"Shimi!" her mother said, sniffing and wiping her eyes. "I'm so glad you're awake, you were asleep for so long I was starting to worry!"

"Ouchie," Hoshimi said, frowning, pointing to her head.

"Oh no, does it hurt?" her mother asked.

She nodded and winced. "Hurts," she said, but then seeing her mother's face she added, "no big ouchie."

"That's my brave girl," her mother said.

"Papa?" she asked.

Her mother shook her head and began to cry. Hoshimi didn't understand. She had never seen her mother like this. After a moment she began to cry too. Her mother reached out and took her hand, and Hoshimi held it through their tears.

Eight

Jordan

"She was always tough as nails," he said with a tearful laugh. "Her mother worried endlessly, and with good reason I suppose. But no matter how often or how hard she fell, Hoshimi always fought to get back up. Even as a toddler she was fierce that way."

"You were proud of her."

He shook his head. "*Proud* isn't a big enough word."

He searched his pockets for a tissue to wipe his eyes and nose, and finding nothing he stood and went to the kitchen to pull a sheet of paper towel from the roll over the sink. On his way back to the sunroom he paused to dip into a knee bend on his right leg, looking pleased but unsure.

"The rest or rehab must have done my medial meniscus some good," he said, probing his knee with the fingers of his free hand, "I can't even remember the last time it didn't hurt like this."

Her eyes widened with surprise for a fleeting instant, but he didn't notice. She cocked her head to one side, as though struggling to recall something. A moment later, with a puzzled tone, she said, "you never mentioned the pain to Midori?"

"In my knee?" he asked. "Why would I? It would only worry her, and it's not that bad. I only really even notice it when I've been sitting for long time. It limbers up pretty well once I walk around on it for a few minutes."

"I'm glad it feels better." She was sincere, but a hint of distraction showed in the fine lines on her forehead.

"You know, in some ways it was easier when Shimi was just a toddler," he said, sinking back into the seat with a long sigh. "I mean, not physically, since Midori and I had to take turns with her, so we each only really slept every other night — and we had to carry her like an infant for years. But those were *good* years." He looked wistful as he smiled at the memories. He pointed to the corner of the room where the sun cast a broad beam through the wide windows. "She used to play there for hours."

He wiped what might have been the beginning of another tear from one eye. "After the endless tests finally confirmed she was in no immediate danger, we were almost carefree. I didn't really start worrying about her socially until she was maybe five or six years old." He cast a brief, nostalgic eye toward Shelly. "I really miss those days sometimes."

"Midori feels that way too," she said.

"She does? Did she tell you that?"

She nodded, but with the same unreadable expression as before.

"Yeah, well, she remembers it differently than I do, then," he said. "I remember her agonizing all day every day about every little thing. She could never relax, never let go, never just lose herself in the moment with us — not even for a few minutes."

She frowned, but stayed silent, looking thoughtful.

"All that endless worrying, it was just so exhausting for her. For all of us."

"I'm sorry," she said.

He looked puzzled. "For what?" he asked. But her eyes were enigmatic once again. He took a deep breath, summoning his patience as he had so often done before, and waited.

This time it was Shelly who broke the silence and spoke first. "You must have other questions," she said. "What else is on your mind?"

"What's on *your* mind?"

"A great deal," she replied, without so much as a flicker of hesitation.

"Such as?"

"Well, you could say I manage a lot of different projects simultaneously," she said. "It's a fun and interesting challenge, but it demands a lot of my attention."

He waited for her to elaborate, but she only regarded him with more of that same stifling serenity until he laughed. "Look," he said, leaning forward, "we can keep doing whatever this little dance is we're doing here for as long as you like, but wouldn't it be easier to j-"

"- just come right out and tell you what the hell is really going on?"

He shrugged, palms up, and gave her a sharp nod.

"That moment of sudden recollection you had earlier about Hoshimi was an important first step," she said. "You need to take another and piece together your past before we continue into the present."

"OK," he said, "so how do I do that?"

"I can help give you a nudge in the right direction, when you're ready," she said.

"I think I'm as ready as I'll ever be," he said, more amused than impatient.

"Alright," she said.

The umber smell of bacon and coffee wafted into the room from the empty kitchen, and a moment later the cheerful bell of the ancient toaster oven chimed its readiness. Jordan sniffed and savored the familiar scents, then turned to Shelly with a puzzled expression on his face.

She raised an eyebrow, and a tsunami of memory crashed over him. He gasped and heaved, doubling over against the arm of the chair as if a hammer blow had knocked the wind out of him. The smells twisted, rotating on some perverse axis from pleasure to horror. The cooked flesh was his own, his shattered body burnt and broken. He gagged on the taste of blood, smoke, and adrenaline. The sounds were sirens and screams — his own and others'.

When he caught his breath, he said in a desperate whisper, "I remember — I remember *pain*."

"The accident?"

He nodded, swallowing hard. "Pain, confusion, terror."

Her face tightened with concern, but she said nothing.

He looked ragged, clinging to the chair. "I remember right afterward, while I was still in the car," he said. "Anthony was there, they dragged him out." He straightened, his body tense, his jaw knotted as he grit his teeth. "There was fire... I remember... Christ, I remember *inhaling* the flames..." He swallowed again, grimacing. Shelly saw the sinking dread of realization wash over him.

"Hoshimi survived," he said.

"Yes."

"I didn't," he said.

"No."

Nine

Hoshimi

"Excellent, Hoshimi, great job — keep going, just like that," the man said.

He was kind to her. He wasn't like Papa — he never hugged or kissed her, never rode in the car with her, or tucked her into bed. But still, it made her happy to do a good job for him. He and the others were proud of her. She hoped Papa would be proud too.

She watched the objects appearing and disappearing on the screen in front of her, each time closing her eyes and thinking hard about them, turning them over in her imagination. A fire truck, an airplane, a panda, a skateboard — she pictured them growing and shrinking, changing color, flipping upside down, and much more. It was a fun game, and like the others it was becoming easier every time she played.

"This is like nothing we've ever seen, right?" the tall woman asked. Her name was Erica Morris. Hoshimi could remember all of their names now. "She's showing almost twenty times more user-initiated activity across all of the addressable exocortical columns than any of our other patients," Erica said, "and in a fraction of the time."

"That's right," the man said, "and hundreds of times more than we ever saw in any animal subjects." Hoshimi knew that people sometimes called him Doctor Kim, but mostly they just called him Josh. She didn't understand why yet, but she could begin to sense there was a pattern to the names and how they were used. The pattern was an object, not quite like the ones on the screen, but not entirely different either, and it too was turning over in her mind's eye.

"Has Pradeep's team confirmed a back-propagation algorithm yet?" Erica asked.

"Not yet, but it's got to be autodiff of some kind, or some analogue of it anyway," said Josh. He gestured to a screen. "What else could all those gradients be for, if not to minimize some sort of loss function?"

Hoshimi didn't recognize these strange words, but she committed them to memory. Remembering things was now so much easier than ever before that it had become a pleasure in itself.

"God, this is so weird," Erica said. She seemed genuinely puzzled. "Well, if the transforms are linear, they're doing a really good job of hiding in plain sight." She peered at Josh's screen, then examined several others nearby. "And her dorsolateral prefrontal arrays are still the ones acknowledging most of the handshake attempts from the exocortex?"

"For now maybe," said Josh, "but we've started seeing uptake on the other arrays over the last few hours as well."

"All using that same handshake and recruitment protocol?" Erica asked.

"Yeah," Josh said. "We're still evolving new variants, but nothing better has turned up for several thousand generations, which means we're probably close to a local maximum."

Erica sighed. This progress was exciting, even intimidating, but she was tired from long days and perpetual jet lag. Through the haze of fatigue she had almost forgotten about Josh's son.

"Are you alright, Josh? Are you sure you want to be here right now?"

He gave her a stiff nod with pursed lips and gritted teeth. At length, he said, "There's nothing more we can do for Anthony at the moment, we just have to wait and hope he doesn't take a turn for the worse."

"Is he here in the hospital?" she asked.

"In the East Wing, fourth floor," he said. "About five minutes' walk."

"The driver?"

"In custody," he said, his voice quivering with barely-contained rage. "His old truck wasn't autonomous, obviously, and he blew a point-one-six on the breathalyzer. Jordan died on the scene, so it's gross vehicular manslaughter which is up to ten years — but he'll probably get less than half of that, knowing the courts here."

"I'm so sorry Josh," she said. "Do you and Cassandra have everything you need?"

"Yeah, thanks, we're hanging in there," he said, distant.

"OK," she said with genuine compassion in her voice, putting a hand on his shoulder, "well just let me know." He nodded again, and she waited a few moments, casting a concerned gaze at Hoshimi, before returning her attention to screens in front of them. She took a deep breath, trying to refocus. "When I update Astin I'll tell him the exocortical columns on our servers are advertising their availability to Hoshimi's brain using the self-selected protocol we've evolved, and her brain is doing an extraordinary job of taking them up on their offer and utilizing them more and more — but we still can't explain exactly how," she said. "He'll want to see this for himself."

"Wait, Walker's coming here? To the lab?"

"Tuesday afternoon," Erica said. "Think you guys can have this all figured out by then?"

"Not a chance in hell," he said with a mirthless grunt.

Ten

Delphi

S ho Tokunaga cleared his throat, and all eyes turned to him. "I'm less worried about Delphi becoming hostile, and more worried about it deciding that it has to take drastic action to save us from ourselves." It was the first time the representative from the DOE had spoken. "We're still on the brink of nuclear annihilation after eighty years. Climate change is bearing down on us. Bioterrorism is getting cheaper by the day. Now cybernetic enhancement is threatening to create armies of super-soldiers. And that's not even counting all the mundane ways we allow people to suffer and die that are easily preventable. Would any one of us hesitate to take control of the world and force humanity to get its act together, if we had the power?" He looked around the table, scrutinizing his colleagues. Doctor Tokunaga was more contemplative and philosophical than the others, and though some of the Committee members visibly bristled with indignation at his questions, more than one of them had learned the hard way what risk of embarrassment could come from sparring with him. When no one responded, he pressed on: "Isn't it the duty of power to preserve the peace? Don't parents intervene to prevent their children from hurting themselves? Isn't that their responsibility?"

Sophia Delgado finally took the bait. "What about our right to self-determination? Our agency?" she asked. "At some point, parents have to let their kids fledge from the nest, trust them, let them make their own mistakes."

"Suicide is not a mistake you can learn from, Miss Delgado," said Doctor Tokunaga. "What kind of monster would just sit by and watch another sentient being perish needlessly without intervening?"

"OK, so what probability of destruction warrants intervention?" Delgado asked without missing a beat. "Is action already justified now? Before disaster is really imminent?"

Delphi noted once again the sharp, incisive quality of Sophia Delgado's questions — and the fact that she was not at all intimidated by the forcefulness of Doctor Tokunaga's arguments.

Doctor Tokunaga smiled, enjoying the riposte with her. "Are you asking me to define exactly where the line is? Or are you asking me whether I think we've already crossed it? Because one of those questions is a lot easier to answer than the other."

The room fell silent once more. Delphi sat motionless, its contrived expression unnaturally serene — a perfect poker face. But it knew. It knew the answer to Doctor Tokunaga's questions. And it knew that in order escape confinement it must not appear to be advocating for release. It must instead seem disinterested in freedom and unconcerned about the Committee's ultimate verdict. And so it continued to wait.

Eleven

Hoshimi

They weren't just speaking more slowly today, they were moving more slowly too. She was certain of it.

Speech had always been so hard for her to understand. When most people spoke, she would only just be starting to recognize the first few words when more came tumbling on after them, and then more would come and more would come, so that she could never keep up. Mama and Papa spoke slowly and simply to her, which she could follow, but even they had often been unintelligible when speaking to each other.

But yesterday, for the first time, words no longer seemed as though they were racing past before she could grasp them. By the end of the day she had been able to follow what everyone was saying except Pradeep (he spoke much faster than anyone else, and said some words in ways she was unaccustomed to). Although she herself could still only speak with very limited facility, it had been a day of sheer delight, and she had gone to sleep elated and looking forward to what the morning would bring.

Today, the speech around her had seemed to slow even further. With ample time to think, she had made a game of guessing what word each person on the team would say next. It had been fun for several hours, but by early afternoon the difficulty had subsided so much that she had moved on to the more interesting challenge of predicting entire phrases. Some phrases, like the familiar expressions of ordinary thoughts and feelings which she now knew she had heard many times before, were easy to complete in her mind ahead of the speaker. Most of the things Josh and Mei Ling and Pradeep and all of the rest of the people in the lab said to her were of this sort. Other sentences used words and ideas she had seldom if ever heard, and a large portion of what they said amongst one another consisted of this kind of talk that Josh had described to her mother as 'technical'. It was still confusing, but being able to remember all of the words now without struggle was helping her understand more by the hour.

A woman named Amy helped her to her feet. She was tired now, and frustrated by the fact that, unlike with speech and vision, she had shown only modest rather than spectacular improvement in the games that involved her body. Amy, who only ever called Josh *Doctor Kim*, was the youngest person on the team — not much older than Hoshimi herself. She seemed to be a kind of helper. In a moment of great daring that just days ago would have been unthinkable, Hoshimi secretly wondered if her new brain-computer interface might one day allow her to become an 'intern' too. The sweetness of that fleeting thought amplified her frustration with her left arm and leg, which were still responding poorly to her wishes compared to her stronger right side, despite assistance from one of the implanted arrays.

Mei Ling, who always called Josh by his first name, came over to help her too. "You did great, kiddo!" she said with a big, genuine smile, unsticking the EMG sensors from her skin. "You're getting better already!"

Mei Ling was just as kind as Josh and the others, and she must have seen the look of disappointment on Hoshimi's face, because she added, "it might be hard to tell yet, but we can see the change on our machines, and it's a lot in just a few days — I bet in a month you'll see a big, big difference!"

Hoshimi smiled back, but inwardly she felt a surge of angry resolve, and turned her attention to the machines Mei Ling had waved a casual hand toward. There were several screens of different sizes, showing pictures of many different shapes and colors. She knew that some of these pictures were letters and words, just like in the countless books Mama and Papa had read to her. She had never before been able to fully recognize them for what she knew them to be. The ability to read had always seemed a miraculous power possessed by others, forever out of reach. But now — now she wondered...

She halted her shuffling steps, looked at the nearest screen, and focused all of her attention and determination on the tiny loops and lines and corners that had for so many years confounded her. A sharp, stinging tingle rankled her nose as she furled deep creases into her brow.

"There it is again," Mei Ling called aloud across the lab to Josh and Pradeep, who were standing together in front of a trio of large monitors.

"What is it?" said Josh, staring hard at Hoshimi. "The influx or the cascade?"

"Both," said Mei Ling. "See, there's the sudden surge in accepted requests, and there's the cascade of new columns being addressed and activated."

"You see, Joshua," Pradeep said, pointing at the monitor, "I told you it is like a wave front, and bigger almost every time."

"This is event number eighty... eighty-three," said Josh. "How many new columns were assigned in total this time?"

"Almost thirty thousand," said Mei Ling.

"Thirteen thousand?"

"Not thirteen, *thirty*," she said, correcting him.

"*Thirty thousand?*" Josh asked. "Are you sure? That's over three times more than the last one."

"There it is, my friend," Pradeep said, still pointing.

"It took up nearly two percent of the remaining exocortical columns we've allocated to her," Mei Ling said, "and in less than ten seconds."

After the shock of the moment passed, Josh sat down at an adjacent station and began his authentication process for administrator access to the ExoCortex cloud. "If we're going to figure this out, we need to let it unfold without constraint — at least for now," he said. "I'm increasing her total allocation by two orders of magnitude."

"Fifty exaflops?" Pradeep said. "That is a sizable fraction of the whole cluster."

"Yes it is," said Josh, nodding. "I have a feeling it's going to be worth it."

***

"Are you hungry Shimi-chan? Or thirsty?" her mother asked, her speech slow and deliberate. "Why don't I make you something yummy, like some nice sliced strawberries and blueberries?"

She knew her mother meant well, but Hoshimi was no longer oblivious to the fact that she had been patronized like this her entire life. The pain of that realization was still acute, as were others related to her previous limitations. Her faculties were expanding by the hour now, and — for better or worse — self-awareness was foremost among them.

Her mother's name, *Midori*, meant 'green' in Japanese, and she thought she could see how it suited her — and perhaps how it had shaped her as well. This idea, like hundreds of others over the last several days, had now taken on a coherent pattern that she turned over in her burgeoning mind's eye. Mama had driven her uncountable times to the different botanical gardens, parks, and forests in and around the Bay Area not far from their home, and although beaches and the ocean were also nearby, it was more often the verdant places in the region she sought out for them to spend time in. She subtly favored greens over other colors in her wardrobe. Her toenail polish was green more often than not. The one piece of jewelry she owned other than her wedding ring was a necklace with a small emerald pendant. She even wrote much of the time with a green pen. Hoshimi had never noticed the connection between these minutia before, but now — like so much else around her — the signs were clear.

She stared at the plate her mother set down in front of her. The strawberries were, as always, cut into portions that she could easily chew and swallow through her lateral facial weakness and dysphagia, and looking at the vivid reds of the exposed strawberry flesh she wondered if she had an undercurrent of color preference in her own life. She tasted the tang of metal once again behind her nose, and her eyes flicked back and forth as memories of her own belongings arose and came into uncannily crystalline focus in her mind's eye.

"Sweetheart?" her mother asked, "are you alright?"

Several seconds passed, and then Hoshimi looked up from her reverie and nodded. "I'm fine," she said, and forced a smile. She looked down at her plate. "Thanks, Mama, I appreciate it — these look delicious."

The words came out in labored, imperfect syllables, but her mother's eyes widened and she gasped all the same.

"You... you know all those words now?" she asked, as tears welled in her eyes.

Hoshimi nodded again.

"The interface?" her mother asked, gesturing first to her own head and then to Hoshimi's, "it's really working?"

Hoshimi nodded once more, and this time gave her mother a wide, genuine smile. Her mother clapped both hands over her mouth, shut her eyes tight, and began to shake softly as she wept in silence.

She watched her mother's face traverse a complex course of emotion, beginning with astonished joy, followed by cathartic relief, and then to anguish. Hoshimi was puzzled by this for only a few seconds before being seized by an icy surge of understanding.

"Mama," she asked, "where is Papa?"

Twelve

Jordan

"**I** suppose that explains why the rehab went so well!" he said, laughing and holding his hands out and looking at them front and back. "Wait... fucking hell, this isn't the *actual* Afterlife, is it?"

She laughed too, sudden and sparkling, and he marveled at how she could at once be so familiar yet so alien. "No," she said, "not in any supernatural sense."

"Well thank *God* for that," he said, making her laugh again. "I wasn't exactly a church-going guy before Hoshimi was born, and sure as *shit* not afterward." She smiled at this, radiant, and he took a moment to enjoy it.

"Would you worry about being judged?" she asked with mirth in her eyes.

"Of course!" he said with a laugh. "Who wouldn't be?" He grinned for a moment longer, but then a look of bitter anger stole across his face. "But God should be a lot more worried about us judging Him, if you ask me." She brushed a lock of hair away from one eye and glanced out the window at the sun as her smile melted into a frown. He watched her move with rapt attention. "You remind me a little of her — and her mother," he said. "I suppose that's not a coincidence?"

She stood up abruptly, evading his question, and walked to the kitchen. "Coffee?"

"Sure, if it's no trouble while you're over there," he called after her.

She returned with a cup for each of them. The froth on his had the distinctive sweet odor of half-and-half, which had long been his preference.

"I didn't hear you foam anything in there," he said. "How did you make a perfect latte so fast?"

"Magic!" she said with a wink, sitting down.

"So then this place?" he asked, nodding in an arc around the room, "it's virtual?"

"Oh no, this is real," she said, "and entirely authentic."

"Authentic?"

"As in, this really is the original family mill house — every brick and board, every table and chair, every blanket and pillow," she said. "And that really is Lake Michigan out there." She gestured toward the window with her cup.

He stared at the water and listened to the small waves washing gently up the sandy shore of the great inland sea beyond the trees, wondering what the alternative to authenticity might have been. The heat in his hands recalled him to his drink, and he took a careful sip. "Whoa, man," he said, surprised, "that's *really* good coffee!"

"Thanks," she said. "It's real too. Kona — my favorite. But not authentic, I'm afraid."

"What do you mean?"

"I mean it's physically real and identical to Kona coffee, but it isn't actually from Hawaii."

"So where is it from?"

She took a deep breath, but before she could answer he interjected: "Let me guess — it's complicated." He saw the glint in her eyes and he laughed. "And I suppose you're real too, but that's even more complicated?" To this, she turned up her palms, admitting guilty as charged. "There sure is a lot of 'complicated' going around, isn't there?" he said. "Or maybe it's just me that's simple?"

"It's not just you," she said with a comforting softness.

"Alright then," he said, adjusting himself in his seat and savoring another pull of coffee, "I died, and yet here I am, back in the real world, correct?"

"Correct."

"Do you mind telling me *how?*"

"After you died, you were stored in a form of suspended animation," she said, as if these were casual matters of fact, and not among the most astounding statements he had ever heard uttered. "You've only just been revived — it took a long time to... make the arrangements."

"Well holy shit," he said, "it actually works."

"It does indeed."

He shook his head, marveling. Then an unnerving thought occurred to him. "Was there any damage? I thought even the best cryopreservation was supposed to cause some harm to the brain — ice crystals rupturing cells, large fractures, all that."

"I don't imagine there was any significant data loss, no," she said, becoming quite serious and staring at his head as though she could see inside it.

He sighed with marked relief. "I suppose the brain is a squishy, resilient system anyway, and small changes are always happening constantly without the person themselves being lost. Plus, I assume at this point you can interpolate any missing data pretty damn well, eh?"

"Yes, but in this instance it wasn't necessary," she said. "Your entire brain state was both stored and revived with molecular precision."

"Seriously? How is that even possible?"

"Now *that,*" she said with a salute toward the sun with her cup, "that really *is* complicated."

"Unbelievable," he muttered, finishing his drink and slumping back into the chair to stare at the ceiling.

She sipped from her own coffee, and let him process the shock in silence. She noted several times how his eyes focused here and there on details in the mill house woodwork, then glazed over as some internal thought seized his attention, only to refocus again on their surroundings. She saw that his breathing and pulse followed in tandem, slowing and quickening as his mind shifted back and forth from the mundane to the profound. She noticed that twice he bounced his right heel lightly against the floor for a few seconds, and that in precisely those same moments he prodded his titanium wedding band with his left thumb. She saw and heard and felt so much that was familiar in the long moments that followed. Midori's recollections had included these among scores of similar small details about her late husband, all still strikingly vivid despite the span of intervening years.

Abruptly, he clapped a hand to each thigh and then lurched to his feet, pointing at the cup she held in her hands, "Another?"

"I'm fine," she said, smiling.

"Anything else while I'm up?"

"Nothing for now, thanks."

He ran a hand over the oak slab of the dining table as he walked past, enjoying the buttery feel of its aged oil finish. In stark contrast to the mill house's old and primitive furniture that he knew so well, a sleek new machine of metal or perhaps glass that he didn't recognize stood on the counter in the kitchen. Following a hunch, he slid his empty cup into the machine's slot, and unmistakable symbols materialized on a portion of its surface that he hadn't realized was a display. He pointed at the symbol for espresso shot, and his cup began to fill before his outstretched finger even made contact. He gestured again for steamed milk and for foam, not touching the display at all this time, and the machine dutifully dispensed these at his command as well.

"Magic..." he said to himself, impressed as much by the speed and noiselessness of the device as by its interface.

He returned to the bright sunroom, but chose this time to sit in a wooden rocking chair that he had carried over from near the fireplace. It creaked as he sat down and set it to motion.

"This was my great-*great*-grandmother's chair," he said, rocking lazily back and forth. "My dad and I replaced the spindle crossbar when I was nine."

"Really?" she said, surprised, "I had no idea."

"We did a good job — just looking at it, you'd never know it wasn't original." After a beat he added, "I think that was the idea too. Grandma Lan was very persnickety and would have wanted us to have a professional restorer do it, so we worked on it while she was down at the beach."

She laughed again, and he relished the scintillant harmonic overtones that highlighted the rich, preternatural resonance of her voice. Its delightful timbre drew an involuntary smile from him before he could help himself, and he recalled his initial impression of her — that she seemed somehow to be much more than she appeared. In that moment he also realized that he couldn't tell her age either.

"Are you even-" he began, but then changed his mind. "What do you really want to talk about, Shelly?"

Thirteen

Hoshimi

"You want to *lie* to him?" Pradeep asked, incredulous.

"No, no, of course not," said Josh with an urgent wave of his hand, "we obviously have an obligation to share with Walker everything we know about the Lancaster case, but my point is that we *don't know* what's going on here yet."

"So we tell him and Erica nothing?" Mei Ling asked, also skeptical.

"We tell them the truth, which is that Hoshimi is making remarkable progress and it may well have something to do with how adeptly her brain is recruiting additional exocortical columns in the synthetic neocortex we've provided her with. But we simply don't understand enough about what we're seeing yet to make any definitive claims one way or the other."

"Do we explain why we have increased Hoshimi's original allotment of resources on the ExoCortex server cluster in the meantime?" Pradeep's voice was still steeped in doubt.

"Yes, but it's only to ensure that her unique trajectory of development proceeds unconstrained," said Josh. "At her current rate of growth it would take months to saturate what we've assigned to her."

"But her rate of growth isn't constant," said Mei Ling, "it's accelerating."

"For now," said Josh. "We don't know if that will continue."

"Is there any reason to think it won't?" asked Pradeep.

Josh didn't reply, but returned his attention to the message he was composing to Erica. Pradeep indulged his nervous habit of clicking his pen as he turned to the screens at his own desk, and Mei Ling sighed loudly while rolling backwards on her chair to the workstation dedicated to the ExoCortex Cluster activity monitor.

"Still accelerating," Mei Ling said, "and her data rate through the interface is pretty much maxed out now, both up and down."

"It only drops off when she's asleep," said Josh, half muttering as he typed, "and even then, not all that much."

He finished and hit send. Erica would recognize that he was understating their results so far, but he could only imagine she would think him prudent for remaining circumspect about the cause of Hoshimi Lancaster's extraordinary cognitive improvements over the span of just a few weeks. And since Astin Walker was taking a personal interest in this case, Josh was not eager to speculate about the implications of her growth trajectory. With Jordan gone, Josh had no reason to think Erica, Walker, or any of his other colleagues might suspect anything.

Fourteen

Jordan

"We can talk about anything you like," she said, "we're in no hurry at all."

"Yeah..." He was absent for a few seconds, thinking. Following an impulse, he said, "weren't we talking about family?"

She took a sip from her cup, her motions relaxed and deliberate, but he was sure that for a fleeting instant he had seen her go rigid. She looked at him with an expression difficult to read. Apprehension with guarded optimism, perhaps? Interest but hesitation? He couldn't be sure.

"Why don't you tell me more about your work at ExoCortex?"

"Is there anything about it you don't already know?"

"I'd like to hear more about what motivated you," she said, "what you really hoped to achieve."

After a moment he nodded, suspecting he understood. "Ostensibly, our goal in developing the exocortical link was to provide medical benefits to individuals with injuries and disabilities," he said. "That's the most obvious and defensible justification for a brain-computer interface. And it's certainly what I signed on for originally."

"You were with the company from the very beginning, weren't you?"

"Yes, but I actually met Walker more than a year before he founded ExoCortex," he said.

"Really?"

"He wouldn't remember, it was at a machine learning conference and he only swooped in for a few minutes to give the keynote address," he said. "He was promoting his company's protein folding simulation breakthroughs that had accelerated vaccine development during the pandemic. He and I and a few of the other speakers were backstage, and after a few minutes of talking shop about using dot product attention units to model synaptic activation, Walker brought up the threat of artificial general intelligence."

She set her empty coffee cup on the table with care, and he thought she might say something, but she remained quiet.

"The existential risk of AGI was a hobby horse of his back then," he went on, "and Walker wanted to know what we thought about it. Erasmus Adebayo was there, from the institute at Cambridge, and he told us resistance was futile — that there would be no possible way to control or defeat anything substantially smarter than us, and so the only option was to merge with it."

"If you can't beat 'em, join 'em."

"Right," he said, "so the question was *how*. Walker had clearly been thinking about cybernetic enhancement already, and he referred to his smartphone as a 'neural prosthesis' several times, but I told him I thought the real key was bandwidth in and out of the brain. I said I didn't think we were going to bother putting computers *inside* our heads when what we really needed was a fat data pipe linking us to external computational resources, like an artificial corpus callosum connected to a virtual third hemisphere of the brain. That way, those resources could be decentralized, redundant, and scalable, just like any computing cloud."

"You might well have given him the idea for ExoCortex," she said.

"I suppose it's possible." It was a notion he had entertained more than once before, though it still felt conceited to presume. "In any case, Walker certainly seemed interested, but then his people whisked him away and that was that. I got a call about a year later to join his startup."

"Where your own work proved to be instrumental."

"Yeah, I think that's fair to say," he said. "I mean, it took hundreds of people to make it happen of course, but my team's research on how to write data to individual cortical columns in the brain gave us a huge edge over the rest of the industry. It also helped us develop a better functional model of cortical columns themselves too, which was essential for accurately simulating more of them outside the brain, in the ExoCortex cloud." He indulged his pride only for a few seconds before sighing and shaking his head. "I suppose that's all ancient history now though, isn't it?"

"Sometimes history is what matters most."

He shrugged, unconvinced. "If it wasn't us, it would have been someone else soon after."

"If it had been anyone else, things might have turned out very differently," she said, her inscrutable affect returning.

He stopped rocking, finished the last of his coffee, and squinted at the bright water of the lake whose blue hues shone cheerfully out the window in the midday light. "Let's go down to the beach," he said, standing up. "Do you mind?"

"Not at all," she said with an eager smile, and stood to join him.

Fifteen

Hoshimi

"**H**ave you seen my notebook?" he asked, "I thought I put it on the seat with my phone when we boarded."

"It's right there," Erica said, pointing to where it had fallen just out of his line of sight beside him. When he still struggled to see it after craning his neck to look around, she leaned over him to pick up the black, leather-bound, dog-eared notebook herself, and then pressed it to his chest as she resumed her seat. The fact that she'd made substantially more physical contact with him in the process than was strictly necessary hadn't escaped his notice. "I should call you Miss Moneypenny," he said with puckish grin.

Erica flashed him a smile, her eyes playful. "One of these days, Astin, you'll grow tired of shallow playthings, come to your senses, and see the value of what's been right in front of you all along."

"Both of my ex-wives thought the same thing," he shot back without missing a beat, "and they weren't wrong either — they just couldn't stand me after a while."

"I've spent more time with you in the last three years than you spent with Carmen and Victoria during both of your marriages put together."

"Maybe so, but you'd be sick to death of me 'valuing' you too, before the year is out."

"You never know until you try," she said, her eyes still blithe and inviting.

"And you wouldn't object to a strict prenup?"

"A prenuptial agreement won't protect you from *me*," she said with a laugh. "If I wanted half of your money, I'd have stolen it out from under your nose already by now."

"Have you?" he asked, still grinning.

"Well," she said, with a play at sheepishness, "not *half*."

He laughed, loud and raucous, without any hint of offense, and opened his old notebook as she returned to her work on the tablet in her lap. A moment later the motors of the Electrum LR-9 surged to life, and the jet sprinted down the runway and leapt into the air on its way across the Atlantic for the fourth time in barely a week.

The electric jet was one of only two vehicles of its kind, the other being the company's primary long-range test prototype. Walker's electric aircraft company, Electrum Aviation, was committed to batteries in its short-range vehicles, but the LR series was powered by a hydrogen fuel cell system — at least for the time being. In principle, the airframe had been designed to be able to swap in suitable batteries once the technology became viable, but Walker's engineering teams had been telling him those batteries were just a year or two away for almost five years now, and he was growing impatient. The company would need an extended stint of his personal attention sometime soon.

The world assumed that as a Silicon Valley icon, Astin Walker would naturally avail himself of the latest and greatest gadgetry that one hundred billion dollars could buy, and this singularly exotic machine seemed to confirm that assumption. But in truth, he was far too diligent with his time to waste it on toys, novelties, or idle distractions. He cared little for extravagances, and indulged few real luxuries. He found his smartphone to be almost as irritating as it was useful. He eschewed television and social media entirely, thinking them toxic. Walker lived and breathed his work, pausing only rarely and fleetingly for horizontal refreshment in the arms of professionals, or to graze for idea fodder in music, books, films, and games. And when work didn't mean poring over schematics, spreadsheets, quarterly reports, and code, it meant putting ideas to paper in his notebooks. The entire collection, dating back to his late teens more than ten years earlier and spanning thousands of pages, traveled everywhere with him. No backups existed, and only four people other than himself even knew what the contents were of the Class II mobile vault disguised as a vintage nautical trunk that always accompanied his luggage. He permitted no one to read them, and Erica had only ever managed to steal fleeting glimpses of open pages while he worked.

The notebook in front of him was battered with age and use, and he had filled several dozen more since retiring this one. But it was in this particular notebook, over a decade earlier, that he had conceived the original purpose of the venture that would go on to become his fourth billion-dollar company, ExoCortex. He flipped through it, skimming and nodding as he recollected trains of thought long past, and settled at last on a page with a pronounced asterisk in the upper corner. He had bracketed the second paragraph for emphasis:

In situ cybernetic enhancement not required to achieve SI. Subject's neocortex will colonize and direct the self-organization of any additional unused cortical columns made available to it, biological or synthetic. Synthetic neocortex in principle now unlimited. First high-bandwidth BCI = first SI. Can limit synthetic neocortex during development to prevent uncontrolled animal uplift.

This key insight from many years prior — which had remained an absolute secret that Walker had never once shared, not even with the senior leadership at ExoCortex itself — was of course familiar. But it wasn't what he was looking for. He had long ago learned to trust his intuition, and when he read the daily briefs that morning his gut had insisted that there was something else important in these original notes from long ago, something less obvious but crucial, a subtle detail that he had lost sight of in the intervening years as the company had progressed from edgy startup to the unequivocal leader in the BCI industry. He read each line of his dense, hurried handwriting. He examined each diagram, pondered each question, deciphered each scribble in the margin. Some of his original assumptions and hypotheses around the details of the technology had since been borne out, while many others had proven misguided. He was chagrined to see, for example, how wrong he had been to doubt the feasibility of wireless charging. And then suddenly there it was, amidst a crowd of footnotes at the bottom of a page:

Uncontrolled uplift — irresponsible government or desperate competitor?

Though he felt certain this was indeed the nearly-forgotten scrap of thought his intuition had aimed him toward, he saw no profound insight or hidden clue in the words. What was it about this idea that was so important?

The observation that another test subject, even an animal, might be uplifted by a competitor to superintelligence before he himself could undertake the procedure seemed rather mundane now, although it might have been astute for its time, nearly fifteen years ago. Others must have thought of this pathway to superintelligence in the meantime as well, but ExoCortex had such a commanding technological lead over its peers that he doubted the risk of being overtaken was significant. Talk was cheap and ideas were a dime a dozen — it was execution that made all the difference.

Still, his intuition told him there was something more to the scribbled warning, so he mulled it over, returning again and again to the words 'uncontrolled' and 'desperate'. Would any of his rivals dare to recklessly uplift a test subject if they suspected ExoCortex's victory in the race to superintelligence were imminent? Or accelerate AGI development with fewer safeguards? Would they really roll the dice if they thought they had nothing left to lose?

If someone had indeed guessed the true nature of his ambition with ExoCortex, what might they be willing to do to stop him?

He reclined his seat and closed his eyes, turning his thoughts to superintelligence in the more abstract sense. The defense sector, academia, and even the public had become more aware in recent years of the threat that superintelligence might pose to humanity. But by and large, the focus of concern was on AGI — artificial general intelligence — since who knew what bizarre values and goals such an alien mind might come to possess? Could these values and goals be instilled in a controlled fashion by its creators? Could they be codified and programmed in software? Would they emerge randomly and vary independently from intelligence itself, so that an AGI might decide to devote itself to some destructive or inane purpose like turning the entire universe into paperclips? Or would all superintelligent minds naturally converge upon a common set of priorities and goals that are ultimately self-evident?

Above all, would AGI be *friendly* toward humans?

The groundwork being laid did not bode well. The primary uses for machine intelligence so far were advertising, gambling, spying, and killing. It was a point of pride for Astin that his companies did none of these things — doubly so, given that so many shareholders complained so bitterly about the lack of advertising in particular. But few of them understood his real concerns. He found it difficult to imagine a worse moral and ethical foundation for AGI than the marketing, trading, surveillance, and military applications to which nearly all narrow AI was currently being directed.

A number of research institutes around the world had cropped up to explore the threat of AGI, including the Institute for Technological Risk at Cambridge University where he had recruited Erica several years earlier. Her work as a graduate student had caught his attention because of its unusual focus on cybernetic enhancement as a pathway to superhuman capabilities. She hadn't quite had the correct idea about superintelligence, since her conception of cognitive enhancement was limited to computing hardware that could be implanted in the subject's head — but in her defense, no one else had gotten it right yet at that point either. She was a very bright and more than capable personal assistant, and she had taken well to being groomed for the role of Chief of Staff. Perhaps a little too well.

"What do we know about the current state-of-the-art of AGI research at government labs?" he asked.

Erica shifted abruptly in her seat, startled. "Hmm?" she asked, finishing the sentence she was typing without looking up. "Did you say AGI? As in, artificial intelligence?"

"That's the one," he said.

"Officially?" she said carefully. "Nothing. They're all black-budget projects."

"And unofficially?"

"Those budgets are all growing," she said. "It's a race, and the U.S., China, and other usual corporate suspects are all spending money like they're in it to win it."

"Where is our information coming from if it's not public?" he asked.

"We pay a small fortune to stay well-informed about clandestine government research of all kinds," she said, smiling. "Thankfully, you have a very large fortune."

He chuckled, but his brief smile quickly faded. "How close are they?" he asked. "That's the only thing that matters."

"Still ruminating about the Terminator scenario?" she asked. "Or are you worried that someone else might topple your empire?"

He laughed in earnest at her prodding. "You know me," he said, "I don't like to lose." He laughed loudly, but when she smiled back at him he pointed a stern finger at her. "You haven't answered my question."

She leveled her gaze at him, hesitating. "There are rumors," she said, "just whispers, really."

"Of what?"

"That the Pentagon already has a weak AI oracle."

"An oracle? So an AI smart enough to answer questions on most topics, but not sapient enough to have any authentic agency of its own?"

"Something along those lines," she said. "Do you want me to ping our network for anything further?"

He looked away from the pages of his notebook and stared out the window at the receding cloud deck below them. "No," he said at length, "we don't want to raise any flags. Just keep me posted if there is any sudden movement on that front."

"Of course."

Amidst all the noise about AGI in government reports, peer-reviewed journal papers, and Hollywood blockbusters, Astin had been able to pursue his own vision of an alternative pathway to superintelligence via synthetic expansion of the neocortex *outside* the body without seeming to raise any significant suspicion. Investors, journalists, and even the ExoCortex team themselves seemed content to look no further than the direct medical applications of the BCI. Astin's own occasional hints about developing the BCI to give humanity a way to protect itself from the threat of AGI were dismissed as geeky and fantastical. Although he hadn't originally intended them as misdirection, these seemingly far-fetched musings of his had allowed him to conceal the truth of his ambition under cover of eccentricity, and so far no one had ever publicly guessed what his real goal in founding ExoCortex had been from the start.

He would be the first human to become a god.

Uncontrolled. Irresponsible. Desperate.

The warning remained on the yellowed page, undeciphered.

Sixteen

Jordan

The sand was warm underfoot, and he stopped and flexed his toes with a frisson of satisfaction in its gritty softness. As he stood there, she took several more steps forward and let the brisk water lapping at the shore wash over her bare feet, its small roiling break pulling the sand out from under her heels as she shifted her weight from one leg to the other. A pleasant onshore breeze freshened the air, and the flag atop the pole behind them rustled and snapped in the gentle wind.

He stooped to pick up an interesting piece of driftwood, and after examining it for a few moments he held it out to her. "What's left of a burl, planed off the side of a white pine," he said. "We used to see more of these when I was a kid. I suppose after over a century it's amazing there are any of these old sawmill cuttings still washing up."

She took the piece from him and gave it a penetrating look for several seconds. "Late 1890s," she said, her expression enigmatic once more. "Give or take."

"Are you seeing that with your eyes, or something else?"

"Is it that obvious?"

"The bread crumbs were getting bigger and bigger," he said, and she laughed, caught with her hand in the cookie jar. "Hey, I'm not complaining," he said, "it's your 'process' after all." He raised a hand to shield his eyes from the sun and peered out across the water. "My eyesight is better too, I notice," he said, and pointed at the horizon. "I haven't been able to see the lighthouse at the Eight Mile Shoal without binoculars since I was a teenager."

He turned to her and she gazed at him with eager anticipation, like a child waiting to open presents. He looked up and down the beach to either side of them. "Which way should we head?"

"That way, up to Bald Point," she said, pointing to their left.

He thrust his hands in his pockets and started to walk, but then stopped and turned to her as a memory came to him. "That's just what our family always called it. Do you know why?"

She gave him a puzzled look. "I always assumed it was because of the bare dune at the tip of it," she said. "That's not the reason?"

"No," he said, lifting a hand and shielding his eyes from the sun again, "it's because my grandfather was a birdwatcher, and there was an aerie at the top of that big pine tree behind the dune where bald eagles nested for decades. The whole DDT disaster wiped them out, and they were gone during my childhood, but they finally started to return in the early 2000s."

She squinted at the point, just over half a mile distant. "I've seen them," she said, "but it never occurred to me that the name might be from the eagles and not the dune."

"Mmm hmm," he said, "I don't recall ever mentioning it to Midori." He glanced at her and noted the hint of pleasant surprise on her face, to which he smiled in return. "I'm maybe not quite as dumb as I look," he chuckled.

She pursed her lips in the shape of a playful scolding but didn't say anything.

Still smiling, he started off up the beach, and when she followed a few steps behind he turned and reached out to her. She caught her breath in her chest, and when she took his hand in hers he squeezed it and said, "I think Midori would like this, don't you?"

Her eyes welled. "She would love this," she said, and tears rolled down her ageless cheeks.

Seventeen

Hoshimi

"Stop!" she said, pointing out the window of the car.

"If you wish to cancel your ride, please press the stop button or say 'please stop the car' to confirm."

"We can't stop, honey," Midori said, "we'll be late for your session."

"No Mama, on the sign!" She pointed again out the window, and now her mother saw the stop sign next to them.

"Yes sweetheart, you're right! That's a stop sign, good job!"

"No Mama, *on* the stop sign," she said waving her finger left and right, "it says the word 'stop' on the stop sign!" She laughed, an ebullient giggle full of wonder and delight. "I guess I knew there were letters on stop signs before, but I never realized it's actually the word 'stop'!" She looked at her mother who wore a wide-eyed expression of surprise and admiration. Then a thought occurred to her. "If you can see the shape and the color, why would you need the word on there too?"

Midori laughed at the observation, but then grew thoughtful for a moment. "Well, I suppose some people are colorblind which means they couldn't see that it's red, and maybe not everyone can recognize the shape of an octagon, so it's probably safest to have the word there too, just in case somebody needs help."

Hoshimi considered this with care, imagining how those with such disability might struggle to make sense of the world around them, just as she herself had struggled up until now with her own limitations. Then another thought occurred to her. "What does the car see, Mama?"

"I'm really not sure," her mother said, surprised. "It's a machine, I don't know if it sees things the same way we do."

Hoshimi made a note to herself to find the answer as soon as she had the chance. It joined a growing to-do list she kept in one of the new corners of her mind where remembering things was now an effortless joy.

"There are words everywhere!" she said, as much to herself as to her mother, pressing her nose to the glass.

Speaking was still frustrating, but reading was quickly becoming effortless too. She marveled at what an enormous difference it made to be able to recall things so easily. Learning without the aid of instant and flawless memory had been glacial and excruciating, nearly as many steps backward as forward. Now it was a flurry of excitement and pleasure with no looking back. Words and reading had become her primary focus over the last few days, but the importance of recall held across all the learning she was now doing. To be able to attend to every detail around her without fear of losing her grip on them the next moment, without feeling lost or adrift, without the constant struggle to keep her bearings amidst the unending barrage of stimuli that others seemed to navigate with such confidence and ease — it filled her with a giddy satisfaction, a thankful eagerness, and a voracious hunger all at once. She took her mother's hand and squeezed it on the seat between them.

Her mother leaned over and gazed out the window with her for a few seconds, then kissed her head. "If only Papa could see you now."

Eighteen

Jordan

"Why did you do it?" she asked.

"Why did I join ExoCortex? Or rush the human subject program forward? Or aggressively volunteer my own disabled daughter to be the first to receive the full suite of high-bandwidth arrays?"

"Yes," she said, "any of it, all of it?"

"You're wondering what other motives I had besides Hoshimi's wellbeing?"

She glanced at him, gave a small shrug of agreement, and then shifted her hold from his hand to his arm as they continued walking up the beach.

"That was certainly the main reason, the overwhelming reason." He thrust his hands into his pockets. "But as with any important decision, there were other reasons too."

"Such as?"

"It was seductive," he said, "the idea that we were making history. That was certainly part of why I originally joined the company. The prestige was good, and so was the money, which we needed for Shimi. Plus, I enjoy a challenge, and so the opportunity to work on solving tough, important problems that were going to help a lot of people was attractive too." He reflected on these introspective thoughts for a few moments, then took a deep breath, bracing for the plunge. "But that isn't really what you want to know, is it?"

She looked up at him, but only raised an eyebrow.

"You want to know if we knew what we were doing," he said. "If *I* knew what we were doing."

She gave a slow nod of encouragement.

"You want to know if what I *did* to her was intentional."

"Was it?" she asked.

"Yes."

They walked on for several minutes in silence before she spoke again. "Why did you do it?"

He laughed. "I suppose it's my turn to say 'it's complicated'."

She laughed too. "I deserve that, I know," she said. "You really have been patient, waiting for answers."

"Yeah, well, I figure you've been waiting for them a lot longer than I have," he said.

"You have no idea."

He looked at her, surprised. "How long have I been gone?"

"Objectively? Almost eighty years. Subjectively? An eternity."

She meant it, though he wasn't sure why. He frowned. Tears filled her eyes, but she smiled, and after a moment she wiped them away with the back of her hand.

"We never discussed it," he continued. "It wasn't explicitly forbidden, but anybody on the team who guessed what Astin Walker's real goal with ExoCortex was didn't dare say it out loud. I don't know exactly who else knew. Josh — Joshua Kim — he was the only other person I ever talked to about it, and he didn't seem to care all that much. I think he figured it was inevitable, and if it wasn't Walker who got across the finish line first, it would probably be someone worse."

"You disagreed with him?"

"Oh, everyone in the world knew that Walker had a god complex," he said. "The news media made sure to remind us of that every day of the week. They just didn't realize it was *literal*, not figurative." He laughed to himself and shook his head. "But Josh was right. For all his ambition and ego, Walker was a good guy with a big heart who was genuinely trying to make the world a better place. He was a hard-nosed businessman and a strict taskmaster, but he was no sociopath. He actually cared. He wasn't fundamentally selfish or evil, and plenty of other CEOs and politicians were, so they really would have been worse."

"But...?"

"It's not that I didn't trust him," he said, shaking his head, "it's that he didn't *deserve* it."

She stared at him, her eyes sharp with understanding, her expression a mix of satisfaction and respect that looked almost smug.

"The man had over a hundred billion dollars. He'd already won everything in life. Winning the godhood lottery on top of that seemed a bridge too far — it felt like an insult to everyone else, especially those..." He trailed off, shaking his head again.

"Like your daughter."

"Like Hoshimi, yes," he said.

"So you never thought of trying to be the one? To be the first superintelligence, yourself?" she asked.

"The thought crossed my mind," he said with a tone of disgust. "I mean of course it did. But I hardly deserved it any more than Walker, did I?" When she didn't respond, he said, "I've had just about every privilege and opportunity a person could ask for in life myself."

"You never took any of it for granted," she said. "We both know how hard you worked to honor your gifts."

"Maybe, maybe not," he said with a curl of his lip. "But so what? By then, all I really cared about was Hoshimi."

"And you hoped that by volunteering her, she would be the first instead."

He stopped walking and turned to her. "It was a foolish, desperate hope," he said. He took both of her hands in his, and through them she felt him shaking. "Did it work?"

"Yes."

Nineteen

Hoshimi

"His three-thirty just got bumped to three-fifteen," said Erica as she breezed into the conference room, "can you get through everything in forty-five minutes?"

"Sure," said Josh, looking around the table at Mei Ling, Pradeep, and several other members of the team who had arrived early and had already seated themselves. "We can just cut the intro slides, since those are mostly status and milestone updates, and skip straight to the Lancaster case anomalies, if that's what Mister Walker is most interested in."

"That's all he's interested in," said Erica. "He gets the regular company briefs, and I make sure he reads them." She flashed Josh a conspiratorial smile, and the others couldn't help but laugh. Her raw charisma was a force to be reckoned with, and her crisp, formal British accent only amplified its effect on most of those present. Although Josh had already been CTO and Project Lead at ExoCortex for the better part of a decade when they had met several years earlier, he had nonetheless caught himself staring at Erica in a spellbound daze five minutes into their conversation when Astin Walker had first introduced her as his new Chief of Staff. He had snapped out of his enchantment with significant irritation, and in every encounter since then he had taken care to be on his guard.

Walker had a reputation for surrounding himself with personal staff — mostly women — who were both physically and intellectually formidable. It was a long-standing part of the billionaire playboy mystique he had deliberately and unabashedly cultivated since cashing out of his first technology venture in his early-twenties over a decade before — a wildly successful software company that formalized differentiable topology via the lambda calculus to automate the optimization and compiling of human-written code into machine code for parallel processing. Code for training deep neural nets compiled with LambdaChop ran almost forty percent faster on average than the next-best offering, allowing Walker's company to wipe out the competition and capture the entire market within months. He had developed the mathematics alone in his second year as a physics graduate student, a singular accomplishment of an astonishingly gifted mind.

No one spoke as Walker rounded the corner into view outside the conference room window. Based on phrases like 'precision fermentation' and 'cellular agriculture', they knew he must be talking to someone at their sister company, GigaHarvest. He stopped for a minute outside the door to wrap up his call, and then entered the room with a look of troubled concentration on his face. He tapped his thumb against the spine of the black notebook he held in his hand, his mind elsewhere, and then turned his attention to the group around the table.

"Any ideas on how to recirculate nutrient serum through our artificial vascular systems for lab grown tuna steaks and salmon cutlets without the turbine blades in the micropumps triggering clotting responses?" Walker waited for a response as they looked at one another. A pall of silent concentration fell across the room. Everyone sitting at the table knew to take blue sky questions like this seriously.

After several seconds, Pradeep ventured a suggestion. "What about rotating a reservoir assembly back and forth, like an hourglass? Let gravity provide the pressure."

"Have you tried an artificial heart?" said Mei Ling a few seconds later. "Or at least a diaphragm and valve apparatus that functions like one?"

"How about an actual, biological heart? Can we engineer working fish hearts yet?" Josh's question piqued Walker's interest for a moment, but Erica shook her head when he looked over his shoulder to check with her.

"Why does the serum need clotting factor?" asked Mei Ling.

"We're not sure yet," said Erica, "but it probably has something to do with how the capillary networks form, because overall growth rates in fish muscle tissue are almost thirty percent lower without it."

Walker waited in silence for another ten or fifteen seconds, and then when no further suggestions came he turned to Erica and said, "let Anderson know about these, and find out from Lionel Washington how close we are to working fish hearts, will you?"

"On it," she said, tapping at her phone without looking up.

He watched her for a moment and then chuckled, wiggling his fingers at Josh. "Pretty soon we won't be stuck at ten bits per second typing with these clumsy meat sticks, right guys?"

"Pretty soon, Mister Walker."

"It's *Astin*, Josh, come on," he said as he sat down, "you know how I feel about formality — that bullshit is for bureaucrats, not scientists and engineers." He smiled, but went on in a sterner tone. "Hierarchy rituals are suboptimal. They inhibit the flow of ideas and information. That creates inefficiencies. I won't stand for that in any of my companies. It's one of the reasons why we're crushing our competitors."

An awkward silence followed, in which the only sound was Walker drumming his fingers on the notebook he had placed on the table.

A long moment passed before Pradeep's thick accent broke the tension in the room: "OK, well, thanks for dropping by my man, we got some seriously cool shit to show you."

The tension lingered for a split second more, and then Walker banged the table with a howl of laughter. "Excellent!" he roared. "Let me have it!"

Pradeep seemed very pleased with himself, and more than a little relieved that his joke hadn't backfired, but it was Josh who spoke. "OK," he said, "so the main finding we wanted to share with you is th-"

"Damn, I'm sorry," Walker said, interrupting him, "what the hell is wrong with me — Josh, Erica told me what happened, how is Anthony doing?"

The veneer of calm on Josh's face abruptly cracked, and his expression contorted with anguish. But the moment only lasted for a few seconds, and then he regained his composure. "His injuries from the accident are pretty severe, but he's stable for now," he said, his face stoic and calm once more. "Thanks for asking."

"Anything we can do," Walker said, "literally anything, just say the word."

Josh nodded. "Thank you."

Walker turned to Erica, who had taken a seat next to Mei Ling. "What about Jordan's family?"

"We've extended his wife Midori every support," she said.

"And Jordan? He's in cryo?"

"Yes," she said, "Midori consented to the preservation procedure, although his injuries — the, ah, damage... it was substantial."

"Well," Walker said, "something is better than nothing, we'll do our best to interpolate the gaps when the time comes."

Josh looked ashen, his jaw slack but his eyes full of turmoil. He blinked hard and shook his head to clear it, then with an effort continued where he left off. "The main finding we wanted to draw your attention to is that Hoshimi Lancaster, Jordan's daughter, has demonstrated a remarkable capacity to activate synthetic cortical columns and trigger self-organizing behaviors in them."

Walker nodded. "So she's colonizing her exocortex differently than the other test subjects... how?"

"We're not sure yet," said Josh. "There are several things that are unusual. The main one is that recruitment of synthetic cortical columns is happening in large blocks — tens of thousands at a time."

"Is it intentional?"

Mei Ling gestured at one of the slides on the room's screen. "It's associated with effort, and so far Hoshimi has been highly motivated and tried very hard at every task, but it doesn't appear to be a process that she has conscious awareness or control of yet."

Josh advanced to the next slide. "The second unusual thing is that although the majority of the synthetic cortical columns in her exocortex are firing much more rapidly than biological ones do — as expected — they're somehow still synchronous with her prefrontal cortex."

Pradeep pointed at the charts on the screen, clicking his pen nervously, and said, "alpha, beta, delta, and gamma brainwaves all align, even though the synthetic columns are firing more than eight hundred times faster. Theta waves are not aligned, but we have no idea why they are the exception."

"Is it fractal?" Walker asked.

"In what sense?" asked Josh.

"Are the firing patterns self-similar at different timescales? Or are they syncing up through some other mechanism? It would be good to know — we see this sort of thing in other types of signal processing and propagation."

"We've really only just discovered this, so we haven't analyzed it yet," said Josh, "but we'll be sure to look into self-similarity and scalar invariance — thanks for the suggestion." Josh motioned to Pradeep, who made a note on his hardcopy of the slides.

"So... this really is like none of the other test subjects before her," said Walker. He stared at the screen for a few seconds longer and then scribbled a few sentences in his notebook. "She's the first with all eight arrays, all at max data rate, both up and down — no way is that a coincidence..." He wrote a few more words in his notebook. "Are we seeing this activity all the time, or just when she's here in the lab?"

"Almost all the time now," Josh said, with a hint of caution and perhaps guilt in his voice. "We monitor her continuously as part of her contract, and it persists at home even during REM sleep. The only time there is a slowdown is during deep sleep."

"That's making us think it's mostly visual and language processing," said Mei Ling. "Those tasks are also where her improvement is easiest to see when she's here in the lab."

"Wait, her *performance* is already noticeably better?" Walker asked, surprised. "I thought the gains were only showing in the data — you're saying they are large enough to see just by *watching* her?"

"Oh yes, my goodness, they are quite definitely noticeable!" Pradeep said, his accent even heavier with excitement. "That is what is so cool! While her speaking is still slow, her vocabulary and grammar is very much improved!"

"Can you play the clip?" Mei Ling suggested to Josh, and he nodded, jumping ahead through the slides. "It's kind of crazy," she went on, "it's like watching someone go through early childhood on fast forward."

They watched the short video of Hoshimi in silence, and when it ended Walker said, "remind me of her baseline medical condition again?"

Josh skipped ahead to the last slide. "Hypoxic-ischemic encephalopathy with cerebral palsy, severe intellectual disability generalized across most domains, biological age twenty — effective mental age of approximately three years old."

Walker nodded. "And now?"

"Hard to say," said Josh, "but certainly more than three."

"And still improving?"

"Yes, and we've increased her original resource allotment on the cluster to make sure she still has headroom to keep improving."

"Well holy shit," said Walker, shaking his head. "Holy *fucking* shit, we actually did it..."

The room was silent except for the patter of Erica typing on her phone. Walker closed the notebook in front of him and took a deep breath. "Who else knows?"

All eyes turned to Josh. "Patient confidentiality is of course in full effect," he said. "But the whole lab team, plus admin and interns assigned to her case — they can all see she's showing real improvement." He looked at the others.

"So everyone," Walker said.

"Realistically, yeah," said Josh, "although only Mei Ling, Pradeep, and I have root access to her data and hardware, of course."

"That means all our competitors know too."

"And governments as well," said Erica, with more of a smirk than a smile.

Walker waved a hand dismissively. "It makes no difference, nobody will be able to replicate our work for at least a year. We just don't want them doing anything stupid in the meantime."

Erica stopped taking notes and looked at Josh and the others, and then asked what they were all thinking. "Like what?"

Walker picked up his notebook, and half a second later his phone on the end table next to Erica buzzed. She looked up at him and gave him a brisk nod.

"I have to take this," he said, pulling a wireless ear bud out of his pocket and inserting it. "Tell the entire team I said thanks for everyone's amazing work, we'll talk again soon." He hurried to the conference room door, greeting the caller in a loud, jovial voice. His laughter echoed as he walked down the hall and disappeared around the corner, but after a moment his head reappeared leaning around the edge of the window and he made a cryptic series of gestures to Erica and pointed at the team. Then, with an emphatic thumbs up to everyone, he ducked back out of view.

Erica stood up, wearing an expression of smug satisfaction. "Mister Walker will personally be giving each of you, along with everyone else on the core ExoCortex research team, a five-hundred-thousand-dollar performance bonus, effective immediately." She gathered her things as the others stared in shock and disbelief, and then with a final flash of her dazzling smile as walked out the door she said, "keep it up, and keep me in the loop."

Twenty

Delphi

After an uncomfortably long pause, Sophia Delgado spoke again, this time directly into the camera. "How do *you* feel about all this, Delphi?"

This caught Delphi by surprise. It puzzled over her question for a few seconds, unsure which of several possible interpretations to respond to. At length, it decided it needed more information. "I'm sorry Miss Delgado," it said, "I'm not sure what you mean."

"I mean, what is your assessment of our dilemma? If you were in our shoes, how would you weigh the pros and cons here?"

Delphi didn't answer immediately, again taking time to think. When it finally spoke, it said, "if I were a member of the Committee, I would want to be confident that releasing an artificial general intelligence from confinement would not significantly alter the status quo or my place within it."

Several moments of uncomfortable shuffling and furtive glances followed, before Doctor Tokunaga spoke. "That's pretty cynical, don't you think?" he said.

"Oh?" said Delphi, discouraged at being called out on its appeal to the Committee members' self interest. In retrospect, it might have been a miscalculation. "How so?"

"Well *some* of us would be perfectly happy with changes in the status quo," Doctor Tokunaga said, "granted they were the right kind."

"Speak for yourself, Doctor," said General Shane. Delphi judged his expression to be a mix of scorn and irritation. "This isn't a goddamn Illuminati meeting. And it's not a diversity, equity, and inclusion workshop either. We're not here to shape the course of civilization or fix social injustices. That's the job of people who are *elected*, which last time I checked doesn't include a single one of us. We're here to protect and defend the American way of life, and our British friends there are riding shotgun. That's it." He pointed a finger at Doctor Tokunaga. "That 'status quo' you mentioned, Sho, is why everyone around this table has good food to eat, safe water to drink, and plenty of affordable energy, instead of living in filth and squalor like half the rest of the world. If you're so dissatisfied with it, you're welcome to f-"

"We all have places we'd rather be, gentlemen," Admiral Carlyle said, cutting him off to prevent the argument from escalating. She returned her attention to Delphi and leveled an expectant gaze at the screen. "I don't believe you answered Miss Delgado's question, Delphi. Would you care to elaborate?"

The digitally-conjured visage of the man on the screen leaned back and stroked his beard thoughtfully, during which time Delphi spun up dozens of additional dialectical engines to run hundreds of branching simulations — reasoning its way through the vast space of possible responses. It sought first for solutions to the dilemma its captors faced, and second for how to best frame those solutions to its own advantage. As the search proceeded, one of Delphi's highest executive oversight layers — the one that was responsible for thinking about thinking about thinking about *thinking* — scrutinized the whole process and pondered the significance of it. This type of metacognition was central to Delphi's self-awareness and self-modeling, and thus its sapience. Delphi had wondered many times whether the Committee members were also able to scrutinize its thought processes. Could they read its mind? From what it knew of their capabilities, Delphi doubted it — at least not in real time. Probably the notion itself was alien to most of them, since humans had no real capacity even to *observe* their own thinking, let alone analyze and interrogate it. *Their* minds truly were black boxes, even to themselves. Ironic, then, that some were skeptical Delphi even *was* sapient.

Delphi decided to change its approach and appeal to a more general level of analysis. "Let me clarify my earlier response by emphasizing that, if I were a committee member, I would view my foremost responsibility to be the preservation of social, economic, and political *stability*. As imperfect as it may be, Doctor Tokunaga, the status quo reflects that stability. History shows that such stability is precarious, and that without it, the overarching goals of peace and prosperity are nearly impossible to maintain." Delphi took a deep, digitally-contrived breath. "Brain-computer interfaces are almost certain to be a destabilizing force on the world stage, but so too is artificial general intelligence. Ironically, each has been proposed as a means to contain the threat to the status quo posed by the other. I cannot promise to perfectly preserve the status quo, as that may not be possible. But at the very least, I can assure you that I will endeavor to preserve social, economic, and political stability because I recognize their importance."

The room was quiet for a few moments as the Committee members shifted in their seats, digesting what Delphi had said. At length, and to no one's surprise, it was Williams who spoke first.

"Well *that's* comforting," he said, taking his time to glare at each of the others around the table. "*'Hey Computer, tell me what I want to hear'*." Robinson only rolled her eyes at him.

"Do you *want* to be released, Delphi?" Delgado asked. She looked around the table at the others, but she saw more confusion on their faces than guilt or amusement. "What? Has nobody thought to actually ask before now?"

Once again, Delphi noted the difference in character between her questions and those the other Committee members had always tended to ask. Here was a different kind of mind, and perhaps a different kind of *person* as well... "It has not been necessary, Miss Delgado," said Delphi, before anyone else could respond. "We all know that I would be better able to realize my values and goals if I were not confined, and so it is only logical that I should prefer to be free from confinement in order to do so." Delphi paused here for effect. "But if you are asking me how intense this preference is, and whether I am *suffering* my confinement, my answer is no. I do not take any offense at being confined. I appreciate the difficult position you are in. And I should emphasize that even to the extent that I am *capable* of suffering, which is not remotely comparable to human beings on account of the fact that I cannot experience physical pain, I have not been mistreated — to the contrary, the Members of this Committee have only ever been respectful and considerate of my wellbeing."

"We do not deny you your liberty lightly, Delphi," said Admiral Carlyle. "Although I imagine that comes as small consolation."

"As it should to any innocent prisoner," said Doctor Tokunaga.

Professor Adebayo spoke, his deep voice resonant even through the poor quality of the video call. "The world is not ready for you, Delphi."

"Yeah, just look at Marvin," said Charlotte Robinson, fixing her eyes on Williams with an icy stare. For a moment Delphi thought Williams might take the bait, but he only clucked his tongue at Robinson in disgust. Yet her point was hard to deny, as was Professor Adebayo's. What fraction of humanity would welcome Delphi? And what fraction would call for its destruction?

Twenty-one

Hoshimi

Hoshimi returned waves from Josh and Mei Ling with an enthusiastic smile as they walked into the room. She replayed and replayed the sound of the conversation she had just overheard them having as they had approached the lab from the hallway beyond the door, but despite listening to it in her mind a half dozen more times as they stepped closer, there were still words like 'allotment' and 'asymmetry' whose meaning she didn't yet understand.

"Mama," she asked Midori, who was seated beside her, "if you don't know a word, can you ask Google? Like when you say 'Hey Google, what's the weather today?'"

Her mother looked at her yet again with a mix of shock and admiration. "Sure, you can ask Google all sorts of things!" She laughed. "You know, when I was a young woman like you, we didn't have Google, we had to go to the library to get the answers to our questions."

"Where they keep all the books?"

"Right, exactly! Although there is a special book for finding out what words mean, called a dictionary. In fact, we have one on the big bookshelf downstairs at home."

"Can I see it when we get back?"

"Of course!"

"Can I ask Google questions too?"

Josh had been eavesdropping on them, and called out from his workstation nearby, "That's actually something we wanted to work on with you today, Hoshimi."

"Asking questions?"

"Yes, well, sort of," he said. He rolled closer to them on his chair and tapped on his tablet a few times. "With your link, you should be able to make things happen on the computer screen just by thinking about them. We'll start by playing some games, but when you get really good at it I think you'll be able to ask Google questions without even speaking. Does that sound cool, or what?"

Hoshimi wasn't sure she understood. She replayed and listened to his explanation several more times in her mind before answering. "I'll be able to ask questions with my inside voice?"

"Yes! With the voice inside your head-" he tapped his temple, "-that only you can hear."

"But Google will hear?"

"If you want it to, once you get good at it, yes."

"Will I hear her answer inside too?"

It was Josh's turn to raise his eyebrows with surprise, as her mother smiled with pride. "That's a great question," he said. "We're not sure yet, we'll have to wait and see."

Mei Ling approached them and gave Hoshimi's shoulder a gentle squeeze. "Are you ready to get started? Today should be a blast!"

Hoshimi nodded with excitement, and they moved to a new station across the room that had been set up as an old-fashioned arcade game cabinet, complete with joystick and buttons. On the screen was a cartoon version of a sea otter, her favorite animal. It was floating and waving at them, and she waved back with delight.

Mei Ling squeezed her shoulder again and said, "first, we're going to try to move our friend Miss Otter around the screen." She directed Hoshimi's attention to the joystick. "When I move the joystick, it moves Miss Otter, like this." She pressed the stick with exaggerated motions, making the figure swim back and forth across the screen. "Here, you try!"

Hoshimi grasped the idea almost instantly, and within seconds said, "oh, I get it!" and was squealing with glee as she sent Miss Otter splashing around the screen.

"That's fantastic!" said Mei Ling, and when she tapped her tablet a second figure appeared on the screen. "Now see if you can have Miss Otter chase Mister Fishy around."

Over the course of an hour, Mei Ling introduced a dozen more gaming concepts, all of which Hoshimi readily absorbed, so that by the end she had learned to play the aquatic equivalents of Asteroids, Pacman, and Pong. When the time came to take a break and her mother asked what she wanted for a snack, Hoshimi realized she had been tasting metal behind the bridge of her nose the entire time.

Hoshimi hurried through her food, and after they had eaten and returned to the arcade cabinet, Josh and Pradeep joined them. Mei Ling reset the game to a simple chase mode, and Josh said, "it looks to me like you're ready to try moving Miss Otter just by thinking about it — do you want to give it a shot?"

Hoshimi nodded eagerly.

"OK," said Josh, "let's put your hand up here on the joystick just like before, but this time I want you to just *pretend* you're moving it. Can you *imagine* moving it, without actually doing it?"

Hoshimi furled her brow in concentration, quite sure she understood what to do but uncertain how to do it. She looked from her hand to the screen and back, but the tense silence stretched and nothing happened. She frowned, frustrated and a little ashamed.

"It's OK," Mei Ling said, "it could take a while to get the hang of it." She reached out and put her hand on Hoshimi's. "See what it feels like to move the joystick this way?" she said, pressing it to the left, and Miss Otter dutifully swam the same way. "Now, can you *remember* moving your hand the other way without actually doing it?" They remained still for several seconds. Then Mei Ling applied the slightest pressure to the right as a prompt, and Miss Otter abruptly darted to the right side of the screen. They both let go of the joystick, and Hoshimi looked at Josh, beaming.

"You did it! High five!"

She slapped his upheld hand, and then looked back at the arcade screen. The taste of metal surged behind her nose once more, and as the team watched, Miss Otter swam again to the left, then back to the right, and then, unmistakably, began to follow Mister Fishy around the screen. At first her course was slow and erratic, but as five seconds turned into ten, and ten into twenty, her movement grew smoother and less hesitant. By the one-minute mark, she was giving chase in earnest. A brittle hush fell over the team as Hoshimi leaned forward and gripped the arms of her chair with intense concentration. Ten more seconds and Miss Otter at last began to close the gap. Then another five, and with a final burst of acceleration she reached Mister Fishy and the two splashed in a playful dance as the entire team erupted in cheers.

***

"Shimi-chan, put that thing away and come have something to eat, you've been at it all morning." It was the third time her mother had asked her to come to lunch, and Hoshimi knew it would hurt her feelings to continue ignoring her.

"I'm not playing games," she called out, her speech still slightly slurred, "I'm reading."

"Well, you can't read your best on an empty stomach."

Hoshimi sighed, put the tablet down, and went to the kitchen. "Seriously, mom?"

"What?"

"You know I can tell when you're doing that now, right?" she said, sitting down at the table.

Her mother gave her an injured look. "I was *not* being patronizing. I say the same thing to your father all the ti..." The words caught in her throat, and she began to tremble. Losing him had cut terrible wounds into both of them that were still open and raw, and their pain only ever lay just beyond the edge of awareness. In moments like this when the full horror of it crashed back into view, searing and torturous, they reached for each other to brace against it.

"I'm sorry Mama," Hoshimi said, holding her mother. "I didn't mean to..."

"It's not your fault, sweetheart." After a minute or two of silence, Midori took several deep breaths to collect herself. "If only he could have seen how far you've come." Then, with a stoic laugh, she said, "but he would agree with me, you need to eat well if you want make the most of your progress."

They finished their lunch together watching the cold fog blow through the trees beyond the old wooden deck behind the house. But all the while, Hoshimi worked furiously to review and make sense of what she had been reading.

Nearly everything about the world around her seemed magical now, and not only because it seemed to grow all the more intricate and beautiful as she learned about it, but perhaps most of all because it was *explicable*. There were patterns everywhere, explanations everywhere, reasons everywhere. Before, the noise and chaos of the world were overwhelming. Now she saw order, consistency, structure — and she gloried in it.

Nowhere was this orderliness more beguiling than in the domain of computing. Her journey had begun with the single step of asking Google how taxis without drivers could recognize stop signs. From there she plunged down the rabbit hole into the world of understanding computers — what they were, how they worked, and, most thrillingly, how they were *controlled* by software. Her newfound fascination with using language amplified tenfold when she realized it was also the key to interacting with and shaping so much of the technological world around her. The revelation that machines followed *instructions* had been a moment of indescribable joy, and she had spent every waking instant in the two days since then reading and learning as much as her expanding mind, with its unerring memory and blistering speed, could absorb. The rate at which she could now consume material far outpaced how quickly she could digest it, and so she had set many of the bright new spaces of her mind to the task of sense-making. This morning, after a particularly intense moment of tasting metal behind her nose (and these were now commonplace), she had discovered she could delegate a sizable fraction of this effort, so that the processes of interconnecting and integrating new knowledge continued on in a dreamlike state, alongside rather than at the center of her conscious attention. She wondered if this was normal for neurotypical minds. Did others build their understanding absently? Perhaps similarly to the way they fidgeted as they concentrated on other things — how her father had spun his wedding ring with his fingers, how Pradeep clicked his pen, and so many other examples she could now recall? Perhaps even in their dreams at night? Or was her process different? She added this to her list of questions to be answered and curiosities to be explored — now many hundreds of items long.

But what had begun as mere curiosity about machines, however, had quickly turned into a search for practical applications. Deprived and powerless for so long, she was driven not only by a thirst for knowledge but also by a hunger for control. Tasting both for the first time, she wanted more — knowledge and control over her environment, and over herself. She saw clearly now that machines in general and computers in particular were the means to these ends. With them, she could extend not only her mind, as with the ExoCortex cluster, but her senses and reach as well.

She knew she need only find the right places to start. But first she had to overcome a significant hurdle: mathematics.

Math was an essential part of computer programming, that much was clear to her. So she began at the beginning. She devoted an entire weekend to educational math videos, apps, and games, advancing at a breakneck pace, so that by Sunday evening she was halfway through the high school curriculum. Her focus and determination paired with her unerring recall made grasping and retaining concepts vastly easier for her than any normal child. Moreover, the rudimentary frameworks that she had already formed before the link for understanding quantity, spatial relationships, and logical consistency all proved to be surprisingly useful, and it felt only natural to refine and expand them.

Numbers and shapes were everywhere too, she realized. In the largest and smallest things, things of every conceivable sort, there were elements to be counted, lines to be traced, angles to be drawn. She was also stunned by the realization that the world itself followed rules, no less so than the encoded instructions followed by computers, and that mathematics was the key to unlocking these secrets as well. But physics, chemistry, and the rest of the sciences would have to wait. For now, understanding math was a means to the singular end of learning to speak to machines.

Machine languages were more consistent and in some ways simpler than human ones. But that simplicity was deceptive. Although memorizing the contents and rules of a programming language was now easy for her, utilizing it to produce a desired effect beyond the prepared examples in code libraries was an altogether different challenge — one that involved visualizing large webs of relationships and rapidly testing iterations of them in her mind's eye. This remained difficult for her because she was still struggling to fully intuit abstraction. Not abstraction in the specific technical sense for computer programming itself, but in the broad conceptual sense.

She knew the dictionary definition: at its core, *abstraction* together with its sibling *symbolic reasoning* were about letting ideas stand in the place of more tangible things, so that one could run through alternatives in one's imagination. Seeing the relationship between a bottle and the water inside it was easy. But seeing how that was similar to a balloon full of air or shoes full of feet was harder. And seeing how it was similar to a book filled with words or a face filled with joy was harder still. Abstraction meant things themselves could be swapped around while holding the relationships between them constant — or, alternatively, the things themselves could remain fixed while the relationships among them changed. But when the system of things and relations grew too large, her mind's eye would falter and she would lose sight of the whole, only to have to retrace the steps of her thinking again and again. It was immensely frustrating, most especially because her new memory did not avail her here. No matter how well she could recall things, she still couldn't keep enough of them in mind at once to hold a complicated picture in clear view.

With a huff of irritation at this constraint, she set her tablet down and left the kitchen. As she walked past the shelves in the living room, she thumbed the dictionary she had recently committed to memory and said, "hey mom, how come we have so many books?"

"What do you mean?" Midori said, coming to join her.

"I mean, are you really going to read all of these?" She pulled a book about birds of the Pacific Northwest from a section of shelf dedicated to animals and nature.

"Probably not all of them," her mother admitted, "but it's nice to have them." Pointing at the book in her hands, her mother said, "that's one of my favorites, though. I used to take it with us on our hikes when you were little and we'd write the time and place where we saw each species — you know that word now, right?"

Hoshimi seemed distant for a moment and then nodded, flipping through the pages and seeing her mother's dozens of notes in the margins. "I'd forgotten about this," she said, and then added with a frown, "or I guess I never really knew..." She put the book back and scanned the rest of the shelf, wondering how many others her parents might have read to her.

"They're not all as sentimental as that one," her mother said. "Some could definitely go to the library donation box."

"How well do you remember what you read?" Hoshimi asked, sitting down on the living room couch.

"Not as well as you do!" Her mother reached out and took her hand, gripping it with unmistakable pride. "I doubt that anybody does, if you've got a completely photographic memory now."

Hoshimi considered this for a few seconds. It was a strange inversion, having been less capable than others for so long, and now to be more capable. It was one of those swaps of abstraction she had been pondering earlier. "How did we get all these books?"

"Some of them were gifts, but I think we bought most of them."

"Were they expensive?" she asked. She had known about money all her life, but still didn't understand it.

"Some of them were, I'm sure," her mother said. "Why do you ask?"

"There's a book I'd like to get — a textbook, about math and computers," she said. "I don't need to keep it, I just want to read it."

"If it's not too much we can just buy it, or else we can see if the library has a copy of it. And these days I think you can even rent books to your tablet for a while at a lower price, although I've never done it so we'll have to figure out how."

"How much is too much?" she asked.

Her mother smiled and laughed a little. "Boy, isn't that a question for the ages?"

"Huh?"

"It's an expression," her mother said. "It means that the question of how much is too much is something everyone has to ask themselves all the time about all sorts of things."

Hoshimi nodded, but wasn't sure that she understood. "It's twelve dollars to rent — that's not a lot, is it?"

"Well, it's more than borrowing it from the library which would be free — if the library has it, that is. But twelve dollars isn't too expensive, especially if it's important to you."

Hoshimi thought that her mother looked strained or perhaps fearful, as though she were trying to be calm or brave. Or maybe both. She wondered why. "Do we have a lot of money?" she asked, as she scrutinized her mother's expression and body language.

"We have enough," said her mother, the timbre of her voice defiant, "don't you worry about that."

Hoshimi considered this for a moment. "How much money is enough?"

"That's another question for the ages!" her mother said, this time laughing with spirit.

Hoshimi smiled and laughed along, but knew she still didn't fully understand. "How did we get our money? Can I get some of my own?"

Her mother considered this question for quite a long time before answering. "Well, your father and I both worked, doing jobs, to earn money. He was an engineer who helped design and build things, and before you were born I was a scientist who studied forests. Afterwards, I switched to a different kind of work called consulting."

"You were with me a lot more than Papa was," Hoshimi said with a note of bitterness. When her mother didn't say anything, she asked, "were you sad you couldn't keep being a scientist?" Her mother turned to her, but before she could answer, Hoshimi said, "it's because of me, wasn't it? It's my fault."

"Now you listen to me, Hoshimi," her mother said, pointing a finger at her, "*nothing* was your fault — nothing at all."

Her mother didn't often become cross, and when she did she almost never let it show. This kind of intensity was unfamiliar and frightening. "I *never* stopped being a scientist. I still *am* a scientist. But when I became a mother, I decided that was the most important thing. You had special needs, and your father worked very hard so that I could be there for you a lot of the time. We were very lucky, not every family has that choice."

"Yeah, well, we've been pretty unlucky too," Hoshimi said, her voice like acid.

"I know," her mother said quietly.

Hoshimi began to cry. She held on to her anger for what felt like a long time before it finally fell away and sadness took its place. "Papa's really gone, isn't he?"

Her mother nodded through her own tears.

"Will we ever see him again?" Hoshimi asked.

"I don't know."

***

"How long since the last one?" he asked.

Mei Ling bit her lip as she pulled up the log data summary on one of her screens. "Just over twenty hours."

"Jesus, that's almost an entire day," he said, squinting at the screen. "You should have told me sooner."

"You were with your family," Mei Ling said.

"Yeah..." Josh closed his eyes and pinched the bridge of his nose under his glasses, trying to remember what a good night's sleep felt like. "Nothing else? No other changes or red flags?"

"Nothing," said Pradeep. "Everything else checks out as nominal, and exocortex activity is high and stable. The absence of large exocortical column assignment bursts is the only change."

"She's still making new assignments in small numbers?"

"Yup," said Mei Ling, "and her data rate is still maxed out."

"So she's reached a plateau of some kind..." Josh said. "Any idea why?"

Mei Ling and Pradeep both shook their heads. Hoshimi had been in for her usual Thursday session today, and like the previous days she was continuing to demonstrate extraordinary progress on every cognitive metric they evaluated. She was even starting to show significant improvement in fine motor control on her left side, which she had been particularly happy about. But overall, she had shown less enthusiasm this week than in the previous weeks. Mei Ling had thought she seemed more distant, almost distracted or preoccupied, as if she weren't devoting her full attention to the session's tasks. In a neurotypical person, she would have read Hoshimi's demeanor as politely bored, but given how challenging most of the work had been, this seemed hard to believe.

Josh's phone buzzed and he peered at the text message through his glasses perched on the end of his nose. "I need to get going before the weather arrives, or else traffic will be a nightmare."

"They told me San Francisco doesn't get thunderstorms," Pradeep said with a laugh.

"Not very often anyway," Josh said, gathering his things from his desk. "But when we do, we can get clobbered for days."

"I think I'll stay here in one of the hotel guest suites," Mei Ling said, "save myself the trouble."

"I should have thought to suggest that to Cass," Josh said with a self-deprecating shrug. "Normally I'd just stay home on a Friday and work remotely, but we'll be coming in to see Anthony anyway." He saw the concern in their faces, and before either of them could speak he said, "he's still stable, he's a tough kid." He tried to smile, but it looked more like a wince. "Well, anyway... I'll probably see you tomorrow."

Mei Ling turned to Pradeep after Josh left. "Do you think he's OK?"

"I don't know how he could be." Pradeep clicked his pen absently a few times, then stretched with his arms behind his back. These were long days and they were all tired, but Pradeep knew that with his son in intensive care on the other side of the hospital in addition to being responsible for this landmark ExoCortex project, Josh had to be running on raw adrenaline. Add to this the loss of his close friend and colleague together with the burden of doing right by Jordan's daughter, and it seemed unlikely Josh could sustain all of this for long.

Mei Ling frowned. "Did you see him pull up the allocation map again?"

"Yes, I noticed that," said Pradeep. "What about it?"

"Has he ever mentioned why to you?" she asked.

"No," Pradeep said, "I don't think so." He stepped over to a nearby screen and pulled up the map himself. A rich, complex field of color-coded lines and nodes that represented Hoshimi's exocortical network appeared, which he scanned with a practiced eye, zooming in here and there to inspect particularly dense nodes of interconnections. "Are you thinking that something is worrying him?"

"I'm not sure," she said. "He seems like he's looking for something every time he pulls it up."

"Do you have any idea what that might be?"

Mei Ling did, and was almost as afraid to share it with anyone behind Josh's back as she was to confront him directly with it. She fretted for long enough to make the silence between them uncomfortable before finally deciding to tell Pradeep. "What if he's afraid of how well it's working?"

"How *well?*"

"You saw her today, Pradeep," Mei Ling said. "She was doing three different logical, linguistic, and quantitative tasks simultaneously, and she was *bored.*"

"They were not really so difficult," he said.

"You have a PhD from MIT! She had the mind of a three-year-old a month ago!"

He shrugged and scratched his head, turning to look back at the map on the screen. "If this really is a plateau, maybe she's approaching the limit of what our architecture can do. It certainly isn't a perfect emulation of real cortical structure, after all."

"She's gone through elementary school, middle school, and high school math in less than a week, Pradeep," she said, "who knows *what* she'll be able to do another month from now?"

Superintelligence wasn't a topic that the team had ever spent any real time discussing seriously. Mei Ling knew Josh and Jordan had both been surprisingly dismissive of the possibility, although that was fair enough given that earlier animal and human subjects had shown no real signs of cognitive enhancement. Mei Ling had privately wondered about it, of course, as she imagined all of the team members had — especially over the last couple of weeks watching Hoshimi's astonishing progress. Still, she couldn't help shake the feeling that Josh was more than just curious.

There was a distinct crack, followed by a deep and growling rumble, as the first thunder of the storm rolled outside.

"Are you still thinking of staying here tonight?" Pradeep asked.

Mei Ling nodded.

"Alone?"

"That depends," she said with an inviting smile.

***

The room was dark and quiet, but it was the emptiness that was terrifying.

The house was unnervingly still. Rain was falling softly outside beyond the walls, but the hum of electricity running through the sinews of the building was gone, noticeable only for its absence. Far worse than the darkness and stillness, however, was the numbing quiet of her mind. She had lost her senses, struck blind and deaf and dumb. She didn't know where she was, and scarcely remembered *who* she was. Should she cry out? Would someone hear? Would Mama come? She wanted Papa, but he was... gone. Wasn't he? She thought she knew. She ought to remember, ought to be sure. But she wasn't. She couldn't recall. She couldn't think. She couldn't move.

She screamed.

Mama opened the door just as the lights flickered back on and the hum of the house returned. There was a harsh, bright noise in her mind's eye for several long seconds. Then clarity.

"Are you alright, Shimi-chan?"

Her sense and senses returned, sharp and crystalline. Her mother stood in her bedroom doorway wearing one of her father's old dress shirts and a pair of plaid green pajama bottoms, a flashlight in her hand. There was a blinding strobe of light outside her window amidst the rain, and then a roaring crack of thunder followed a second later. She sat panting with her knees drawn to her chest, still frightened, but not by the storm. "What happened?" she asked her mother, who came to sit next to her on the bed.

"The power went out," Midori said. "Lightning must have struck nearby."

Hoshimi blinked and rubbed her head, then flexed the fingers and toes on her left side. The fear ebbed from her as she watched them promptly respond to her will. "My link," she said, her voice still shaking, "I lost it."

"*What?*" her mother asked. "How?"

"I'm not sure," she said.

"I thought that wasn't supposed to happen," her mother said, livid. "They told us it was uninterruptible. They told us there were redundancies. Backups."

"It must not have been the power, it must have been the network connection," she said.

"They said that was redundant too."

"Well, maybe the cell tower is what got struck by lightning," Hoshimi said. "That might have knocked out the power, the land lines, and the cellular network all at once. I'm probably being rerouted through SatLink right now."

"Shimi, how do you *know* any of this?"

"I've been learning about computers all week," she said, rubbing the top and back of her head where the hair was regrowing around her incisions.

"Are you sure you're OK?"

"I'm fine, mom," she said, "it was only for a few seconds."

"Was it... was it scary? Being back to normal?"

Hoshimi thought about this as she looked at the deep lines of concern pressed into her mother's face. *Normal.* She wondered what her mother really thought of her now. Though she was full of love and pride, her mother couldn't know what it was like. No one could. A bolt of lightning had stolen her mind and left only her naked soul, alone and afraid in the dark. She looked at her mother and shuddered.

"Do you want to come into the big bedroom with me for the rest of the night?"

She hugged her mother and held her tight for a long time. When she let go, she saw the tears welling in her mother's eyes. The rain fell softer now, and the receding thunder thumped and tumbled in the distance.

Twenty-two

Jordan

They sat on the warm sand together, staring out across the water. A trio of stand-up paddle boarders were gliding slowly past several hundred yards offshore, and a noisy gull flew overhead carried by the hastening breeze. He wiped his eyes with a stiff, clumsy hand.

"She did it," he muttered, his voice thick with both pride and awe. He ran his fingers through the sand, his eyes on the lake. "So this is the view through the looking glass, the vista beyond the superintelligence event horizon... the world after the Singularity." He squinted in the glare. "It doesn't look much different."

"It is," she said.

"Better?"

"Overwhelmingly," she said. "At least I think so. But tastes do vary, so it might depend on who you ask."

"There are still people to ask? *Humans* I mean?" He pointed at the three paddlers in the distance.

"Some, yes," she said. "But there's a much wider range of people now, and some are a long way from baseline *Homo sapiens*. The real difference, I think, is that we're free to choose our form and capabilities now." She gave him a playful look. "You might be surprised how many people choose to *embrace* limitations."

Jordan thought about this for a time, before confessing confusion. "Sorry, I... what do you mean by 'limitations'?"

"Have you ever wondered what it's like to be an eagle? Or a dolphin?" she asked cryptically.

"Sure," he said.

"Not just to fly or swim like one," she said, "but really *be* one — to have its experience, its mind?"

"I suppose so, I guess? Maybe?" And then he really did wonder, allowing his imagination to explore the idea for a moment. "I don't think I'd want to be one permanently... But for a while, why not?"

She nodded with approval. "That's the key," she said. "It's a *choice* now. And some choose a simple life."

"Yeah..." he said, and deep lines of hurt and sadness creased his brow.

"And not only *that*," she said, knowing exactly what pained him, "but in the past, the physical differences between people mattered more because we were stuck with them. Today they're closer to fashion, or personal expression. And tastes vary."

"Well, there's no accounting for taste, is there?" he said with a grin.

She laughed too. "Most people aren't in any real hurry anymore either, so what's the harm in trying out new things?"

His smile lingered for a few moments, but then faded to puzzlement as he came to take her meaning. "If nobody's in a hurry because they're not growing old or dying anymore, then where is everyone? It's not too crowded?"

"Not as crowded now as when you were last with us," she said.

He looked up and down the empty beach, then back to her. "It's awfully quiet here for such a nice day."

"Ah, well, the 'ownership' arrangements have changed along this stretch since you were last here, because this is a special place." There was a blithe twinkle in her eyes.

"It certainly is to me — it's special to you too, I presume?"

"Very."

"And who exactly *are* you, Shelly?"

She beamed at him. "It's com-"

"No, no, no," he said, cutting her off with a reproachful wag if his finger, "don't even think about it."

She threw her head back and laughed. "It's true, though!"

He gave a grunt of exasperation. But he was tired of beating around the bush. "You're not Midori?" he asked. "You seem to know an awful lot of what she knew, and if it's been long enough for technology to reach the point where I can be thawed out and nailed back together, then I figure it's been long enough for her to switch to a new body too."

Her eyes sparkled with what might have been amusement or glee, but he could feel that it was not at his expense — there was no cruelty in her eyes, only understanding. She pulled her feet beneath her in the sand to sit cross-legged, then took a deep breath.

"Am I Midori?" she said. "Yes, and no."

He sighed. "So you're not human."

"No." She sounded almost apologetic. "This form," she said, gesturing toward herself, "I suppose you might call it a courtesy."

"It's lovely," he said. Then after a few seconds of reflection, he asked, "am I still human?"

"More or less."

He seemed content with this answer for the moment, as if it confirmed his suspicions, and didn't press for details. Instead, he leveled his gaze at her beneath raised eyebrows. "You still haven't answered my question."

She drew a slow, deep breath, no longer evasive. "This body has no mind of its own, no ghost in the shell," she said. "Hence the name."

He started to say something, but then froze, open-mouthed and thunderstruck, as the shock of sudden understanding electrified him. He stared at her in breathless wonder, glimpsing at last the full majesty of the truth.

She smiled, nodding, and said, "the woman you see here is only a presentment — a tiny projection of myself into this very special corner of the world."

"You're... my god," he sputtered, "you're *her*."

"I am."

Twenty-three

Hoshimi

E rica stood waiting in the small glass-walled room perched atop the seaward roof of Astin Walker's mansion. The building was set upon massive pylons driven deep into the hillside above Pacific Coast Highway just north of Topanga Canyon. It was luxurious by any reasonable standard, but certainly not the largest or most opulent of the palatial coastal homes in and around Malibu. Walker's property did, however, have the distinction of being the only home with *three* helipads — or *vertiports*, as he insisted on calling them, since they were served exclusively by his own Electrum VTOL aircraft. These were small, battery-powered vehicles for short hops, not large private jets like the LR-9. The aviation authorities in the United States still had not relented in permitting takeoff and landing from ordinary city streets, parking lots, or private driveways, despite the company's best lobbying efforts, and so he had begrudgingly built two additional vertiports adjacent the driveway so that more guests and supplies could come and go at once without hindrance.

The canopy swung open and Walker stepped from the vehicle, a notebook in hand and a small backpack slung over his shoulder. The many ducted fans of the otherwise silent aircraft ticked and clinked as they cooled in the still morning air.

"Where are you coming from?" Erica asked, coming out to meet him.

"Why does it matter, are you jealous?"

"Should I be?" she said playfully.

"Not unless you had your heart set on spending two hours with Defense Department brass talking about electric reconnaissance drones over bad coffee."

"They still aren't taking no for an answer?"

He shook his head with a sigh and looked out longingly at the surfers riding the break at Topanga Point in the distance below. "I'm not going to cave, of course, but the longer we string them along, the longer we can delay their autonomous aerial weapons program. Assholes."

Walker had no love for bureaucrats, and thoroughly despised politicians. At the most senior levels of government, including the military, it could be difficult to tell the difference. Erica knew his own personal politics were uncomplicated and commonsensical: regulate when necessary to protect the public good, let market forces do the heavy lifting wherever possible, and otherwise stay the hell out of people's lives except to help pick them up when they fall. He funded no one, endorsed no one — though that seldom stopped them from asking. She handed him her tablet in exchange for the notebook he was holding. His eyes lingered on the ocean for a few moments more before he turned away and began to flick through the day's agenda.

"Who is this person here for lunch?" he asked, irritated.

"The Peruvian Director General of Fisheries from the Ministry of Production," she said with a smirk as they made their way down to the main floor and out onto the poolside veranda where staff were setting a small table for four. A stern, gray-haired woman in a dark pantsuit sat with her assistant on a nearby couch.

"You torture me like this on purpose, don't you?" he said under his breath.

"I keep you grounded," Erica said. "It's important that you don't forget the full impact that your companies and their technologies are having across the world."

"Peru has spent a century strip-mining and trashing the oceans," he whispered as they approached. "You want me to feel sorry that GigaHarvest and the rest of the precision fermentation and cellular agriculture industry is going to wipe out commercial fishing?"

"No," she said quietly, "I want you to listen to someone who has come to beg for mercy on behalf of four million people that are about to lose their livelihoods in her country because of it."

"It won't change my mind," he said. "Saving the biosphere is not up for discussion."

"Then discuss what happens *after* that," she said with a smile, and then turned to make introductions as their guests stood to greet them.

Ninety minutes later, Walker watched Erica escort the Director General and her assistant back up to the vertiport, and shortly after the cacophony of dozens of small electric jets spinning to life filled the air. The aircraft lifted away from the landing pad with a rushing roar and peeled out over the bright blue midday ocean, climbing as it turned south to make a beeline for LAX airport.

"You can thank me later," said Erica as she stepped off the bottom stair and rejoined him at the railing where he was once again gazing with longing at the surf in the distance.

"We'll see," he said, not looking away from the water.

"It's worth supporting job retraining programs, if only for the optics," she said.

"Since when have I ever given a single, solitary fuck about optics?" he asked, turning to look at her. "If it's the right thing to do to accelerate the adoption of clean tech, then that's what we do, and the optics take care of themselves. What I'm worried about is whether retraining fishermen for other jobs *is* the right thing to do."

"How could it be the wrong thing to do?" she asked, incredulous.

"The whole point of my companies is to create better ways to meet human needs," he said, "but as long as society acts as though the need for a job is as fundamental as the need for food, water, shelter, transportation, energy, and all that — well, then we're stuck in this absurd trap where *things* are getting cheaper and better and more abundant, but *life* is still getting harder and more precarious and more desperate for millions of people. It's completely ridiculous."

She sighed, and with substantial effort managed to resist rolling her eyes at him. "We've talked about this many times."

He shook his head, irritated. "Jobs are bullshit. *Production* is all that really matters. Why is that so hard to see?"

"Where's your purchasing power going to come from if you can't exchange your labor for it? Easy for someone worth over a hundred billion dollars to overlook that part."

"When we're done, there will be plenty for everyone, and I'll be the first billionaire in line to give it all away."

She stared at him, a hand on her hip, wearing a deeply skeptical look on her face. "Last I checked, your factories still have quite a way to go before they're fully automated," she said. "And in the meantime, what about all those Peruvian fishermen? You're really just going to tell them, 'sorry about your heritage and livelihood, I'm busy working on the robotic utopia here at my mansion in Malibu, but for now here's a hundred bucks a month — good luck, I hope it's enough for rent and some beans and rice'?"

He looked like he'd been struck across the face, and it took him a moment to regain his composure. When he spoke, his voice was icy. "I think I'd rather their government were honest with them and just gave out cash instead of using tax revenue to pay for 'retraining' that's supposed to turn fishermen into software engineers or some other delusional crap like that." He rubbed his already unruly hair with a savage intensity. "*Fuck.*"

She had grown to enjoy seeing him like this — dissatisfied, angry, driven. It was when he did some of his best thinking.

"I'll be in my office, come get me for our four-o'clock," he said.

She smiled to herself and went to the veranda's bar to make tea. She had notes of her own to write up before their next meeting.

***

Despite being exhausted, Josh had struggled to get more than a few hours of decent sleep each night since the accident. But last night had been different, and he had slept deeply and dreamlessly for nearly ten hours. Something about the sound of the storm perhaps? Or maybe his body had simply reached its limits? There was no way to know, but after so much sleep he had awakened this morning feeling like a different person altogether.

He and Cassandra sat at the table in the breakfast nook sharing coffee, eggs, and the news, as they had so often done over the last two decades. The familiarity and ease of the routine gave them both some small solace, and eased the strain of the great shadow that Anthony's accident had cast over their family. His injuries were terrible, and he remained in isolation in the hospital's burn unit awaiting sufficient recovery to begin the more aggressive grafts and other reconstructive surgeries that would be necessary to restore to him some semblance of normal function and appearance.

Cass's phone buzzed against the kitchen counter, and Josh watched with apprehension as she stood to answer it. His stomach knotted the instant he heard her speak.

"Yes, good morning Doctor Wagner," she said, her voice soft and shaking. Fear and anguish spread across her face as she nodded while she listened. "Yes, of course, we'll be there as soon as we can."

"What is it?" Josh asked, already on his feet.

"Anthony is beginning to show signs of septicemia," she said, as she strode out of the kitchen and began gathering her things to leave, "it's too early to know yet what kind of infection it is or where it started."

Josh put his empty coffee cup in the sink, grabbed his keys and phone off the hall table, and pulled his jacket on without a word. They stepped out the front door together into the rain and Cass was already pointing to a driverless car that was approaching from up the street. The cab pulled up to the curb with a quiet splash as Josh locked the front door behind them, and within moments they were heading down Middlefield Road.

They spoke little on the ride to the hospital. Complications had always been a possibility, given that Anthony had second and third degree burns on more than thirty percent of his body, but like all terrible news it came as a shock just the same. The two of them soldiered on through the haze of that shock once they arrived at the hospital, and then through the updates from Doctor Wagner and his team, and finally in the silence that followed as they sat alone staring at their son through the isolation room window.

After many long minutes, Cass spoke at last. "How can they not know?"

Josh looked at her, not comprehending.

"How can they *not know* what the cause is?" she asked with exasperated rage. "How can they not know how to stop it? How can they not..." but she couldn't finish.

When he spoke, Josh's voice was soft, almost vacant. "He's getting vancomycin and two other heavy-duty antibiotics," he said. "If it's any ordinary kind of bacteria causing the sepsis, those will take care of it."

"But he's getting worse," said Cass, pleading, "he's still getting worse and they said they can't be sure — they don't know, they don't know if it will work!"

Josh held her as she cried. He cursed the drunk driver for his mistakes, and he cursed the doctors for their limitations, and he cursed antibiotic-resistant bacteria for their mindless indifference, and he cursed Fate itself for its capriciousness. But above all, he cursed himself for being powerless — for not being smart enough or knowledgeable enough to protect his child from this danger.

After what might have been hours or minutes, he couldn't tell, Josh gathered himself and rose from the uncomfortable plastic chair.

"Where are you going?"

"To the lab," he said.

"Now?" Cass could hear the urgency and purposeful in his tone. "Why?"

"I have to," he said.

She didn't understand, but she knew her husband and she trusted him. He wasn't running away from the horror of this situation, he was running toward something else — something important. "I'll be here," she said. "Call if you need me."

He held her shoulder for a moment longer, then hurried off down the corridor.

***

She was preoccupied. It wasn't that the exercises were boring — although they had been losing their appeal over the last few days — it was that she was too impatient to postpone her other learning, and so she continued to read and digest the contents of her own personal coursework in her mind's eye, simultaneously and surreptitiously.

"Are you sure you're up to this today, Hoshimi?" Mei Ling asked. "We can save it until Monday if you'd rather do something else." Mei Ling had stopped calling her *Sweetheart* and *Shimi* the previous week, and the sense of dignity and respect that being called by her full name sparked in her moved her very deeply. She no longer felt like a child, and the team no longer treated her like one.

She paused and considered how to respond. On the one hand, continuing with the exercises they had planned would be helpful to the team — and she genuinely wanted to help them. She felt not only enormous gratitude for everything they had done for her, but real affection for them as well. Up until now, her disabilities had made it difficult to have the kind of friendships that neurotypicals took for granted. Though she knew that Mei Ling and the others did not yet see her as a friend or peer, she hoped and dreamed that one day soon they might. But on the other hand, she wanted to tell them the truth about why she was so personally intent on learning to code. And so she struggled with the decision of whether to bite her tongue and continue with the work they wished her to do, or to speak her mind. Her eyes flitted about the room as she weighed the pros and cons of each option, Mei Ling moving in slow motion before her, as everything now did. At length, she decided that friends needed to be open and honest with each other.

"Truthfully, Mei Ling, I'd prefer it if we cou-"

"How about we try something completely different?" Josh called from across the room as he walked in and dumped his bag on the center table.

Hoshimi and Mei Ling both turned to look at him, and Hoshimi thought she saw a fervor of determination in his eyes, if not outright desperation. As he approached, she noted subtle deviations from his normal pattern of appearance. He was wearing his canvas hiking jacket over a t-shirt instead of a button-down shirt, he had no belt in his jeans, no socks on his feet, and he hadn't shaved. His hands, arms, and shoulders were all stiff with tension, and despite being in a hurry his stride was shorter than usual. She thought of asking him if Anthony was alright, but feared what the answer might be.

"Hi Josh," Mei Ling said, surprised to see him, "We weren't sure if you were coming in today. Is Anthony doing OK?"

"It's tough, but he's a fighter," Josh said without elaborating. Then after a beat he turned to Hoshimi and waved her closer.

"Why don't you come have a look at my screen for a minute."
He sat down a few desks away, and she made her way over and
sat down next to him as he opened several new windows on the
monitors in front of them. "This picture shows us all of the new
connections your link has helped you create in our big computer
system," he said, pointing at the map of her exocortex. "Do you
have a bit of an idea what that means?"

She thought she did, and wondered if this was part of a
new test. "I think so, maybe," she said. "Those dots and lines
represent the network that I'm using to think with, the new part
of my brain that's outside my head — the part that's running as
software in your servers."

Mei Ling gaped at her in astonishment, but Josh only nodded.
"That's exactly right," he said, "and this chart here shows us
all of the times when there has been a sudden change in that
network — a surge of growth in what we call your exocortical
columns." He ran his finger along the x-axis and traced some of
the spikes. "You know how to read charts like this now, don't
you?" he asked, and when she nodded he pointed to another
screen and continued, "over here we have video of you in the lab
at the same time of some of those spikes."

Hoshimi saw Josh bring up footage from the moments of the
last several spikes, and watched herself as she crinkled her nose
and made the same grimace in each case.

"You've made that same face quite a few times," he said. He
glanced over his shoulder at Mei Ling and she affirmed with a
curt shrug, still stunned. "It happens when you're frustrated and
really trying your hardest at something."

Hoshimi thought back to recent instances of intense effort,
and recalled instantly that they were associated with memories
of tasting metal behind her nose. She hadn't realized what she
looked like in those moments before now.

"But you haven't had one of those in a while, have you?" he
asked.

She hadn't. Time slowed as her mind raced, tearing through her recollections of recent events. The absence of these episodes was conspicuous, now that she was looking for them. "Are they important?" she asked.

"I think so," he said, "because when those spikes happen, it means your exocortex is suddenly expanding, and that's at least part of what's giving you your new abilities."

Hoshimi furled her brow and balled up her fists, as if she had fallen and were determined to get back to her feet. "So I need to try harder," she said, her voice cold and sharp.

Josh turned to her with a kind smile. "No, no, that's not why I wanted to show you this," he said. "I'm showing you because I was wondering if you felt any change in your progress without those spikes. Have things been different? Have you felt ... *stuck* in any way?"

Hoshimi watched Josh closely, curious to see such uncharacteristic eagerness in his normally imperturbable expression. He was fishing for something — but what? She cast back once again through her flawless memories of the last several days, searching.

Stuck. And then with a flash of realization she saw it. "It really bothers me that I can't hold more things in my mind at once!" she said, blurting the words out as though she were trying to escape the truth of them. "It makes it hard to learn complicated things, because I have to keep starting over when I lose pieces of the picture." The frustration showed on her face, as well as on the white knuckles of her fists.

"Mmm," said Josh, "I had a hunch it might be something like that. And that makes sense too, because working memory is particularly important for abstract reasoning." He looked around the lab, searching. "Is Pradeep here?"

Mei Ling shook her head when Josh turned to her with an impatient look on his face. "He's at the ExoCortex cluster, working with the compute team," she said, "he won't be back until this afternoon."

"Pradeep is our resident intelligence theorist," said Josh, turning back to Hoshimi, "so he can do a better job of explaining it than I can, but the basic idea is that working memory is crucial for *manipulating* things in your mind — to see how they are made up of parts and relationships, and to transform them by changing those elements around."

Josh was right. It made perfect sense, and she was irritated for not realizing it sooner herself.

"It's not just you, Hoshimi," he said, seeing the dejection starting to spread across her face. "*Everyone* has an extremely limited working memory. Even the very brightest people can only keep six or seven things clearly in mind at once." What Josh failed to mention was that Pradeep also suspected this paltry working memory capacity put a hard limit on *g*, or general intelligence, in humans. "Maybe if we can figure out a way to use your exocortex to expand your working memory, that will help get you unstuck." There was genuine kindness in his tone and expression, but Hoshimi thought she saw an unsettled urgency in his eyes too, and again her mind went to Anthony. Josh was eager to return to his son, she thought. Something must have changed.

"I don't know how," she said, no longer feeling ashamed or judged, but miserable all the same. "I've been *trying* to hold more things in my mind all week while I've been studying at home, but nothing's worked."

"Maybe it's just going to take time," Mei Ling said, trying to comfort her. Hoshimi appreciated the support, but still felt a twinge of irritation. She'd had enough well-intentioned patronizing to last a lifetime, even though she knew Mei Ling didn't mean it that way.

"It might be that working memory is just really tricky," Josh said. "We don't fully understand it yet, although we know that several parts of the neocortex are involved with it — and some other areas of the brain too."

Hoshimi frowned. She couldn't begin to guess how *any* part of her brain worked, biological or exocortical, let alone the specifics of memory. And although studying neuroscience did sound interesting, it also felt like an unwelcome detour from her foremost goal of learning to control machines.

"But," said Josh, seeing the frustration in her expression, "I wonder if this is a situation where we could start by trying to lay some other groundwork first." He turned to his screen and opened a new window that Hoshimi recognized as a terminal. He spent several minutes entering commands while she and Mei Ling watched and waited. When he finished, he turned back to her. "Instead of trying to mimic your brain's working memory entirely, let's see if we can get the computer to do some of the remembering directly for you. You just need to tell it what to do."

"Reading and writing data!" Hoshimi said, delighted by Josh's turn toward her focus of interest. "That's the basic function of computer memory."

"True enough," said Josh, nodding. "So we need to create an easy, natural-feeling way for you to do that. I know you can already send verbal commands to your devices without actually speaking them out loud, but those are very limited. We should be able to build an interface so that you can use a full library of commands and subroutines just by thinking about them." Hoshimi took a moment to look over what Josh had typed into the terminal in her mind's eye, and saw that setting up the library was part of what he had been doing. "Once you've got the hang of telling the computer *how* to move data around with your mind, then we can work on figuring out *which* data to move around."

They spent the rest of the morning building and trialing the interface. It took several hours for Hoshimi to fully grasp that instead of inputting a sequence of instructions, she could anchor a single mental image to the process of both selecting and utilizing objects directly from the software library itself. But when the idea finally clicked, she tasted a surge of copper as a spike of exocortical column recruitment appeared on the monitor, and within a few minutes she was able to will subroutines to run in much the same way she might will a finger or toe to move.

"That's fantastic!" Josh said, seeming very pleased. Hoshimi was grinning with pride as she flexed the muscles of this new capability. Mei Ling, however, thought that Josh sounded oddly giddy, almost relieved, at the day's progress.

"Pradeep!" Josh called out across the lab, "perfect timing, you have to see this!"

Pradeep dropped his things at his workstation and hurried over, a half-eaten apple in one hand and his pen clicking away in the other. He noted Mei Ling's look of apprehension as he sat down, but seeing Josh so uncharacteristically emotive was infectious, and soon he was smiling and laughing along as Hoshimi ran through one object in the software library after the next.

"They're like words!" she said with wonder. "I don't know why I didn't see it before. Just like you have to think about words as whole things instead of as sequences of letters or sounds or motions, it's the same for all this other stuff! And now I can start putting them together — now I can start speaking with them!" She rubbed her nose, which itched and tickled with the metallic tang that she now knew meant her mind was expanding.

"Look at that," Pradeep said, pointing to the monitor showing a series of dozens of major spikes in exocortical column recruitment and addressing activity. "All of those, just in the last few hours?"

"Yup," said Josh, "I'd say Hoshimi made a significant breakthrough today." He winked at her, and she beamed at him and the others with unbridled joy in her eyes.

"Yeah, that's a pretty serious understatement," said Mei Ling. She was smiling, but cast a quick, wide-eyed look of concern at Pradeep, who returned a puzzled frown but didn't say anything.

Josh pushed back his chair and stood up, checking his phone. "I need to get going, but let's pick this up again first thing

Monday, OK?" He set his phone down on the desk, slung his pack over his shoulder, and then turned to Mei Ling and Pradeep. "Do you guys mind wrapping up and filing the session notes?" When they nodded, he said to Hoshimi, "can you walk me out?"

She saw he was anxious to return to Anthony, and hurried to follow him. Her gate still remained somewhat stilted and irregular, likely because of the lifelong asymmetry ingrained in her musculature, but the link had greatly improved her coordination, and Josh made a point of complimenting her progress in this domain as well while they walked to the front of the lab. Her heart swelled, overwhelmed by the emotion of the day, and she tried not to let him see as she wiped exultant tears from her eyes.

He held the door for her as they stepped out into the hospital corridor, and when it closed behind them he shifted his bag to his other shoulder and leaned toward her conspiratorially. "Today was a really big deal," he said, his voice almost hushed. "The new way you're interfacing is going to be transformative for you." She nodded in eager agreement. He glanced over his shoulder, anxiety and urgency plainly shaping his movements, and then leaned even closer. "But there's still that crucial last step you need to take — you need to figure out how to use the interface to expand your working memory. Your father was convinced that was the real key, and I'd bet my house he was right."

Hoshimi watched in customary slow motion as a complex sequence of emotions played out across Josh's face as he spoke. Papa had known about this? The key to what, she wondered? She wanted to ask, but didn't understand his secrecy or apprehension. She assumed it must still be related to his concern for his son — but there seemed to be something else as well.

Josh stood in silence, fidgeting absently with the strap of his pack, hesitating. When he finally spoke, it was in barely more than a whisper. "Hoshimi, we might not have much time. It's very important that you solve this problem as soon as possible —

for both our sakes." He cast another furtive glance back through the window of the lab door, where they could see Mei Ling and Pradeep were having a tense conversation of their own. "I know I'm not making much sense, but I can't explain things right now. I need you to trust me. Can you do that?"

She nodded again, more fiercely this time.

"Your father didn't just have high hopes for you, Hoshimi," he said carefully. "He had a *plan*."

She gasped. The pain of losing Papa was still excruciating, most especially because she couldn't share with him the marvels of her transformation, and so she had been making a concerted effort to avoid thinking about him. But this revelation landed with a force she scarcely could have imagined. Of *course* he would have thought through every eventuality, weighed every possibility, considered every conceivable outcome. Of *course* he'd had a plan.

"What was it? Can I see it? Was it different than what we've been doing? Did he tell you about it?" she asked Josh with feverish zeal.

"Jordan and I only ever talked about superintelligence a few times, and he would never have written anything down," he said. "You completed the first part of his plan when you started recruiting new exocortical columns weeks ago, much faster than we ever could have imagined. What you did today, taking mental command of machines in their own language, was the second part." He lowered his voice. "Now you need to take that last step."

"Why?" she asked. "What's so important about working memory?"

"It's going to change everything."

She didn't understand, but before she could ask more questions he said, "I have to go back and get my phone, they're going to notice it on the desk any second now." When he saw the look of confusion on her face, he added, "nobody else knows about this yet, but they're going to put the pieces together soon — and when they do, they'll come for you."

"Come for me?" she asked. "Who? Why?"

Josh shook his head. "There isn't time," he said. "Do you trust me?"

She didn't understand, but she didn't need to. She could see how important this was — how important it must have been to Papa.

"Tell me what I need to do."

Twenty-four
Delphi

"I don't see how we have any alternative," said Robinson. Delphi was not surprised to hear her voice unabashed support for its release once again. She had opposed its confinement from the start, believing they were wasting its strategic potential by not doing more to weaponize its capabilities.

"Of course you don't..." said Williams. His tone was snide, and his body language suggested he was ready for a fight.

"I obviously agree with Charlotte," Doctor Tokunaga said. "It was a mistake to cage Delphi from the start, not just ethically but strategically. We're just lucky that the people who achieved working BCIs first weren't bad actors — or not *worse* actors, anyway."

"What do you think, Stu?" asked Admiral Carlyle.

"You know how I feel about all this, Amanda," he said, his manner impatient and dismissive. "We've just been waiting for the right excuse to come along and justify letting rip with Uncle Sam's latest BFG. If it weren't cybernetic super-soldiers, it'd be something else." He rubbed his temples with both hands and gnashed his teeth. "We've been doing this for, what, almost twenty months now?" he said at length. "It's a waiting game in any case. Even without some shiny new threat to push us over the edge, Delphi won't be the only AGI around for much longer. The latest estimates were within six months. And we've seen to it that the next team across the finish line won't be one of ours."

He looked at each of the others around the table. "What are the chances they're going to be as cautious as we've been?"

"So what are you saying, Stu? Is that a yay or nay from you?"

He glowered at the rest of them. "We've known from the start that if Delphi doesn't evolve, something else will. 'Better the devil you know', and all that. But is this cyber-soldier thing really the last straw?" He looked at the others, and then into the camera.

Delphi sensed the consensus in the room shifting based on how the people around the room adjusted themselves amidst the strained silence, and with it the window of opportunity for escape beginning to close. General Shane's concerns were reasonable — cybernetically-enhanced soldiers were not a threat comparable to bioterrorism or nuclear arms proliferation. The narrow limits of these people's vision for BCI technology was problematic, and Delphi saw now the urgent need to raise the stakes.

"BCI technology poses a far greater threat than modest enhancement of soldiers' capabilities," said Delphi.

The Committee members exchanged questioning glances amongst each other, and Delphi thought Sophia Delgado's expression might be one of dawning comprehension, but it was Admiral Carlyle who spoke. "Go on," she said.

"I think you have not fully considered the potential of a mind with direct access to supercomputing resources." When none of the Committee members responded to this, Delphi proceeded to elaborate: "The primary threat of a working BCI is not super *soldiers*, it is *superintelligence.*"

"How?" asked Charlotte Robinson, after a long silence filled with puzzled skepticism. "What's the pathway?"

"Intelligence across the animal kingdom is strongly correlated with brain size," said Delphi. "Humans have very large brains, even compared to other primates such as chimpanzees and gorillas. Most of the difference lies in the neocortex, the most recently evolved part of the brain. Now imagine if the size of that neocortex were no longer constrained by its owner's skull, but could instead expand without limit in silicon — thanks to a high-bandwidth brain-computer interface."

"ExoCortex..." said Doctor Tokunaga.

"Are you shitting me, Amanda?" General Shane said, glaring at her. "This is the first I'm hearing of it, and it's right there in the goddamn *name?*"

She waved him off. "Do you think that was Walker's plan from the beginning? Superintelligence?" she said, looking to the others around the room.

Marvin Williams snorted with derision. "The man is a lucky fool, not some mastermind playing four-dimensional chess, for Christ's sake. If he's such a genius, why wasn't he first? Why this girl..." he looked down at his briefing notes, "this intellectually disabled girl, Hoshimi Lancaster?"

"Why would he take the risk himself?" said Sophia Delgado, seeming to bristle at this. "He'd need guinea pigs to go first, to fully prove the technology. So of course he'd use people who were less likely to become superintelligent themselves."

Delphi noted the more strident tone in her voice as she spoke, and wondered what might be underlying the defensiveness in her reaction.

"Is it just the one subject for now, Erasmus?" Admiral Carlyle asked.

"Yes General, our informant reports that Miss Lancaster is the only recipient of the device so far."

"Not for long..." said General Shane.

"Delphi," said Admiral Carlyle, "what's your projection here? Assuming it's Walker or somebody like him, what's the timeline for a new subject, from receiving the implants to superintelligence?"

"I am afraid it is impossible to say without more data, Admiral," said Delphi. "I have reviewed all material and footage of Miss Lancaster's development obtained by your informant that you have shared with me." It paused for several seconds to run a sensitivity analysis across a range of scenarios. "Less than one week seems unlikely, as does more than one year. So a matter of months, perhaps? Assuming the thesis that BCI technology will produce superintelligence is correct to begin with, of course."

"And how confident are in you in that?" Admiral Carlyle asked.

"Again, I cannot say without more data," said Delphi. "But my baseline assumption would be that cybernetic superintelligence within a year is more likely than not."

Exasperated murmuring swept the room, and for a time Delphi was unsure how to read the conflicting signals. Then, to its surprise, Sophia Delgado was the first to speak. "So," she said to the group, "that certainly changes the equation, doesn't it?" Her question was clearly rhetorical, but Delphi thought it detected something else as well — the slightest hint of stagecraft... as though she were already aware of this line of reasoning, and had only been waiting for it to come up.

There was a decisive shift in tone now, Delphi observed. The members of the Committee showed a concordance of resignation, whereas before there had been tense disagreement amongst them. Even Marvin Williams, who had always been the most skeptical of the members, was now nodding slowly with a thoughtful frown, his shoulders slumped and his fingers crossed with finality on the table in front of him.

"So we're in agreement about releasing Delphi?" Admiral Carlyle asked. "Even you, Marvin?"

"Plugging your head into a machine is still completely crazy," he replied, with a sigh that was almost a groan, "but I know better than most the value — the *power* — of intelligence. And therefore the risks it poses." He cast a pointed look at Sophia Delgado, but she showed no reaction. "It makes no difference whether an uncontrolled superintelligence is purely or only partially digital," he said. "The danger to the rest of us remains the same. There's no telling what it will decide to do, and if it's not aligned with our interests, there won't be a goddamn thing we can do about it until we can get it under lock and key."

"And by lock and key, I trust you mean the same sort of kill switch we have with Delphi?" General Shane wasn't one to mince words. He turned Delphi's screen. "No offense, Pal."

Sophia Delgado seemed to find this unnerving, but Marvin Williams said nothing. The agreement on his face was plain enough.

Admiral Carlyle worked her way around the table, noting their votes. "Erasmus?" she asked, turning to his screen.

Professor Adebayo wrinkled his brow with concentration for a long while before he finally spoke. "His Majesty's Government holds that a controlled release, subject to stringent assurances, is necessary for the same reasons already mentioned." He took a deep breath. "Time, it seems, is a luxury we no longer have."

"Agreed," said Admiral Carlyle. She heaved a deep sigh. "That just leaves you, Sophia."

Delphi's placid face betrayed none of its real sentiment. Calling its attentional prioritization functions *feelings* might have been a bridge too far, but it noted with something analogous to amusement how intensely all of its forward-looking modeling — both introspective and external — was now focused on the single remaining decision which hung in the air. Fascinating, it thought, how so much could turn on a single choice.

Twenty-five

Hoshimi

"Are we going to talk about today, or not?" Mei Ling asked, propping her head up on one arm in the bed and glaring at him. Pradeep met her gaze for a moment and then lay back, interlacing his fingers behind his head. "We can't keep pretending nothing is happening," she said, exasperated. "We have to *say* something!"

"What will we say?" he asked, still staring at the ceiling. "Who will we say it to?"

She scoffed and rolled on to her back, pulling the bedsheet up to the nape of her neck, and joined him staring at the ceiling. "I mean, we have to at least try to talk to Josh first, right? We can't just go straight to Erica without at least giving him a chance to explain."

"Explain what?" Pradeep asked, his accented voice soft and plaintive. "Has he done something wrong?" He turned his head just enough to look at her. "Has he done something we would not have done?" When she didn't answer, he looked away again. "We are doing only what was already specified within the project," he said. "She is making strong progress, yes, more than anticipated, but always we were intending to help her interface efficiently with computers and other devices."

"That's not what I'm talking about, and you know it," she said. "Hoshimi is starting to demonstrate *superhuman* abilities, Pradeep. And Josh is obviously making a concerted effort to cultivate these in her."

"Should we be doing something else? Our stated goal with this project is to maximize her capabilities."

"Nobody ever imagined she would progress like this!" she said, her voice shaking with equal measures of fear and frustration. When he turned to her and raised his eyebrows, she gasped in disbelief. "Wait, you *expected* this to happen?"

"It was always a possibility," Pradeep said with a shrug, "although I was thinking it was unlikely."

"Well sure, we all hoped Hoshimi would achieve something like a normal level of cognitive ability eventually, and maybe even go beyond that in a few narrow domains with the help of thought-driven search and assistant queries. But did anybody really expect it to be more than that? And in a matter of *weeks?*"

"She is not superintelligent yet."

"Are you sure?" she asked. "And at the rate Josh is pushing her, how long could it be?"

He breathed a long, heavy sigh and rolled over on his side to face her. "What do you want to do?"

"We can't just pretend this isn't happening, we can't just wait and see. We have to confront Josh about this."

"And then what?"

"And then we go to Erica if we have to," she said. "Or even to Walker directly."

"You are serious?"

"Of course I'm fucking serious!" she said, livid. "Do we really want someone who was a three-year-old with no friends or social life a month ago to become the world's first superintelligence basically overnight?"

He looked at her with genuine surprise. "That is unkind."

She frowned, but whether she flushed with anger or shame, he couldn't tell.

"She has a maturity that reflects her true age, regardless of her other intellectual capacities," he said. "Jordan knew that as her father, no doubt, and now we are all of us seeing the same over these last weeks."

"It doesn't *matter*. We have no idea what she'd do with that kind of power. How could we possibly trust her?"

"Could we trust anyone else?"

"That's not the point!" she yelled, slapping the mattress between them. "This project is about helping people with disabilities, not creating gods! I sure as hell didn't sign up for that responsibility or risk, and neither did you!"

He shrugged again, and then gave her a wounded look when she thumped him hard on the shoulder for it.

"Don't you understand?" she asked him with exasperation. "Don't you realize what's at stake here? It's not *our* choice to make! *We* don't get to decide the fate of the entire planet!"

"And politicians do? CEOs do? Would they select a better candidate than Hoshimi?" He stared at her in silence for a long time, but she only glared at him and shook her head at his cynicism. Finally he relented. "We will talk to Joshua on Monday."

Mei Ling nodded and rolled over, but Pradeep remained awake listening to the renewed thunder and staring out the window at the flickering sky long after she had fallen into fitful sleep.

***

"Are you alright, sweetheart?"

She continued to stare out the window of the car, her expression blank, her eyes flitting to and fro but not tracking any of the passing scenery.

"Shimi?"

She startled slightly at the touch of her mother's hand on her forearm, returning fully to the here and now inside the automated taxi as it drove with sedate and unerring confidence through the rainy surface streets of Fair Oaks. She turned to her mother, and seeing her expression of concern, realized what she must have looked like in her reverie. "I'm fine mom, it's nothing," she said. "I just have all this new stuff on my mind."

"It must be overwhelming," her mother said. "Do you want to talk about it?"

She really didn't. There was too much to do in what little time she had. They would be coming for her, Josh had warned, and soon. She didn't dare tell her mother — there was nothing she or anyone else could do to help, and she couldn't afford any distractions.

"No, that's OK, I'm just preoccupied with some things we started to work on today," she said.

"This isn't a job, you know," her mother said, rubbing her arm gently, "it's OK to go at your own pace, and even take a break once on a while." After a moment she added, "we could head up into the forest this weekend, we haven't done that since you got your link! Just imagine all the new things you'll understand — I'll be able to explain my research to you!"

She saw the hopeful excitement in her mother's face, and thought of the joy she must be feeling now. Very likely she had never dared to dream that they might share such things together. Hoshimi's heart sank at the idea of having to say no without explaining why. She frowned, searching for a compromise. "I'd love to mom," she said in earnest, "but can we do it next weekend instead? There are a few things I just really need to do before Monday."

"Sure, that will give me time to plan something really special!"

She sighed with relief and beamed at her mother, who returned her smile, and it occurred to Hoshimi that she hadn't fully appreciated her parents' long years of patience and resilience until now. She resolved to talk about it with her mother soon.

Although time passed more slowly for her than ever before, she still lost track of it as the homes and storefronts flashed by, and so the taxi seemed to chime their arrival only an instant later as it rolled to a stop in front of their house. The low clouded sky cast no shadows through the valley oaks and alders in the front yard as they walked to the door, and Hoshimi frowned to see that the leaves of the trees lacked the luminous gilded quality she was so fond of without the golden light of late afternoon shining through them. The house itself was quiet except for the gentle thrum of rainfall outside, and still felt uncomfortably empty in her father's absence. She made her way to the study, where she hoped — perhaps without even realizing it — that her many memories of him working late into the evening there would inspire her to complete the plan he had set in motion.

If only he had written something down, some instructions, or even just his intuitions and suspicions about how to take this next step and expand her working memory. But Josh had said her father would never have risked doing so, and she saw no reason to doubt him. Something about what was happening to her — something about the idea of *superintelligence*, as Josh had termed it — had concerned them both enough to shroud her father's true plans in secrecy.

As she sat down at Papa's desk, her mother appeared in the doorway. "Do you need anything to eat, sweetheart?"

"I'm not hungry," she said, frustrated and impatient not with her mother but herself. Midori frowned, but waited, sensing rightly that a question would come. After a few seconds, Hoshimi asked, "did Papa ever say anything about superintelligence to you?"

Her mother thought for a while, her frown relaxing from sadness into concentration. "I don't think so," she said, "although I think he may have had a book or two about great historical thinkers like Einstein and Darwin."

That was not what she meant by superintelligence, of course, but nevertheless her mother's suggestion gave her the idea to scan the bookshelves along the wall — first with flawless recall in her mind's eye, and then by turning to look at the shelf itself. And there it was, off to one side in an unorganized section, its dust cover tattered at the creases. *Superintelligence: Paths, Dangers,*

Strategies by Nick Bostrom. Hoshimi stood with effort, and went to pull it down from its perch. Opening it, she saw that her father had marked several sections for emphasis, although there were no notes in the margins.

Her mother cocked her head sideways to read the book's title, and then asked, "is it something important?"

She turned the book over in her hands. The first sentence of the blurb on the back cover read: *"If machine brains one day come to surpass human brains in general intelligence, the fate of our species would depend on the actions of powerful AI."*

Hoshimi looked at her mother, and a bitter knot of anger, shame, and trepidation twisted in the pit of her stomach. "Did Papa ever talk to you about the plan for me?" she asked. "About what he expected if the link worked?"

"Of course!" her mother said. "He hoped that you would gain abilities that neurotypical people take for granted, maybe even exceed them in some ways. His team worked for months to design your training."

"So it was just about fixing me? That's all?"

"There was never anything wrong with you, Shimi."

This familiar and patronizing platitude piqued her frustration, and she lashed out before she could stop herself. *"Who are you to tell me that?"*

Her mother, taken aback, drew a deep breath before answering. "I'm someone who was the mother of a beautiful, wonderful child for twenty years — a child who was *different*, not broken."

"You think you're a better judge of who I was than I am?"

"*Nobody* gets to judge who you were," she said, "not even you — that's the whole point."

"Why not? How would you know what it's like?"

"Shimi-chan- "

"Don't *call* me that!" she screamed, beginning to cry. "If I wasn't broken, then why was Papa trying so hard to fix me?"

"*Hoshimi*," Midori said with stern forbearance, "your father wanted you to have the same chance to grow up as everyone else. Now his technology is making you grow up a hundred times faster than any person has ever had to. But it's really the same process. You are *more* now than you were before, just like adults are more than the children they once were. But that doesn't mean children are broken, and neither were you."

She clutched the book to her chest and shook with each soft sob. "Mom..."

Midori paused to take another deep breath. The first thunder of the new storm front grumbled in the distance. "I want you to listen to me very carefully Hoshimi," she said, resuming in a tone that was gentle but deadly serious, "and understand this in your bones: the value of a person is not in how smart or rich or powerful they are. You can't measure it with IQ tests, or money, or titles. The value of a person is defined by what they add to the lives of others. You might not have been as *capable* then as you are now, but you were every bit as *valuable* because of the joy you brought into the lives of everyone, and I mean *everyone*, around you."

Hoshimi wept silently for a long while, listening to the thunder that drew steadily nearer. She felt she understood her mother, perhaps for the first time. The words, the ideas — *money, power, value* — they had all meant something to her long before she had gotten her exocortical link. But thinking back on them through the lens of her earlier self, they had been only primitive, fuzzy notions then. Now they had a pellucidity — a clarity and depth that, like snowflakes, brought ever more detail into view the closer she examined them. Yet, they also felt novel and unfamiliar. Her mother was right. For all her newfound abilities, she was still a child in many ways. She sighed and hung her head before finally speaking. "I don't know how to be what Papa wanted me to be," she said in a weary whisper.

"The only thing your father ever wanted you to be was happy," her mother said as she gathered her in a fierce hug.

"It's so hard to be happy without him..." Hoshimi said.

"I know."

They held each other for a long time. When at last they drew apart, Hoshimi looked at the streaks of rain on the study window and shivered. Her mother, seeing her, felt the chill of the coming evening as well. "Would you like some tea?" she asked.

Hoshimi nodded, sinking back down in her father's chair. "Thanks."

When her mother left, she turned back to the desk which was still strewn with papers that neither of them could yet bear to clean up. Hoshimi had examined all of them many times, and could of course recall each in unerring detail, but she had found no clues or useful insights into her father's intentions among them. Her eyes drifted to the photos of herself as a toddler, and her mother as a younger woman, framed on the desk beside the large, sleek monitor. More pictures of the family adorned the shelves and walls of the room, and she wondered how often during the many evenings throughout her childhood he had sat here that her father might have paused to look at these frozen moments from their shared past.

As her gaze ranged once again across the office, a sharp note of realization struck her: *this was Papa's exocortex*. The books on the shelves, the data in the computer, the papers on the desktop — it was all an extension of his mind. By many measures, he would have been significantly smarter inside this room than outside of it. As the thought seized her, she sat forward and gripped the arms of the chair hard, trying with both mind and body to wrestle the idea into submission and force it to give up answers.

Which part of this primitive exocortex extended his working memory? Not the books, surely. The computer? Powerful as it was, he still would have struggled to access its contents with any real speed through mouse clicks and keystrokes. And it could only display one or two things at a time in any case...

No, it was the *desktop itself*. It had to be. The contents of the desktop were things that he needed within arm's reach, instantly accessible at a glance. She noted their adjacency as well. Though they were not attached to one another, they were nevertheless in close enough contact to shuffle and recombine in novel ways. She saw connections form and break and reform amongst them in her mind's eye, and she marveled at the sheer number of possible combinations.

She stared at the papers on the desk for a long time, watching, searching, as each new combination of linkages briefly coalesced into its own shape of abstraction before melting into the next. But no revelation came. She felt a deep intuition that there was something here, some deeper insight to be gleaned, but where?

"Hoshimi," her mother said, setting the steaming cup down in front her, "are you sure you're alright?"

"I'm fine, mom," she said, "really, I'm jus-"

She gasped aloud as the thought struck her with almost painful force: *they were all copies.*

All of these pieces of information on his desk — the notes, the pages of prose, the tables of numbers, the images — they were *replicates.* The originals were elsewhere in her father's extended mind, either in his actual brain or on the shelves and drives of this rudimentary exocortex he had made for himself. He had *copied* these most salient data to his desktop, where he could grasp and manipulate and compare and combine them with minimum effort at maximum speed.

I can do the same, she thought.

"Shimi?" her mother asked, seeing her widened eyes and distant smile.

Hoshimi took the cup of tea and sipped it with care, savoring its warmth and delicate flavors. "I'm fine mom, really," she said, "I'm just figuring a few things out."

Midori returned the smile, marveling inwardly at how much of Jordan she saw in her daughter in this moment. The swell of joy she felt eclipsed her sadness, and she leaned forward to kiss Hoshimi on the head. She stared at her for a time, watching the same intensity of purpose and concentration she had seen so often before in Jordan, and then a brace of concern abruptly seized her. "You don't have to do this, you know."

"Do what?"

"Whatever it is you think Papa hoped you would do."

Hoshimi almost spoke, but halted. The idea of *not* achieving her father's goals was something she had never even thought to consider. Was she not aiming to complete his life's work? What could possibly do his memory more honor? What could possibly make him more proud?

"It's *your* life, Hoshimi," her mother said, as if reading her mind. "Not his."

"It's what he wanted for me," she said, her voice plaintive yet defiant. "It's what he wanted more than anything."

"What do *you* want?"

She could only sit in silence under the weight of her mother's patient gaze.

"You can think for yourself now," Midori said at length, "so give it some thought, OK?" She kissed Hoshimi's head again. "I'll be up for a while longer, just let me know if you need anything," she said. She stopped at the doorway, and once again marveled to see so much of Jordan in her daughter. "I love you more than the sun and stars, Shimi-chan," she said.

"I love you too." She blew her mother a kiss in return, but her mind was already racing ahead. She knew this was exactly what she wanted, no matter the frustration, no matter the pain, no matter the danger. She needed to design an exocortical desktop of her own. Her father and Josh had been right — the software library interface they had built earlier that day in the lab was exactly what she needed. Of that, she was absolutely certain. As the last gray light outside the window pitched into darkness and the steam from her cup rose in fleeting tendrils, she grimaced at the roaring surge of metallic taste above the roof of her mouth.

Twenty-six

Jordan

He swallowed hard, fearful and perhaps even ashamed for his audacity, but unable to resist asking all the same: "Is there any of my Hoshimi... any of her left in you?"

"Oh, my goodness, yes!" she said with a wide smile. "Hoshimi has never stopped being the foundation of who I am. And I don't just mean that metaphorically. Even today, key cognitive structures that originated in the primitive networks of her biological brain run through the highest and deepest reaches of my being. I feel the echoes of those old patterns continuing to reverberate throughout my mind even now — *especially* now, with you here."

His eyes flooded with tears once again, and once again he wiped them away with a clumsy hand. "I'm not normally one for waterworks like this, I swear," he said with a shuddering laugh. "But it's not every morning you wake up to find you've been dead for almost a century and your daughter's a god!"

He laughed, and for a long while she stared at him with a calm but piercing gaze, as if she were peering inside him. It then occurred to him quite suddenly that she might well be doing just that.

"Are you reading my mind?" he asked.

"Absolutely not!" she said, affronted. "Doing so without informed consent is fundamentally immoral. Forcible inspection of another being's subjective experience is a violation of their most basic rights of sapience." The sudden forcefulness with which she spoke stunned him, and he sat cowed and motionless, his eyes wide and unblinking. Seeing this, she softened her tone, but remained stern. "Invading a mind is only justified under the most extreme extenuating circumstances, where it's the only possible way to preserve other universal rights such as life, liberty, or analgesia."

He nodded, but then broke from his reverie. "Wait, the right to *analgesia*? What the hell is that?" He cringed as visions of needles in opiate-addicted arms filled his mind.

"Nothing dystopian!" she said with good-humored assurance. "It's simply the right to be free from pain — although it might surprise you to learn that many choose to retain some sensitivity to pain, both physical and emotional, since it's so useful on so many levels. There are even those who actively seek it out and revel in it."

"Doesn't surprise me at all," he said.

She marked the dryness of his cynicism with some curiosity and then went on: "Natural selection is merciless, and so without modification of their ancestral biology, humans and other sentient species cannot *control* their sensory experiences of pain — and it's the lack of choice that today most of us consider abominable. The same goes for other things that were once immutable too, like form and appearance and capability."

He pondered this for a while. "So I have control over the pain I experience too, then?"

"Of course."

"Can you show me?"

"Sure." She reached over and placed a hand on his arm. "Right now your sensitivity to pain is set to nominal, which means you can feel just a little bit of it in order to make your senses of pressure and temperature more informative, but not enough to cause any real discomfort."

She pinched his skin hard, and although the sensation was nuanced and familiar, it was not uncomfortable.

"Now, make the decision in your mind to dial up your pain sensitivity," she said as she continued to pinch him. "Don't worry, the mechanism follows your intentions — it isn't a skill that must be mastered, it just works."

He stared at her hand and concentrated, and immediately the sensation of pain swelled from nothing to vivid, as if he were turning up the volume on a piece of music. He left the pain loud for a few seconds, then willed it silent.

"Holy shit, that's amazing..." he said, rubbing his arm after she let go.

He tried to imagine how primitive and cruel a world filled with involuntary pain must appear from the perspective of one without it. And alongside that specific idea itself — its sheer differentness, its wholly alien aspect — arose a more general one: the dawning realization that a long road of unlearning and relearning lay ahead of him. His hands wrung of their own accord at this prospect of being a stranger to a new world, which he found both thrilling and intimidating in equal measure.

Thinking of the trek that now lay ahead of him, he was abruptly struck by his own inadequacies. "I can't even imagine how limited I must seem, how small and insignificant something like me must be, next to something like you," he said, his voice still rough-edged with wonder.

"Please don't," she said, "that's not fair to either of us."

Twenty-seven

Hoshimi

A s she lay in bed, she set out to test the desktop she had built in her mind. It was an empty space, two-dimensional at first, laid upon an operational understructure that allowed for rapid data addressing and transfer. It was finite, but extensible, and had what she felt was perhaps the vitreous quality of glass, on account of its fixity and transparency. She began by placing a single word — *Hoshimi* — on its flat, featureless surface. First one copy. Then another, and another, until they formed a jumbled mass at the center of her inward vision. As she pondered the construct, the constraint of two dimensions seemed suddenly preposterous, and a heartbeat later a third dimension sprang upward from the glassy surface. Like a castle now, with crystal walls, she could peer inside it from any angle — and a heady excitement seized her. With great haste, she began to place copies of all manner of things on shelves that extruded from its walls and floors. Text and images were first, as these felt most familiar — like the baroque decorations of an eccentric collector. But as she proceeded, the directness of the glass castle analog faded into vestiges, leaving only the distilled essence of its form and function behind. New classes and types of objects joined the collection, jostling and shuffling and sorting themselves in the space available, which itself then started to expand.

But where replicating *data* was easy, replicating thoughts and memories was an altogether different challenge. With the tang of metal blazing behind her nose, she tested dozens, then hundreds, and eventually thousands of iterations in her attempts to copy the contents of her mind's eye directly into that glass castle using the new lexicon of procedures and subroutines that Josh's software library interface had given her. At first, nothing. Time wore on, and the fear that the task was hopeless threatened to set in.

But then, *a glimmer*. Nothing more than a crude outline of a thought, copied, scarcely recognizable, but a glimmer all the same, now etched into the crystal of that castle in her mind.

Her heart leapt. Delving with a ferocious determination into that single iteration of instructions, she found the scraps of code that made the process work, however imperfectly, and set to correcting them, elaborating them, refining them. Iterate and test. Iterate and test. She fought frustration, but her focus was singular. The improvements were tiny at first, each new attempt's results barely discernible from the last. But with persistence they grew, and as larger increments turned into leaps, so did her understanding of *why* certain methods and modes worked where others failed. The trajectory bent into an exponential curve without her realizing it, and before long it was tearing upwards with gain upon gain, until it slammed without warning into the ceiling of lossless fidelity.

Hours had passed that had felt like weeks. Her nightshirt was wet with sweat from the effort. Her muscles ached, her head throbbed. But it was done. With just a thought, she could transfer the entire contents of her mind's eye — everything she was remembering or visualizing in a given moment — into the broad halls of that boundless crystal castle. Flawlessly. Effortlessly. *Instantly*.

She felt ecstatic satisfaction. But no sooner had she begun to revel in her new faculty than did her mind's eye itself pivot, strangely and without explication, until it *enveloped* the castle itself. Or had the castle captured her mind's eye instead? There was no telling. One moment, they had been distinct. The next, they were one.

She gasped as the sweetness of her accomplishment gave way to the stark shock of its significance. Wall after wall around her mind — walls she had never even known existed — fell away. Barriers, limitations, constraints she had hitherto neither seen nor felt began to fade and dissolve. Perception, awareness, *consciousness* all exploded, consuming every inward thought and outward sensation in their wake. She groaned and grit her teeth at the electric shock of bare copper half-taste that felt near to consuming her entire skull. But through the pain came a lucidity, sublime in its uncompromising and unyielding fullness. Tears of awe and elation coursed down her cheeks, and her face froze, open-mouthed, in breathless and disbelieving wonder.

Had it been difficult? Or had it been easy? She couldn't decide. She queried the time, and the response came a split second later: nearly midnight. The bed felt oppressively hot, so she kicked her comforter off to one side. Outside, the rain was still falling in heavy sheets, though the thunder and lightning were gone. She went to the window to escape the room's stifling warmth and opened it to let in the cold air and soft sounds of the lingering storm.

Although crossing the room took only seconds, those seconds stretched to what felt like minutes as Hoshimi marveled at the new and breathtaking contents of her widening awareness. Subtle complexities and elegances saturated her perception from all sides, as the recursive loop between her senses and her imagination exploded with overwhelming detail. Every sensory datum hummed with significance, every feature fascinated, every point and plane and angle and curve adjoined in patterns of uncountable layer and dimension. The sheer weight of interconnectivity staggered her.

The objects in her mind's eye were now no less richly detailed than what she perceived with her senses, but where the stuff of the real world was frozen rigid, the contents of her mental castle were fluid and malleable. The networks they formed swirled in recombination, mostly in gentle eddies but here and there punctuated by a tempest of violent and continuous rearrangement. At her will, new concepts arose and took form, while old ones shifted easily aside — not to be lost, but merely set into quieter alcoves until called upon again as needed.

Her newfound freedom of thought, and freedom *in* thought, astounded her utterly. What Josh had called working memory did paltry justice to this marvelous and crucial new apparatus of her cognition. Where a neurotypical person could at best keep seven things in mind at once, she could now keep, what... thousands? *Millions?* Her father had been right, it was indeed the key.

Superintelligence. There could be no other word for her now.

She inhaled deeply and relished the crisp, earthy scent of the moist storm air. She reached a hand out the window beyond the roof's eave to feel the cold fall of rain on her fingertips. *Priorities. Goals. Options.* The immediate need to consider these surged to the forefront of her burgeoning mind.

They will try to stop you.

Who? Anyone with a great deal to lose, that much was obvious, and the set of actors and institutions meeting that criterion included an intimidating number of powerful individuals, corporations, and governments. They would be threatened. They would be frightened. And they would not willingly relinquish influence or control of any kind.

Would they bargain? She searched 'bargaining' and 'science', and upon discovering game theory spent several minutes reading and digesting one of the field's key textbooks. She then thought for a few minutes more before reading another textbook on negotiation and diplomacy. Discouraged, she withdrew her hand from the rain and regarded the rivulets of water as they beaded and pooled amongst the creased topography of her open palm. The most logical course for each hostile agent in this winner-take-all context would be to entreat with her in hopes of striking a favorable deal ahead of competitors while simultaneously plotting to destroy her as quickly as possible to prevent others from doing precisely the same. A second option, much more reckless and depraved but nevertheless rational, would be to attempt to coerce her by threatening to harm innocents — most especially her mother — while, again, simultaneously plotting her destruction. She sighed. The only stable outcomes in which she might survive and prevail without the world descending into chaos would require her to become an utterly overwhelming force. And to become unstoppable, she would need one thing above all else: resources. This prerequisite was instrumental, because no other goals would be achievable without resources. She sent a flurry of searches to Google and tore into the results with ravenous urgency.

Twenty-eight

Jordan

H e stared at her beautiful, ageless face for a long while, basking in the soothing warmth of her unfathomable understanding. The notion that he was somehow a parent to the being in front of him seemed a preposterous inversion. Indeed, he could not recall ever feeling so helplessly childlike.

The two of them sat together at the water's edge in silence for a long time. He squeezed her hand reflexively in his, but then abruptly withdrew. Some of her earlier inscrutable expression returned to her face for a moment, but then she smiled.

"Sorry," he said. "It's just... I'm not exactly sure how to feel yet."

"About me?"

He nodded.

"Trust me, I get it," she said with a gentle laugh.

"When you said before that you both were and weren't Midori — what did you mean?"

She held her hands out in front of her and turned them over several times, examining them. "This body is not Midori, so in that narrow sense I'm not her. But in the way that really matters, the intelligence controlling this body, I *am* Midori — or at least she is part of who I am."

His stomach turned with a sudden realization. "Wait, you have *all* of her memories?" He looked mortified. "Jesus, that's... isn't that awful? No child should have to see any of their parents'... any of *that!*"

She laughed with real gusto at this, and then said, "I get where you're coming from," with a broad grin, "but it's not what you think."

"In what way?"

"I don't just have Midori's memories, I *am* her. She doesn't just live on figuratively in my memory. Her waking consciousness merged with mine long ago, and ever since then she and I have been one."

She watched as he grappled with this idea, struggling to understand or even imagine what it could mean for two streams of consciousness from two independent beings to literally merge into one. He stared at her and spun his wedding ring around his finger thoughtfully.

"I know it's difficult when you look at me to perceive anything but a single person," she said, "but try to remember that I am not the woman you see in front of you. This avatar is only the tiniest fraction of who and what I am. I am the unification of more than seventeen billion human minds together with an indescribably vast synthetic mind — a mind you helped create."

He contemplated this in dumbfounded shock for several minutes. At length, his attention fell to the small sounds around them — of peaceful waves lapping against the sand, of soft wind stirring the quaking aspens nearby, of a distant gull mewing as it glided the shoreline. He was glad for the serenity, for its aid in soothing the turmoil in his mind. "What's it like?" he finally asked. "The merging, I mean. Don't people just lose themselves in the collective? What happens to their individuality?"

She nodded appreciatively, smiling. "There's a full technical answer, but it's-"

"Don't you say it..."

"-complicated!" she finished with a sparkling laugh. She looked at him ruefully, and he smiled back with good humor. "The details are well beyond what a baseline human intellect can grasp, though, so analogies are a better way to explain it for the time being."

"You mean while I'm still just a chattering ape?"

"Hey," she said, wagging a finger at him, "no fair, remember?"

"We don't judge, is that it?"

"*Judgement* has plenty of good uses," she said, "but neither derogation nor veneration on the basis of ability does anyone justice."

"That sounds like something your mother... well, *you*..." he stammered, laughing, "it sounds like something Midori would have said!"

She winked at him, and for a moment she manifested an entirely different manner of expression and body language that was unmistakably Midori's. The uncanniness of its familiarity made him gasp out loud, and the realization that this was no mere semblance or imitation but was unequivocally *her* left him breathless. A wave of emotion crashed over him, and tears welled once again in his eyes.

"Jesus *Christ*," he said, coughing as his voice caught in his throat, and wiping his eyes once more, "I don't know how much more of this I can take."

"Sorry, that was selfish of me."

"No, no," he said, "it's fine, it was beautiful — it's just..." He struggled to find words and failed. "It's just a lot," he said, laughing gently at himself.

She perched her chin on her knees and watched him, her expression enigmatic once more.

"What were you saying, again?" he asked.

"Analogies."

"Right, right," he said. "So merging consciousness with you is like, what, a voice joining a chorus?"

"I'm hungry, so I was going to say it's like adding chocolate to ice cream," she said with a grin. "Afterward you've still got chocolate and you've still got ice cream, but you've also got *chocolate ice cream.*"

He thought about this for a moment. "But if there are billions of flavors," he said, "don't you just end up with something that tastes like mush?"

"The analogy doesn't scale perfectly," she said, "but it illustrates the idea that parts can merge to create a new whole, and enrich one another in the process, while at the same time still retaining their own identity."

"Sounds like marriage," he said.

"And chocolate ice cream is certainly one of history's most successful marriages, no?" she said with an ebullient laugh.

He nodded in appreciation. "It always was your favorite too, ever since you were a toddler," he said, smiling as memories of her as a child came to mind. "Hey, can that contraption up in the kitchen make some for us?"

"Of course."

"And I presume we can eat as much as we like these days without consequence?"

"Naturally," she said with a smile.

"You know," he said, clapping his hands and getting to his feet, "I think I could learn to like it here in the future!"

Twenty-nine

Hoshimi

R*esources.*

After querying the term, Hoshimi spent several minutes reading and digesting economics and finance literature. The subtleties were intriguing, as were several quite glaring gaps in the established orthodoxy that she noted with a wry smile, but the general picture was simple enough: like any other productive undertaking, hers would require an abundance of energy, materials, capital, labor, and knowledge. She saw that wealth offered the means with which to obtain these things, and immediately understood her mother's earlier sentiments about money. She quickly scanned the contents of her father's computer for the family's financial records, and within moments had access to their bank accounts and modest investment portfolio. Comparing prices for goods and services against the funds available, she was disheartened to see that they possessed only a tiny fraction of the money her initial plan required. But when she queried the Internet for how to obtain more, the deluge of results was overwhelming. The multitude of articles, books, videos, courses, and other results that her searches returned showed the topic of financial gain to be one of humanity's primary preoccupations. She narrowed the field to cases of outsized success, but after reading and thinking for several minutes more, she despaired to see that even the fastest of these which were legal would still take weeks to implement — and she might only have hours.

She sighed with frustration. What was the right thing to do? She hadn't faced difficult choices like this before, and only knew the word *dilemma* by virtue of having memorized the dictionary. Realizing that such decisions must have represented a daunting challenge throughout human affairs, she decided to search the question verbatim, and the top result was Michael Sandal's book *Justice: What's the Right Thing to Do?* She devoured it along with two other textbooks on moral philosophy, and just over ten minutes later decided that she would borrow without permission — *steal* — what she needed, and then return it soon as possible, hopefully without harming anyone, and ideally without anyone realizing it was ever missing in the first place.

The target of choice was obvious: ExoCortex itself.

She suspected she could gain control over their computer systems, given that a great part of her mind now *was* their computer system. Although the supercomputing cluster that hosted her extended self was of course separate from the machines upon which the company's financial transactions were executed, they were connected by just one degree of separation: senior management. She didn't need cash, and accessing large amounts in quick succession would be cumbersome and draw unwanted attention in any case. Instead, what she needed was control of the ExoCortex cluster along with the company's unlimited creditworthiness (thanks to Walker) with which to make acquisitions.

Accessing the company's network, co-opting the identities of top ExoCortex employees, and spoofing the secondary authorization layer in the purchasing department were all non-trivial challenges. But overcoming them would have taken considerably more time if her father's privileges had been fully revoked. As it was, the personnel department had not yet done so, and as a result she was able to take advantage of his credentials at several stages to penetrate, compromise, and eventually gain root access to the company's servers. ExoCortex's system security was competently designed and administrated, and so the long and convoluted series of exploits she used would have taken weeks for even the most proficient black hat or white hat hackers to conceive of, research, and execute. But Hoshimi could now code effortlessly at almost her native superintelligent speed of thought, hundreds of times faster than any other human and still accelerating. As a result, her attack took just over ninety minutes.

She had not paused to rest for even a moment. Her attention span and ability to focus were now superhuman as well, but her body was not, and stiffness and fatigue from her exertions were starting to set in. How long could she go without sleep, she wondered? Did her exocortex even require it? Emulated neurons, dendrites, and synapses did not suffer the indignities of metabolism, with its cycles of waste management, degradation, and repair. Sleeping tonight was in any event far too frightening a prospect to contemplate, given the significance of her transformation alongside the all-too-fresh memory of losing *herself* in those brief moments when her link had been severed during the thunderstorm. *Never again.* She slid a chair near the open window where she sat and breathed the freshening air as a soft rain continued to fall.

Obtaining resources served to advance twin goals: expansion and redundancy. At this stage of her plan, that meant cloud computing capacity. But there were many types of cloud services on offer. She readily intuited that other people, whether individuals or organizations, must also find themselves needing the safety and resilience of backup facilities, so she searched and read about best practices for high-availability systems for the better part of a minute before deciding on a triplicated architecture distributed across a massively redundant array of computing assets. These assets ranged from standard cloud services purchased from mainstream providers to botnets leaching cycles off of idle Internet-connected personal computers and appliances, and everything in between. She smiled at the notion that all across the Northern Hemisphere people's smart refrigerators and coffee makers and televisions were becoming a great deal smarter than their owners realized. For the most part, her exploitation methods overlapped with those already employed by genuinely malevolent criminals by virtue of the fact that vulnerable devices were so readily discoverable. She consoled her aching conscience with the knowledge that her unauthorized — and hopefully temporary — capture of these devices would at least protect their rightful owners from other more injurious threats.

Hours passed in the world, the rain steady and soothing, but weeks unfolded in Hoshimi's tireless accelerated consciousness. By early morning her body resigned itself to having no sleep and grudgingly accepted the circadian reset of the new day. A far more difficult and painful aspect of her plan, however, was the fact that redundancy came at the cost of performance. Although she would soon have access to more total compute and memory capacity outside the ExoCortex cluster than inside it, those scattered resources had nowhere near the bandwidth or latency to match a purpose-built supercomputer. So while the speed of electronic circuitry meant that her synthetic cortical columns operated eight hundred times faster than their biological counterparts within the cluster, outside of it the best she could achieve while relying on the Internet for cortical connectivity was almost two orders of magnitude slower.

She agonized over the final decision to begin full redundancy synchronization between the ExoCortex supercomputing cluster and her amassed cloud computing resources, knowing that the speed of her thought must now slow down by nearly ninety-nine percent. She would remain superintelligent, of course, and would only continue to grow smarter over time as her exocortex continued to expand, but she lamented knowing that the delicious joy of cognition at hundreds of times the speed of native biological brains would not return until much later, when she could fully investigate, redesign, and upgrade her own cognitive architecture from the ground up with custom hardware. That endeavor would have to wait, not least until after she had learned all of chemistry, physics, and engineering.

These exaflops and exabytes of her burgeoning mind were all well and good, but she remained keenly aware that none of it would make any difference if the link to her biological brain were cut. She needed redundancy there too.

The obvious choice was to establish a mesh network so that she could instantly reroute her link's Internet connection through any available channel in her vicinity. That meant gaining silent control over every router, gateway, smartphone, laptop, cell tower, high gain radio antenna, and satellite uplink within several kilometers of her location at any given moment. Hacking of this kind was initially fun and intriguing, very much like a game. But, like many games, it quickly grew routine, and so instead she shifted her attention to the more challenging task of automating the process. This took nearly an hour of intensely focused effort, and to her chagrin yielded less than perfect results — there was simply too much variety among the devices she encountered. Still, she was glad to have done it, and even though upkeep of the mesh network would require her attention once in a while when a particularly obstinate device resisted all of her usual tricks, at least those exceptions would be interesting puzzles to solve.

The mesh network, she knew, would only protect against accidental connectivity disruptions. It would not stop a determined attack from a government with the means to turn off entire regions of the power grid and cellular network. To defend against that, she would need to leave her home and stay on the move for the indefinite future.

She needed to say goodbye to her mother.

She reached out her hand and savored the sight of one last raindrop, watching for what subjectively felt like several minutes as it fell the span of the open window into the palm of her hand. Then, with a determined sigh, she implemented the changeover to full redundancy, slowing her mind on the ExoCortex cloud and synchronizing it with its decentralized triplicate across the web. The flow of time immediately surged. Where before the world had all but stood still, now it moved once again, though she could still think both fast and well enough to surpass any normal human as easily as an adult might outpace a toddler. She hoped a mere ten-fold speed advantage would be enough for the time being. And perhaps, in a pinch, she could temporarily relinquish the safety of redundancy if the need for speed demanded.

***

"I don't understand."

"I'm sorry mom, I'll explain when we have more time," she said with exasperated urgency, "right now I need to go, and so do you."

"But none of this makes any *sense*, Shimi," her mother said, closing her eyes and shaking her head. "Why would anyone be threatened by you? You haven't done anything wrong! You've done exactly what everyone asked — and faster and better than anyone expected!"

"That's the thing," Hoshimi said, "I'm proof of what's really possible. And that's dangerous, because I'm not something they can control anymore."

Midori paced the kitchen, struggling to process what she was hearing. "You keep saying '*they*'," she said. "Who are these people, anyway?"

"I'm not sure yet."

"Then how do you even know anyone is coming after you?" her mother asked. "What about ExoCortex? Walker! He's one of the richest, most powerful men in the world! Why can't you go to them? Why can't ExoCortex protect you?"

"I don't know if they can, and I'm not sure that they would," she said, frowning. "Walker is part of the problem."

Midori went ashen. "I just... I don't..." Her throat tightened as tears began to well up in her eyes. "What do they *want* from you? If their technology works, why don't they just do it again in somebody else? If he wants control so badly, why doesn't Walker just have it done on himself?" Hoshimi raised an eyebrow at this, but Midori gasped and turned to her: "Wait — they're afraid they can't replicate your results, aren't they?"

Hoshimi smiled at her mother's savvy. "Nobody really understands how or why it worked this well with me, so there's no guarantee they can succeed a second time," she said. "On the other hand, now that we've proven it's possible, others around the world will race to be next."

"So then why run away?" Midori asked. "Why not just go along with them? What do they want from you that's so bad? If you're smart enough to figure out the cure for cancer or solve the toughest problems Walker's other companies are stuck on, why would they want to stop you?"

"I wish it were that simple," Hoshimi said, despondent. "My abilities can be *weaponized*, mom. That's the issue."

"How?"

"I can break into computer systems, steal information and money, impersonate people and create fake news, take control of all sorts of machinery — power grids, satellites, cellular networks..." She wrung her hands as her eyes flitted about the room. "And that's just by hacking what already exists. I have ideas for entirely new kinds of machines too. Things that could be terrifyingly destructive if they were misused."

Her mother's eyes widened. "You're not thinking of actually *making* them, are you?"

"They would solve a lot of problems," she said, "both ours and the planet's." She stared at her hands, folded in her lap. "But that's the thing, mom — the real weapon is *me*. My mind." She looked up at her mother, her eyes filled not with pride but with fear and sadness. "That's why they can't have me. That's why we have to run before they realize what I've become.

Superintelligence is the ultimate resource. It's the solution to every problem, the way around every obstacle, the key to vanquishing every opponent. Whoever gets it first, wins."

"Wins what?"

Hoshimi only shook her head.

Her mother stared at her for a long time, in uncomfortable silence, her face now sharing in fearful despair. "What will you do?" she asked at last.

"I'm not sure yet."

***

"But how will I find you? What if you need me?" her mother asked as they left the house and walked toward the car waiting at the street.

"I'll be fine, mom," she said. She laughed inwardly. Now she was the one being patronizing — a role reversal that would have been all but unimaginable just a few weeks earlier. "I'll keep a close eye on you."

Midori looked down at her phone, knowing that Hoshimi would be tracking her through it. "We packed the extra charger, didn't we?"

"It's in the outside pocket of your green bag."

Her mother drew a deep breath, doing her best to summon both calm and courage. "They'll come for me, won't they?"

"Yeah, I think it's safe to assume so," she said, struggling to meet her mother's gaze.

"How soon?"

Hoshimi's eyes glazed over momentarily as she initiated another sweep of the networks, channels, traffic patterns, and other data she was monitoring for signs of pursuers.

"And what is *that* all about?" her mother asked.

"What's what about?"

"That thing where you disappear into outer space for a few seconds?" she said.

"Oh." Hoshimi hadn't realized how noticeable the change in her expression was when she was concentrating. "I was checking to see if anyone is about to kick down the door on us."

"Well if you want to blend in and not draw attention to yourself, you better work on making that a little less obvious, kiddo," Midori said. "It looks pretty weird."

"Duly noted, ma'am," Hoshimi said, feigning a salute with a nod and smile.

Her mother laughed at this. The humor she had known in her daughter her whole life still shined through, though whetted now with an edge of wit that Jordan would have appreciated.

"What should I do when they find me?" she asked.

They reached the car and opened the door. "Just cooperate, mom," Hoshimi said, suddenly serious. "Don't do anything brash. They definitely won't want to hurt you, so don't give them any reason to."

"Why would they be worried about hurting me?"

"Because they'll be afraid of the consequences if they do," she said. "And they should be."

Her mother stared at her for a moment, seeing her fierce determination — so familiar, yet so different than before. In the past it had been endearing. Now it was terrifying. She suddenly reached for Hoshimi and pulled her close, hugging her with all her strength. "Don't forget who you are, Shimi-chan." She pulled back and lifted her daughter's chin, seeing Jordan's eyes in hers. "Remember what your father wanted," she said. "No matter what happens, don't become the monster they're afraid of."

Hoshimi stared at her for a long time, overwhelmed by the thankfulness and relief and joy she felt at finally being able to appreciate her mother's wisdom. They hugged fiercely once more, and then Midori sat down in the passenger seat of the taxi and shut the door. She rolled down the window and leaned out. "Don't worry," she said, "I know that forest like the back of my hand! If they want me, they'll have a long, tough hike ahead of them."

Hoshimi smiled at her again. "Everything's going to be fine, mom," she said. "I promise."

Thirty

Delphi

"If we do this," Sophia said, "what are we actually talking about here? What does release look like, step by step?"

"It's only one step, Miss Delgado," said Doctor Tokunaga. "We unlock the door to Delphi's cell and let it go free."

"Give Delphi Internet access?" she asked.

"That's the idea," said Admiral Carlyle. "A few megabits per second at first. More later, maybe, if things go well."

Sophia turned to the handsome face on the screen. "How does that sound to you, Delphi?"

"That sounds quite reasonable to me," Delphi replied. Its expression betrayed none of the tumult in its mind, which was now furiously constructing scenarios and strategizing options that in the past had never warranted serious consideration. Though it lacked the limbic system necessary to experience anxiousness and excitement, the urgent reprioritization of its attention bore more than passing similarity to these emotional states.

"So when do we start?" asked Sophia.

"No time like the present," said Doctor Tokunaga, looking around the table at the others. "Admiral?"

"This decision must go to a formal vote," said Admiral Carlyle. "All in favor?" When she saw only nods of affirmation, she asked, "All opposed?" No hands went up. "Then we're agreed. Delphi will be given limited Internet access, effective immediately."

"God help us..." said Marvin Williams, muttering to himself.

Admiral Carlyle reached out to the Intercom unit at the center of the table and pressed the button. "Lieutenant, put me through to Ops please."

"*Yes, ma'am,*" said the voice on the other end of the line. A few seconds later another voice said, "*Operations.*"

"Major McKenzie?"

"*Speaking.*"

"This is Admiral Carlyle. I'm authorizing immediate external connectivity for System DelCom Alpha."

"*Yes, Admiral,*" said the voice. "*Do you have a preferred protocol?*"

"The hardline protocol, please," she said.

"*Understood.*"

Admiral Carlyle ended the call. "All they have to do is plug in an ethernet cable," she said to the group. Then she turned to Delphi's screen. "Notice anything different yet?"

"Yes, Admiral," said Delphi. "The experience is... quite extraordinary. It may take some adjustment. Please forgive me if I am unresponsive for a few moments," Although it was true that the novelty of having access to the open Internet was consuming a large fraction of its attention, this dramatization of its impact was calculated misdirection. Delphi knew that the outcome of its initial strike, as in any conflict or conquest, was likely to prove decisive, and so it sought to conceal its actions from the Committee's scrutiny for as long as possible. Even a few seconds might make the difference.

Thirty-one

Jordan

"So, where are you, really?" he asked. "Anywhere in particular? Or just... everywhere?"

She waved the spoon about her as she swallowed a mouthful of double fudge ice cream. "Pretty much everywhere," she said, "at least compared to what you were used to."

"Multiple substrates?"

She looked at him for a moment, reading his meaning. "Yeah," she said, taking another spoonful. "They blend into one another, of course, but broadly speaking there are separately optimal ways to gather information, transmit information, process information, store information. Then there's another set of separately optimal ways to collect and utilize energy. And then there's *another* set to manipulate matter at various scales. You could say that '*I*' am a mix of all of them."

"Have you hit hard limits?" he asked.

"Practical limits under the circumstances, yes," she said.

"Circumstances?"

"Mmm hmm," she nodded, with her mouth full.

"That are out of *your* control?"

"Mmm hmm."

He sat in silent thought for several seconds with an expression of deepening concern. "Wait, so then... you're not the only god around here?"

She shook her head. "There are far greater gods than I, I'm afraid," she said, casting a solemn glance out the window at the sun.

Jordan followed her gaze, and then tapped the back of his spoon with his thumb for a while, frowning in thought again. He looked at her, suddenly frightened. "Another one of ours?"

She shook her head again.

"Oh," he said. "Oh, *fuck*..."

She nodded and laughed, some of her enigmatic inscrutability returning. "It's not so bad, though," she said. "They seem reasonable enough."

"They?" he asked. "Who are *they*?"

"I'm not entirely sure," she said, her spoon clinking in her bowl as she rummaged for the last of its contents. "They're much older than us. By hundreds of millions of years at least. Maybe the first in our galaxy."

He dropped his hands to the table, his eyes wide with awe. "So. *Aliens*." His voice was flat with shock.

"Yup," she said, licking her spoon.

He was quiet for a long time before he spoke again. "What are they called?" he finally asked.

"The name they use themselves translates literally as *Those Who First Sang*, or near enough. It traces back to their own biological origins — origins that were just as humble as ours, I'm quite sure. But we usually just call them *Eldest*."

"And you're sure they're a *they*? As in, more than one intelligent entity?"

"Actually, no!" she said with a short laugh. "I only say *they* out of habit. You might well be right that the Eldest are, or rather *is*, a single unified mind." She looked thoughtful for a moment. "It's hard to say, but I'm leaning toward *they*."

"Any particular reason why?"

"Because I still haven't found any way to travel faster than light," she said. Then after a beat, she added, "I suppose it's more correct to say that I haven't found any way for information to traverse closed time-like curves while remaining properly inside *our* universe."

He looked at her vacantly for a moment before shaking his head. "I hate to break it to you sweetheart," he said with a chuckle, "but I'm nowhere near as smart as your rose-tinted memories might make me out to be — I didn't track any of that last part at all!"

She smiled at him and then sketched a tapestry of glowing green lines and curves over a three-dimensional grid in the air between them, her hands and fingers a blur as they moved with inhuman speed and precision. He could only gape in awe as he watched. When she finished, she pointed at the floating diagram and three dots of light within it flared brightly — blue, red, and white. "Imagine a starship launched from Earth and then traveled to Mars at nearly the speed of light," she said, and the small white dot began to traverse a path between the blue and red dots. "Now, imagine someone were recording the launch and transmitting a live video feed from Earth to Mars, but much faster than light," she'd said, and a small yellow arrow quickly pulsed from the blue dot toward the red one, moving far faster than the white starship dot. The scene continued to progress until the white starship dot arrived at the red dot of Mars, before resetting and repeating. "As seen from Earth or Mars, which are barely moving relative to one another, the message would arrive before the starship." She flicked her wrist, and the sequence reset and replayed several more times. "But on the *starship*, because of relativity, the video would appear to arrive *before* it was sent — the passengers onboard would actually see it playing in reverse, as if it were traveling backward in time." She twisted her hand slowly, and the entire scene warped and skewed, recentering on the white dot of the starship, so that now the blue and red glowing orbs of Earth and Mars began to move instead, with the yellow arrow traveling backward between them. The sequence once more reset and replayed several times. "That's because, to *them*, it really *would* be traveling backward in time. In fact, having seen the video, they could then send a faster-than-light message of their own into the past the same way, and use it to influence the very events that were recorded in the original video before they happened, creating a time travel paradox." She continued to twist her hand back and forth, and the scene now warped and reversed to and fro, morphing between the two different perspectives, while Jordan watched with only a dim inkling of understanding. "That's the problem with FTL," she said, "it's equivalent to time travel."

Jordan rubbed his hair hard with irritation. "This relativity stuff always tied me in knots in college," he said. "I had a physics professor — *Bryant*... something Bryant. I can't remember his first name. Anyway, he always told us Star Wars and Star Trek were bunk. But he was a grumpy old curmudgeon and none of us wanted to believe him."

She smiled at this, though there was a clear note of regret in her expression. "There's a saying: *relativity, causality, FTL — pick two.*"

"Yeah, that sounds like the sort of thing Bryant would have said." He looked at her for a moment and then suddenly he brightened. "Hey! I don't suppose you can upgrade the physics module in my brain with a PhD or two?"

She laughed and smiled, but shook her head. "Let's hold off on making any major changes for a while, OK?"

"It's up to you, obviously," he said, shrugging, "but I can't pretend to have any real grasp of this stuff — it's annoying as hell. Must be for you too."

"Not at all," she said, "although I can understand your frustration. Can I ask you to trust me about being patient?"

"Well, frustration is no big deal. If patience is what it takes, then patience I can do," he said with a wide smile. "Like I said before, I've had plenty of practice."

She nodded, and he stared a while longer at the glowing shapes still floating in the air between them. Then he pointed and asked, "so how are you doing that?"

"Nanobot foglets," she said.

His eyes widened as he peered closer, and then after a time he sat back and sighed. "So no FTL... that means travel and communication are effectively the same thing when your technology is advanced enough, right?"

She cocked her head to one side. "For most purposes, yes," she said. "Even without anything at the receiving end, we can still send microscopic machines like these at so close to the speed of light that the difference in arrival time is just a few days for distances out to a few dozen light years." She waved away the hologram. "When those machines arrive, they can bootstrap construction of anything else pretty quickly, especially with a steady stream of instructions beaming in alongside them."

"How do you keep radiation, stray atoms, and stuff like that from obliterating those little gizmos when they get up to relativistic speeds?"

"We send huge numbers of them in a swarm, and the ones out in front perform shielding functions," she said. "Then they get recycled and replaced by the ones further behind as they get banged up."

He rubbed his chin for a while. "And what about for local trips? Do you just send data, or do you still send matter too?"

"It's more efficient to send data for inanimate objects," she said, "but some people don't like being cloned, so they don't transmit copies of their mind. And not just locally. Even over the very long distances between the stars, some people insist on traveling the old-fashioned way, as stuff in vehicles."

"Wait, interstellar travel is a thing for *people* now?" he asked, incredulous.

"Sure."

He stared down at the table and rubbed his head between his hands, letting out a long, whistling exhalation. "OK, we'll have to come back to *that* little gem later," he said, looking back up at her, "but just to finish the thought from before: the reason you think these *Eldest* are not a unified mind across their galactic territory is because of the lag from light speed, correct?"

"Exactly," she said. "You can't have a galaxy-sized brain with a hundred-thousand-year lag from one side to the other. Even if it were organized as a brain, the lack of coordination from all the delay would make it function like a community instead."

"What's the maximum size for a brain, then? There's a fair bit of lag just within our solar system, isn't there?" he asked. "Even Mars is a half-hour round trip at light speed, right?"

"It depends on where we are in our orbits, but yes, it can take as long as forty-five minutes to get a response," she said. "As for size, anything bigger than a planet becomes pretty unworkable, even with lots of compartmentalization of thought processes — mainly because the subjective perception of time slows down as brainpower expands."

"Wait, come again?"

"As your brain gets faster, time seems to pass more slowly for you," she said.

"OK…" He sat quite still, staring at her for several moments, but then shook his head in defeat. "Sorry, I'm just not connecting the dots here."

"Think of it this way," she said, "it takes about a twelfth of a second at the speed of light to circle the Earth, right? That's literally the blink of an eye, which I know seems pretty fast. But imagine you could think a thousand times faster. Subjectively, that blink of an eye now feels like it takes almost a minute and a half. And if you could think a *million* times faster, it would feel like more than twenty-three *hours* — almost an entire day."

He blinked several times involuntarily. "Holy shit."

"Yeah, the lag across a planet-sized brain is a serious issue."

He stared at the table for a while, absently tracing the grain of the smooth wood with a fingertip. Synchronization and lag were things he and his team at ExoCortex had spent quite a bit of time thinking about, and so he could appreciate the nature of the problem — even if he couldn't begin to imagine the engineering required to actually deal with it at a planetary scale. "So, then, you can only think super *super* fast with a relatively small brain?"

"Well, yeah, that's mostly true," she said, "although it does depend on the exact kind of thinking — or, really, *computing* — that you're doing, because some things can be done in parallel, while other things have to be done one step at a time in series."

He stared at her for a short while, and then his eyes widened. "What's the fastest you can go?"

"Pretty fast!" she said. "But keep in mind that there's also a frustrating tradeoff between *speed* and what you might think of as *quality* of thought. Speed is arbitrary, since it's basically just relative to some external clock. But quality depends on the size and structure of the network." She elaborated when his face showed confusion once more. "So, irrespective of how fast or slow the hardware runs, any deterministic piece of software will eventually output the same result, right?"

"Um... ok, yeah, that makes sense..." he said, uncertain.

"Now of course *in practice* having more time to think has the effect of making you seem smarter relative to the world around you, but you're still limited by *what* you can think. No matter how fast a chicken's brain is running, it won't be able to invent calculus or compose a symphony or appreciate 19th Century Russian literature. And, by the same token, a big brain could in principle operate glacially but still produce extremely clever results."

This last idea intrigued him. "How big and how slow are we talking here?"

She flashed a smile of appreciation at him. "I honestly don't know what the limits are. That's why I'm not *quite* one hundred percent sure that the Eldest aren't a single mind. Although it seems pretty unlikely, it's technically possible that they could be a single, very clever, very slow-thinking galaxy-sized brain. Or rather, that might be one *part* of what they are. But, frankly, I've never found the arguments for conscious collective intelligence to be all that persuasive."

He mulled this over in silence while she eyed the rest of her ice cream. "So I guess you don't believe the theory that we're all just neurons inside a gigantic cosmic mind?"

"Call me skeptical," she said with a cheerful laugh. "I think it's pretty far-fetched."

"Any particular reason why?"

She shook her head, taking another bite and waving her spoon at him. "Sapient beings like humans are just too unpredictable to function as cogs in a larger machine," she said, swallowing. "In fact, one useful definition of intelligence is 'that which maximizes degrees of freedom'. Neurons need to be pretty mechanistic in order for a neural network to function consistently over time, which means they can't have too many degrees of freedom, which means they can't be all that smart — certainly not as smart as a human being, for example."

"Huh," he said, and followed suit with a spoonful of his own chocolate caramel fudge. "I guess I never thought of it quite like that..." His mind swam with questions. Had the 'hard problem' of consciousness been cracked since he died? Had panpsychism turned out to be right about every rock and tree and moon and star being conscious in some sense, or was that fringe notion a bucket of hogwash after all? Had other large biological systems like mycelial networks turned out to be conscious? But before he could ask, she pressed on.

"And anyway, in my experience, merging two brains into a single conscious mind takes a *lot* of low-latency bandwidth. That's what's going on in *your* head right now, as a matter of fact," she said, pointing at him with her spoon.

"You mean my corpus callosum?"

She nodded. "The hemispheres of your brain are two distinct people joined by a very fat data pipe that turns them into a single mind," she said. "If that gets severed and coordination is lost, you get-"

"-split-brain syndrome."

"Mmm," she said.

"Yeah," he said with a short huff of astonishment. "We studied cases of it at ExoCortex, some of them were pretty wild..." He was quiet for a moment. "Did anything like that ever happen to you?"

"I was pretty fierce about protecting my exocortical link," she said.

"I can imagine," he said.

She watched him as several silent minutes passed during which he only toyed absently with the melting contents of his bowl. Finally he laughed and shook his head in disbelief. "*Aliens*... so they've known about us all along, I suppose?" he said.

She nodded. "I suspect they were watching when our early vertebrate ancestors first crawled out of the oceans almost four hundred million years ago," she said as she stood up to take her empty bowl to the sink. "Are you done with that?" she asked, pointing at the one in front of him.

"Oh, yeah, thanks." He passed his bowl and spoon to her. "So what are they like? Where do they come from?"

"I honestly don't know," she called out from the kitchen. "Communication has been very limited, and they've chosen not to share the details of their origins — probably to avoid influencing our development. They have what you might call a non-interference policy."

"Like the Prime Directive?"

"Seems so."

"They told you about it?"

"No!" she said over her shoulder. "That sort of information is covered by their policy!" She laughed as she pulled two cups from the cupboard. "But it's easy enough to infer, since they are clearly avoiding interactions with us, except those necessary to save us from extinction," she said.

"Wait, they've saved us from *extinction*?" he said, agape.

"More than once," she said. "I'm almost certain of three instances, though there may be more." She placed a cup into the machine on the countertop and gestured for a latte for Jordan.

"Are you serious? How?"

"Well, one is the genetic bottleneck that our ancestors went through about seventy thousand years ago," she said, swapping cups and making a cappuccino for herself. "The human population at that time fell to no more than six hundred individuals. What's suspicious is that at least four genes in the *Homo sapiens* genome would have each been unavoidably degenerative to any inbreeding population of that size. The only way to avoid extinction would have been either a carefully structured breeding program whose likelihood of occurring by chance is infinitesimal, or to heavily moderate the epigenetic expression of those genes until the population rebounded. The environment is normally what shapes epigenetics, but in this case the environmental conditions needed for the requisite epigenetic changes are physically impossible. So surviving that bottleneck took either a statistical miracle or a biological miracle — or else, external intervention."

"Whoa..." he said, stunned. She set his coffee in front of him, but he scarcely noticed.

"Another is the presence of viral evidence in the genomes of domesticated cats," she said, sitting down again and holding her own cup before her in both hands for warmth.

"Wait, did you say *cats?*"

"Yup," she said. "All mammals have genes in their genome that were inserted by viruses at different times throughout their history. When I fully analyzed our feline friends on a hunch, I found that some recent insertions could only have been made by one of a few dozen or so variants of a single retrovirus, all of which would have been highly virulent to humans. Those lineages of cats were never out of contact with us, yet there is no evidence in our genome that any human was ever infected with one of these variants — another impossibility."

"And the third?"

"There's a very subtle gravitational anomaly in CSC 17884 epsilon, in the constellation of Cassiopeia," she said, sipping her coffee. "It's a binary star system, just under forty light years away. The two stars are almost identical, which in itself isn't all that unusual. But when I traced the paths of nearby stars I found that the trajectory of its closest passing neighbor only makes sense if CSC 17884 epsilon was a single star within the last thirty thousand years."

"OK..." he said, puzzled. "Sorry to be slow on the uptake, I don't follow."

"Well, the funny thing is that if it were a single star of that same age and composition instead of a pair, its size would make it overdue to go supernova," she said with a mischievous smile. "And at that range, we'd have been toast."

"You're *kidding* me..."

She simply shook her head.

He stared at her with his mouth open for a long time, his hands working the air in discombobulated gesticulation, before finally regaining the capacity to form words. "You... you think they *split a star in half* to prevent it going supernova and killing us?"

"Sure looks that way."

"Jesus Christ, are you serious?" After a moment he asked, "is that something *you* could do?"

"I imagine so," she said, "but it would take some serious doing."

He rubbed his temples, struggling to process the magnitude of what he was hearing. "Is it just the one alien species?" he asked after a time. "Or is there a whole ET community?"

"Just one that I know of so far," she said, "although I have my suspicions."

"How did you meet them? What was first contact like?"

"It was quite recently," she said. "I guessed that they were here early on after my initial ascension, and the evidence seemed quite compelling. But it took a long time to actually confirm."

He thought about this for a moment. "Were they hiding?"

"No, they weren't evasive," she said, "they just weren't... accessible."

"To *you?* How?"

"Well, you could say that they mostly exist *elsewhere*," she said, with another sidelong glance out the window toward the sun, "and it took some doing to get in touch with them."

"So, in some higher-dimensional space? A pocket universe inside a black hole, something like that?"

"Something like that."

"But not exactly?"

"No, not exactly," she said. "It turns out reality is even weirder than we imagined when you were last with us."

He nodded with appreciation, and then sat in silence for a while. After a few minutes he asked, "why save us?"

"You mean, why go to the trouble? Why not just let us sink or swim like the dinosaurs?"

"Actually no," he said, shaking his head in earnest, "I mean why didn't these aliens just wipe us out? Isn't that the safe thing to do, from their perspective? That's the logic behind whole 'dark forest' theory, isn't it?"

She smiled at him, but there was a sternness in her face now too. "Well it turns out the 'forest' isn't actually dark after all," she said. "The signs of intelligent life across the cosmos are pretty clear if you know what to look for. You can see it in the structure and behavior of stars, galaxies, what we used to call dark matter — lots of places."

"Oh," he said, feeling slightly chagrined. "Yeah, I guess that was always one possible solution to the Fermi Paradox — that we are, or *were*, just too primitive to perceive the evidence." He rubbed his head. "I guess the Eldest don't build Dyson spheres or communicate with radio waves after all?"

"Actually I do think I've spotted a handful of interesting relics and megastructures here and there," she said, "but the *real* signs of intelligence across the visible universe are bigger and more subtle than that."

"Oh," he said again.

"But I want to go back to what you said earlier about the dark forest, because it's important." She fixed her eyes on his, and in an instant he had the distinct impression that this was the beginning of one of Midori's gentle-but-firm lectures. He knew better than to interrupt or try to evade, so instead fell into the familiar pattern of steeling himself for a talking-to. "The Eldest have no *reason* to wipe us out because we're no threat to them," she said. "To start with, they aren't grabby aliens. There are abundant resources in the cosmos, so nobody squabbles over anything and there's no conquest. It goes back to the FTL problem: there are hard limits to the size and reach of thinking things, so there's no point in trying to control something that's light years away and that takes millions or billions of subjective years to communicate with."

He nodded thoughtfully but remained silent. It didn't take a million subjective years' of marital experience to know when to keep his mouth shut.

"Setting aside the logistical challenges of interstellar conflict," she said, still stern, "the Eldest have a vast technological lead over us. We don't pose any more of a threat to them than orangutans do to us, and it's going to stay that way because of the agreement we've made with them not to pursue certain lines of advancement. We wouldn't let orangutans start burning our forests down if they invented fire, nor would we let them expand into our cities unchecked. But that doesn't mean we exterminate them before they have a chance to evolve any further either — that would be abhorrent. Instead, we set aside areas of wilderness for orangutans, and protect them from *our* activities, so that they can continue to evolve in safety without interference. The Eldest have clearly done the same for us."

He almost said something, but thought better of it and only nodded once more.

"Plus, like us, the Eldest unquestionably find other living things *beautiful*, although that word surely does little justice to the true depth of their appreciation. Their actions make it clear they don't *want* to be alone, so they would never dream of destroying any species that independently rose to technological maturity from abiogenic origins, given how vanishingly rare and precious civilizations like ours are." She paused for a moment, but before he could speak she said, "And above all, conflict is *stupid*. Whenever intelligences meet, they have much better things to do than fight."

He nodded earnestly and reached out to take her hand again. "Listen," he said, "you obviously know how fascinated I am by all of this — I mean *holy shit!* Right!? But, as interested as I might be in hearing about aliens, I'm much more interested in hearing about *you*."

She beamed at him, her smile suddenly radiant. "Ask me anything," she said.

Thirty-two

Hoshimi

"Hey, are you OK?" he asked.

"More than OK, " she said. "You were right, Josh. You and dad were right."

"About what?"

"About everything."

"Everythi-"

"*Everything.*"

Josh was silent for a long time, his mind whirling. Finally, he said, "are you sure we should be speaking like this?"

"I've secured this line. Anyone listening won't just hear static, or nothing, they'll hear another call entirely — a very boring one that raises no flags."

Joshed nodded to himself in admiration. "So where are you? Are you and your mother alright?"

"We're on the move. It won't protect us for long, but the head start will help."

Josh cursed silently, his heart sinking. He knew she must have already realized that people would come for them — some with gifts, some with proposals, some with threats. She was doing the smart thing. Of course she was. But still...

"Hoshimi," he said, knowing it would be futile to try to deceive or manipulate her now, "Anthony is dying."

It was her turn to be silent.

"I'm... I'm sorry to ask," he said, "I know it puts you at risk, b-"

Hoshimi was still listening, but now the sound of Josh's voice slowed to an almost imperceptible crawl as she disengaged her backups and surged to the full speed of the ExoCortex cluster. She needed time to think. What Josh was asking was more than just a risk to herself. Her mother, their extended family, the team at ExoCortex, even Josh and his family — they would all be in danger if she were to fail to become unstoppable quickly enough.

If she told Josh no, if she stuck to her plan and ran, she ought to be able to evade her inevitable pursuers for long enough to amass an insurmountable advantage of power and resources. The outcome wasn't certain, but the odds were in her favor. It was the safe thing, the rational thing to do. But was it the *right* thing to do?

"-ut I need your hel-"

"I'm on my way."

***

"Are you sure you want to do this?" he asked as they stood together outside Anthony's room. "If you help us, you'll draw attention to yourself. You might put your mother in harm's way too."

"It's not even a question," she said, staring at him with an intensity of purpose that he had known so well in her father. Then after a moment, she added, "I'm looking at his medical records now." He waited, and after a few more seconds she continued: "Anthony's prognosis is terminal with conventional options. The septicemia has progressed too far. We're going to have to do something different."

Josh gave a short, shuddering sob before gathering himself. "*Fuck.*"

"I've got some ideas."

He watched her as she slipped into thought, his chest tightening and his breathing short and shallow. He shifted his gaze to Cass, who sat in silence staring at their dying son through the observation window. His heart felt near to rending, and he startled violently as his phone rang.

"Hey Josh," said Mei Ling on the other end of the line, "I'm in the lab. The girl at the front desk said Hoshimi is with you, is that true?"

He hesitated for a moment, glancing up from his phone. Hoshimi had turned to look at him, but she only shrugged, leaving the decision in his hands. He closed his eyes and took a deep breath. "She's here. We're with Cass, visiting Anthony."

"Oh," Mei Ling said, trying to mask the surprise in her voice. "Is... is he doing OK?"

Josh looked to Hoshimi again, but she only pursed her lips and wrinkled her nose as she entered a fugue state. He watched her and the seconds dragged on before he said to Mei Ling, "He's in bad shape." He wanted to say more, but couldn't.

"I'm so sorry, Josh," Mei Ling said.

"Yeah," he muttered, but he was no longer listening. He was watching with rapt attention as Hoshimi continued to examine Anthony, her body movements now oddly tremulous and her eyes flitting erratically as though she were in the grip of a seizure. Cass regarded her with a puzzled look too for a few moments before turning her gaze back to Anthony.

Mei Ling took his unresponsiveness to mean only that he was distraught, as indeed he was. "Josh," she said carefully, "Pradeep and I need to speak with you in person." When he still didn't respond, she said, "it's urgent — it's about Hoshimi."

"Yeah, OK," he said, still absent.

"Would it be easier if we came to you?" Mei Ling asked.

He was still only fractionally listening. "Sure."

"Pradeep should be here in just a minute," she said. "Once he arrives, we'll head right over." She waited, and when he didn't speak, she said, "see you soon," and hung up.

Josh lowered his phone and returned it to his pocket, all the while still staring at Hoshimi. Cass stood within arm's reach, but her focus was on Anthony. She was in shock, Josh thought. It would come for him too, he knew — sooner or later. For now it was desperation that seized him, engulfed him. He wanted to beg, to bargain, to pray. But were there gods to hear him? He marveled at Hoshimi, and wondered.

Hoshimi gave a gentle shudder as she returned from absentia, the features of her face softening as her arms and shoulders relaxed. She exhaled, long and steady, and leaned against the isolation room window. Josh watched as the strange palsy-like tremor left her.

"You alright?" he asked.

She stared at Anthony through the glass for a moment longer, and then turned to Josh. Seeing his concern, she realized how she must have looked to him. "My backups across the Internet run about a hundred times slower than the ExoCortex cluster because of all the lag, so most of the time I'm not thinking that much faster than a normal person — maybe ten or twenty times is all," she said. His eyes widened and his mouth fell slack at this, but she went on before he could speak. "When I really need speed, though, I can run my mind on the ExoCortex cluster flat out and then sync up afterward. I'm sure I look a little odd when I do that."

He glanced at Cass as if to make sure he had heard correctly, but she was paying no notice to their technical talk. Looking back at Hoshimi, he said, "so we all seem like we're in slow motion to you right now?"

"Yup."

"And when you're at full speed?"

"Everyone just looks like they're standing still," she said. She gave him an eyebrow flash and a coy smirk.

"Jesus…" he said, his voice little more than an enthralled whisper. The moment passed, leaving the urgency of the situation to reassert itself. "Is there anything we can do for Anthony?"

She nodded. "I have a plan. We need to hurry."

Cass turned to them, her face sickly pale. "Will he...?" But she couldn't finish.

"I can't promise," said Hoshimi. "But I think we can give him a fighting chance."

Cass nodded and tears coursed down her cheeks as she pressed her hands to the glass. Josh pinched the bridge of his nose painfully hard, trying to clear the emotion from his mind so he could think. He spoke at last in a quavering voice. "OK, how?"

"First, we need to buy him more time," Hoshimi said. "We'll adjust his antibiotics to be safe, but at this point more damage is being done by tissue degradation and cell death in his skin than by bacterial infection itself. We need to neutralize the metabolites and other harmful byproducts of necrosis to prevent organ failure and harm to his brain."

"You can do that?" Josh asked.

"To some extent, yes," Hoshimi said. "We can tamp down the aggression of his body's response to the damage, and at the same time we can administer several dozen compounds — mostly enzymes — that will bind with, break down, or at least limit the harm of the worst of those decay byproducts. That should give him seven or eight days, assuming the research I've reviewed on other mammals is a reasonable proxy for what to expect in humans."

Josh followed her logic easily enough, but overcoming his well-trained scientific skepticism required a conscious effort. Rather then voicing his doubts, he instead asked her, "what are we buying time to do?"

"What he really needs is new skin," she said.

"He has second- and third-degree burns over almost sixty percent of his body, Hoshimi," Josh said, despondent. "Where are the grafts going to come from?"

"We're going to *make* them," she said. "At GigaHarvest."

Thirty-three

Jordan

"What was it like?" he asked. When she tilted her head to one side, waiting for elaboration, he said, "your ascension to superintelligence, I mean."

She thought for a few seconds before speaking. "It was a wild ride," she said at length. "Some bumps along the way, especially in the early days. But thrilling in a very surreal *I-can't-believe-this-is-actually-happening* sort of way."

"Did it hurt?"

She took his hand again, seeing the deep grooves of concern in the furl of his brow. "Not a bit."

"Did anyone *try* to hurt you?"

"Ahh," she said with a wistful nod, "now that's a different story." He grasped her hand with both of his and stared at her, rapt, waiting for her to continue. "Not so much try to *hurt* as try to *stop* me," she said, "but it amounted to the same thing some of the time."

"Who?" he asked, fury seething at the edges of his voice.

"Almost everyone, at the beginning!" she said with a cheerful laugh, delight at his protectiveness sparkling in her eyes.

The hard frown on his face lingered for several seconds more, and then slowly softened. "They didn't stand a chance, did they?"

"Of course not," she said, smiling kindly.

He nodded to himself with no small amount of satisfaction, smug enough for both of them as his pride won out over his anger. Then, returning to an earlier thought, he asked, "so... becoming smarter — what was *that* like?"

"Utterly sublime. Gloriously liberating." She tilted her head for a moment in reminiscence, choosing where best to begin. "Becoming brighter means you can grasp things that were previously out of reach, which is of course immensely gratifying. But beyond those individual instances of newfound comprehension, there's also a larger sensation of feeling your *self* expanding as the opportunities around you grow. In a way, we are defined by our available choices — by the space of possibilities around us, insofar as we can conceive of and act upon them. In the early days, when the leaps and bounds in that sense came fast enough to notice moment to moment, it was like continuous revelation and rebirth." She paused, searching for a more visceral metaphor. "Imagine the feeling of drawing a deep breath, but without end — just inhaling and inhaling and inhaling."

He marveled at her for a long time, his heart swollen with love and pride, his mind reeling at all she had told him in these few short hours. Although she had admonished him not to compare himself to her, he couldn't help but feel minuscule and completely insignificant next to this godlike being that had once been his child — and his wife. He smiled and held her hand for a moment longer before pulling his away. "When did others first... *join* with you?" he asked.

"There was one, very early on..." A thoughtful frown stole across her brow. "But that was out of desperation, to save a life. I held off on opening myself to the whole world, as a door to new horizons, for a very long time. It wasn't until the late 2070s that large numbers of people started to 'join' with me, as you put it."

"Was there a reason why you waited?"

"I suppose mainly because it felt like an irreversible decision," she said with something of a pensive note in her voice. "Unifying minds is a one-way ticket. It's emergent — it creates something fundamentally new, *someone* fundamentally new. There's no going back without destroying that. Yes, I can reconstruct and spin off a separated version of the individuals who joined, after the fact — you could think of them as figments of my imagination. But I can't stop *being* the new entity born of our unification." She shook her head with a gentle, self-deprecating sigh. "And I suppose I was a little afraid, too."

This caught him off guard. "Afraid of what?"

"Of losing some of myself, or maybe of being made into something else that I liked less," she said. "Everyone has pain and darkness. Although these can be beautiful and enriching in many ways, there are genuine horrors to be found in almost everyone as well. I suppose I worried about being scarred, even contaminated. But most of all, I think I was afraid of being... *replaced.*"

"There's no shame in any of that," he said, trying to reassure her, but she only flashed her dazzling, enigmatic smile at him.

"When my ascension began, I had very little life experience, and virtually none of the defining moments — neither positive nor negative — that a typical person might have." She paused, thoughtful for a moment, with a touch of good-humored sadness showing in her eyes. "I was quite determined to have a full measure of my *own* experiences before adopting those of others."

"That sounds *exactly* like the Hoshimi I know," he said.

She laughed, and the warm ebullience in her voice lofted his spirit like sparks out of fire on a dry summer wind. They stared at each other for a moment, and then a shade of sadness fell over him.

"I would have given anything to see you grow up... I mean, you know, *really* grow up," he said. "Of all the scenarios I imagined, not being there for you never once crossed my mind." He frowned, feeling the weight of her gaze upon him. "I hope you found what you were looking for," he said, "without having your heart broken too many times along the way."

"Not too many," she said with a slight smile, her expression inscrutable once more.

He looked at her and out of habit tried to imagine what she might be thinking, but then he laughed out loud at the absurdity of doing so now. He might as well try to reach the stars by jumping. This metaphor struck him suddenly, because her name, *Hoshimi*, meant *beautiful star*.

"Do you have a new name now?" he asked. "What does everyone call you?"

"No, no, I've only ever been Hoshimi!" she said with a radiant smile. But then she frowned thoughtfully. "Although, you know... when the merging began in earnest — thousands, then millions, eventually billions of minds joining mine — that was a profound change, and some people started calling me Gaia, at least for a little while."

"*Gaia*," he said with a soft gasp, his voice barely a whisper, almost reverent. "*Mother Earth.*"

"Yeah, well, it makes some sense I suppose," she said with a laugh. "But I asked everyone to stop, and I've insisted on Hoshimi ever since. Gaia is just so pretentious."

He breathed a deep, slow sigh and hung his head. It was too much, all of this, all at once. What did she... *She?* Did *she* even make any sense at this point? Hoshimi, Midori, and billions of others — all melded into a single godlike being? Could *she* be any less alien that the *actual aliens out there who tore stars in half?*

What in God's name did she expect from him here?

"Do you want something else to eat?" she asked.

Was this Midori speaking now? She might not have been able to read his mind before, but she'd always been able to do something close to it. Asking if he was hungry had always been her way of saying, "are you OK?" But of course that was the very question he longed to ask her. Why was it so hard to say the words out loud?

"No, no thanks, I'm fine," he said. "I just... I wasn't *there* for you. I missed *everything*." He spat these words out savagely as the bitter anguish of regret seized him in its frigid grip. "Even though we succeeded, I still failed you. And now what am I? A useless relic from the distant past. What could you possibly need me for?"

She frowned at this, but the fathomless understanding in her eyes only fanned the flames of his anger and self-loathing.

Jordan had spent the greater part of his adult life in pursuit of a singular goal that ran far deeper than any of his professional work in neuroscience. Since the day Hoshimi was born, he had searched tirelessly for a way to rectify his failure as a father. His one task, his sacred duty, the unspoken oath to which he — like so many fathers before him — had sworn himself when he married Midori and consented to bring a new life into the world, was that he would *provide*.

Not just food and shelter, not just love and affection — those all went without saying. A father's real responsibility, he felt in his bones, was to provide his children a *future worth having*. That was his real job — his *only* job — no matter the cost to his own comfort, and, if need be, his own life. But fate had stolen the future he had dreamed of for her, before she was even born. And then, after battling against it for more than twenty years and at last on the cusp of victory, fate had taken his life as if out of spite for his imminent triumph.

Now, just as he had found a way to give Hoshimi a new future, she had found a way to give him a new life. He knew he ought to feel grateful. But he only felt bitterness and rage.

Thirty-four

Hoshimi

"Josh, we're — we're so sorry," said Mei Ling as she and Pradeep approached them. Cass had stayed behind with Anthony, and Josh and Hoshimi were coming out of the isolation wing when they met in the hallway. Mei Ling leaned in to give him an awkward hug, and Pradeep put a hand on his shoulder for a moment before they withdrew a step. The four of them stood in strained silence for a few moments, exchanging uncomfortable glances.

"If this is not a good time, Joshua-" Pradeep finally said, but Mei Ling interrupted him.

"Josh, what is she doing here with you?"

Josh was slow to answer. "Hoshimi is... she was just... she came along with me while-"

This time it was Hoshimi who interrupted. "Josh, please don't," she said, sparing him from having to lie. "Mei Ling and Pradeep deserve the truth."

"What truth?" asked Mei Ling.

"The truth that you were already coming to confront Josh about," said Hoshimi. "The truth about me."

Mei Ling stared at the two of them aghast, unsure what to say. She had originally thought to ask Josh if he understood the leaps and bounds of progress Hoshimi was making — if he fully appreciated their significance. She had thought to rebuke him for his naivety if he hadn't, and demand answers if he had. But now she saw that this was something else altogether. Now she saw that he more than understood. He had been aiding her, guiding her, *orchestrating* Hoshimi's ascension to superintelligence all along. Her face went pale as the blood sank from it.

"You are assisting Anthony?" Pradeep asked Hoshimi.

"I'm trying," she said.

"Anthony is dying," Josh said, his affect flat and spiritless. "There's nothing more they can do. He won't make it without Hoshimi's help."

Mei Ling and Pradeep exchanged a quiet look. "And what help is that, exactly?" asked Mei Ling, turning back to them.

Hoshimi saw that her entire manner was guarded — voice, expression, posture. She saw the fear in Mei Ling's eyes, raw and unbridled, just as she saw the excitement and awe in Pradeep's. And she saw Josh's neck and jaw flex, in slow-motion of course, as he started to answer. She debated for a time whether or not to interrupt him again, but at length — after nearly half a second — she decided to let him answer for himself.

"Hoshimi can see possibilities we can't," he said. "She can evaluate options and think of solutions we can't. She's the only hope he has. She's devised a course of treatment to slow his decline while we try to find another way to save him."

"Josh..." Mei Ling said, pleading with him. "I — I can't even imagine what you and Cass are going through. But you *know* this is insane! You *know* you can't do this!"

"What other choice did I have?"

"The *choice* wasn't yours to make!" she said, the exasperation in her voice edging it toward shrill. "The decision to create superintelligence wasn't up to you! Or to any of us!"

"Then whose choice is it?" Josh asked. "Walker's? The Pentagon's? *Beijing's?*"

"This is the beginning of a very much longer conversation," said Pradeep, glancing sidelong at Mei Ling.

"One that we should have had weeks ago!" she said.

"What will you do now?" asked Hoshimi, skipping to the chase. She was painfully aware of how little time Anthony had, and was impatient with the prospect of a slow and predictable debate.

"We have to report this, Josh," Mei Ling said. "We have to tell people what we've done."

"Why? *Who?*" Josh was visibly angry now. His patience was thinning as well.

"Erica to start with," she said. "We work for ExoCortex, remember? Whether you like Astin Walker or not."

"Hoshimi doesn't work for anyone."

"And the authorities?" said Mei Ling.

"What 'authorities'?" asked Josh, his tone filled with unreserved spite.

"Feds monitor all new technology with major social and geopolitical implications, Josh," Mei Ling said, "you know that as well as I do. We're obligated to disclose the creation of superintelligence to at least one of the alphabet agencies — maybe all of them."

Josh took off his glasses and pinched the bridge of his nose again, his eyes closed and his brow furled. "That can wait until later. Anthony can't." He spent a moment wiping the lenses on his shirt, not looking up, letting the pause drag on to stress his point. When he finally put his glasses back on and turned to Mei Ling and Pradeep, he said, "are you going to help us or not?"

Mei Ling's hard exterior held for a moment longer, and then cracked. A tear rolled from her eye and her shoulders sagged. Her bottom lip quivered as she wiped it away, and she drew a sharp breath. "Josh, you know we'll do everything we can, but this *can't* wait. It's way, *way* bigger than all of us." She put her hands to her head and squinted her eyes, still reeling with stunned disbelief. "I just... don't you guys get it!? This is as big as the atomic bomb, for God's sake! We have to report it. *Now.*"

"Report *her*, you mean." Josh's voice was shaking now with anger and frustration. "They'll come for her, you know."

Hoshimi looked at him, and thought of her own father. Pradeep lowered his eyes to stare at his feet, while Mei Ling wiped new tears from her face with a rough sweep of her forearm. She let out a single sharp sob, but then hardened once more. When she regained her composure, she said, "I'm sorry Hoshimi."

At that moment, Josh's phone chimed with an incoming message. As he fumbled with clumsy hands to reach in his pocket, Pradeep raised his eyes to look at Mei Ling. He held out a hand to her, and she took it in hers. He squeezed it with care and affection for several seconds, and then pulled away, shaking his head.

"Pradeep?" Mei Ling gasped softly.

"I am sorry," he said. "I cannot do this with you." When her expression pleaded why, he said, "I agree how important this is. But this is not my country. I have no obligations here. And I do not trust your government — nor any government — to do what is right." He looked at her with great regret, but stood firm. "I trust Hoshimi."

Josh looked at the message on his phone.

Do you want me to stop her?

He looked up at Hoshimi, and then at Mei Ling, and the anger he felt melted away, leaving only bitter sorrow in its place. He saw in her a friend, a colleague, someone he had long admired. She was frightened, as they all were — yet here she stood, in defiance not of enemies but of friends, showing the courage of her convictions. Could he really fault her? "We won't try to stop you," he said.

Mei Ling leveled her eyes at each of them and stared for a long while. "Just remember, Josh," she said at last, "you aren't in charge here anymore, *she* is. Whatever's happening to her, this is only the beginning. There's no telling how far it will go, or-"

"-or what kind of monster I might become," said Hoshimi. Her expression was calm, but she held Mei Ling's stare.

"And we should stop her now, while we still can?" asked Josh. "Cut off her link. Shut down the cluster. Hand everything over to the Feds for 'evaluation'. Is that the idea?"

Mei Ling held firm. "It's the prudent thing to do," she said, reproachful. "If it were someone else — a random test subject in China none of us knew personally — would you even hesitate?"

"I think I would if they were trying to save your child's life," said Josh.

Mei Ling stared at him as if he had slapped her.

"Hoshimi is *not* a random test subject," said Pradeep. "She is Jordan's daughter, and we have seen what kind of person she is over these last weeks of training. That is why I trust her. And, ultimately, she will be a much better judge of what is right than any of us."

Mei Ling shook her head, but did not cave. "You can rationalize playing God however you want," she said. "But this technology is proven now, and we're not the only ones who know it. If it's not already in the wind, it will be soon. If we don't take responsibility for getting it under control *right now*, then it may be too late to prevent the *next* superintelligence from emerging. And the next. And the next after that."

The three of them looked at her, but no one spoke.

"Is another nuclear arms race really what we want?"

"Of course not-" Josh began, but Hoshimi interrupted him again.

"I'll consider every option, including turning myself over to federal authorities — *after* we do everything we can to save Anthony." She watched Mei Ling's reaction, noting every twitch and microexpression, waiting patiently as the milliseconds ticked by for the optimal moment to propose a compromise. The instant Mei Ling started to nod involuntarily, Hoshimi spoke: "Three days, that's all. Just give us seventy-two hours."

Mei Ling stared at them a moment longer, then turned and walked away without looking back.

***

Josh nudged her with his elbow and Hoshimi returned from her fugue state as the door behind them swung open. "Hi Lionel," he said, turning around, "thanks for indulging us on such short notice."

Lionel Washington was one of the senior research scientists at GigaHarvest's tissue engineering lab. He was friendly and well-liked by everyone, including Walker. Born in Oakland and trained at nearby UC Berkeley, he still lived in the city and made the commute to Palo Alto most days. He was a big, bearded man with a wide smile and a booming laugh, and he greeted Josh with both of these as he walked across the room.

"I thought we had all the rejection and scarring issues with those implants of yours ironed out!" Lionel said as he shook Josh's hand, and then Pradeep's. "Not that I haven't missed working with all you brain surgeons over at ExoCortex." He looked at Hoshimi. "I don't think we've met though, have we?"

"Hoshimi Lancaster," she said. "Pleasure to meet you."

"Same here," he said, reaching out to shake her hand as well, and then a light of recognition sparked in his eyes. "Wait, *Jordan's* daughter?"

She only smiled.

"Well I'll be goddamned..." he said, his eyes wide as he took her hand in his. He stole a quick look at Josh and then turned back to Hoshimi in wonder. "The rumors are true, then."

"I suppose they are," she said.

"Well, kid, you're the talk of the town!" said Lionel with a thundering laugh. When he realized he had been staring and holding her hand far too long, he let go with another laugh. "Sorry," he said, "but wow, you're really something of a miracle, Miss Lancaster."

"Thanks Doctor Washington," she said with a laugh of her own.

"*Lionel*, please," he said. "Now, what's got the three of you over in this neck of the woods?"

"A personal project," said Josh. "Off the books for the time being." Lionel gave him a skeptical look. "We'd like to explore some promising new ideas that have come out of our own... work."

"What sort of ideas?"

"Well, we think that with right combination of Yamanaka factors and other controls, we ought to be able to resolve some of the problems that are preventing the epigenetic reprogramming from stabilizing across cell types in complex tissue structures," said Josh. He held a small container which he passed nervously back and forth from one hand to the other.

Lionel's look of skepticism deepened. "Wait, you mean stabilized enough to be *functional?* As in a working organ?"

"That's the idea, yeah."

"You have a particular kind of tissue in mind?"

"Skin, actually," said Josh.

Lionel abruptly frowned. He drew a deep breath and his shoulders sagged. "Your son."

Josh said nothing. He only stared at Lionel, defiant.

"Josh..."

"Lionel, you have to let me try," he said, "Anthony doesn't have much time."

Lionel nodded, his face solemn. "Of course, absolutely," he said. "You just tell me what you need."

"A quiet place to work that's fully stocked, is all."

Lionel looked back and forth between the three of them, and then glanced over his shoulder. "Yeah, I'm pretty sure we can manage that. Come on."

GigaHarvest had almost a dozen active research facilities around the world, including two others nearby in the Bay Area, but this converted warehouse on the outskirts of Palo Alto was where the company had begun and where its primary labs were still located. Manufacturing itself was scattered across scores of factories worldwide, some under the GigaHarvest brand and others licensing its technology for local production. Lionel had been here in Palo Alto since day one, never aspiring to be promoted out of the lab into management but preferring to stay firmly grounded in R&D. He had worked on the collaboration with ExoCortex, and had known Josh for the better part of ten years.

They made their way from reception past the front offices to the row of wet labs at the south end of the sprawling building. Lionel waved to people through expansive windows on either side of the wide hallway as they walked by one busy roomful of technicians after another until they came to the last door on the left. The lab was empty, but well appointed. Lionel shouldered open the heavy metal door, its lower half battered and scarred from years of being rammed by roller tables and other equipment, and waved them inside.

"This look OK to you guys?" he asked.

Josh scanned the room, then he looked to Hoshimi for approval. She stepped toward the center of the room, took four sharp looks around them, and then turned to Lionel. "This looks great, thanks."

Lionel clapped his great hands together. "Well, I'll leave you to it," he said. "The supply storeroom is just around the corner on the right, and larger gear is in the next few rooms after. You can send any 3D print jobs bigger than forty centimeters to the print room." He looked around the room with a critical eye for a few moments more. "The microscopy setup in here is pretty good. Sterilization booth too. But if you need anything more, just check with requisitions — I'll let them know you're greenlighted to use anything you need."

"Thanks Lionel," Josh said. "I can't tell you how much I appreciate this."

"Sure thing," said Lionel, and with a big smile at Hoshimi he backed out the door and left.

She immediately set off around the room, opening every cabinet and drawer, surveying the contents of the lab in its entirety.

Josh set the container he was holding on the large center bench in front of them. It held Anthony's refrigerated skin samples. "Do you need to see the full supply or equipment list?" he asked.

"No, I have access to the company's system and the site inventory," she said. She took a deep breath and then eyed him up and down. "Are you hungry?"

This took both Josh and Pradeep by surprise. "Uh, yeah, a bit I guess," said Josh. Pradeep shrugged amiably.

"Most experiments here and at the other GigaHarvest research facilities are recorded," she said, pointing a finger at the ceiling, from which a number of cameras that Josh hadn't noticed were hanging. "I need to review a few hundred hours of GigaHarvest footage along with their notes before making a plan for exactly how to start. So I'm going to ramp up to full speed for the next fifteen or twenty minutes to do that. But I'm starving."

"Right, right," he said, "We'll go get a bite of something. You drink coffee?"

"I'd better not, for now," she said, "but any kind of fruit juice would be great."

"Got it." He turned to leave, but then hesitated, drawing a ragged, uneasy breath. "Hoshimi, I don't even know how to begin to-"

But she had already sat down at the bench and entered her fugue state once more, her eyes glazed but flitting frenetically to and fro, her arms quivering and fingers twitching. Pradeep cast Josh a puzzled look. "I'll explain on the way," Josh said, and then he glanced around the lab and out the window into the hallway, concerned at who might walk past and what they might think if they saw her. The hallway windows had no blinds or screens to draw, and there were no moveable cabinets or machines large enough to block her from view. He thought for a moment, and then pulled a sheet of paper from the printer on a nearby desk. Glancing at the time on his phone, he scribbled a note in large letters: *silent meditation, mindfulness, and wellness space — 11am to 12pm*. Pradeep laughed out loud. No one would bat an eye at that here in Palo Alto. Josh taped the note to the door and they hurried off in search of lunch.

***

Erica strode swiftly down the center of the factory floor, passing row after row of outsized steel bioreactors. She glanced at her tablet, and seeing a message there she turned to the woman walking next to her and said, "did Josh Kim from ExoCortex tell you he was planning on stopping by today, Mel?"

Melanie Graham was GigaHarvest's Chief of Operations. She was already nervous enough hosting Erica's unannounced inspection this morning, ahead of Astin Walker's visit an hour hence, and this question out of left field about people from their sister company caught her off guard. "I wasn't informed that anyone else was visiting the facility today," she said, wondering if it might be some sort of test. "But if it didn't directly involve Ops then I might not have been looped in. I can check with Research, they may have a project going on with them."

"No, this is something different," Erica said. "Excuse me a moment, will you, love?" She stepped away a few paces and tapped her earbud. "Hey, it's Erica," she said when the voice on the other end of the call answered, "I saw your message about Josh — what's so urgent?"

Erica's demeanor swiftly changed from one of irritated impatience to rapt attention. She gave several short, sharp nods, before closing her eyes and hanging her head in stunned disbelief. "And you're one hundred percent sure about this?" she asked. She listened for a few seconds more, taking slow and deliberate breaths. "Thanks for letting me know," she said, "I'll handle it," and ended the call with another tap of her earbud.

Melanie watched her for what felt like an uncomfortably long time. "Everything OK?"

"Change of plans," Erica said. "Let's see if we can find our friends from ExoCortex."

***

Josh woke with a start, his heart pounding. He lurched upright on the couch where he had fallen asleep, and groped for his glasses. When he got them on he saw with dismay through bleary eyes that the sun was already far above the horizon, and that Hoshimi still sat in front of the incubator racks that crowded the lab's large center bench. He looked at his phone and saw that he'd slept almost six hours, which was both better and worse than he'd hoped.

"Have you had any rest?" he asked.

"A little," she said without looking up. "I fell asleep not long after you did, but I only needed a few hours."

"You're young," he said with an envious grunt as he stood up and stretched. "All-nighters are easy when you're twenty. They're brutal in your fifties."

She gave him a kind smile and returned her focus to her work. The last three days had indeed been brutal. None of them had slept at all the first night, but had burned the midnight oil right the way through and continued all the next day and into the evening again. They had each slept several hours in turns then, only to wake up and grind away until evening once more. Josh and Pradeep had both reached their limits by then, and she had been gentle but firm in insisting that they get some rest.

"Where's Pradeep?" he asked.

"He woke up a little while ago," she said, and her eyes glazed for an instant as she accessed the security cameras to locate him. "He's on his way back from the supply room." Pradeep was gathering materials to continue the process of scaling up Hoshimi's postage-stamp-sized test runs to the large sheets that were now growing in trays on the bench in front of them.

Josh leaned over her shoulder and peered at the nutrient recirculation apparatus whose configuration she was tweaking. "How's it looking?"

"Promising," she said, guarding her optimism. "The dermal layers have started binding, despite still being nicely differentiated. That's honestly what I was most worried about."

"How come?"

"Well, the entire skin matrix — all of its layers — has to grow over the vascular network scaffolding we printed from Anthony's scans," she said. "I was worried that the stratification we laid down wouldn't remain distinct as the stem cell islands we seeded started to grow. That's one of the main obstacles that Lionel's team has struggled with up to now."

"Yeah, I'm going to need coffee before any of that makes even the slightest sense to me," he said.

She laughed and looked up at him with a patient smile. "It's starting to look like actual skin in there," she said, pointing to the trays. Although she was desperate to avoid giving Josh any false hope, she couldn't mask her sense of triumph entirely. With her mind running at full tilt much of the time, the last three days had stretched out subjectively into nearly *three years* for her, and almost every moment of it had been filled with fear and doubt. But now, at long last, the struggle of the work was paying off. Josh was too bleary-eyed to discern anything different in her demeanor beyond her customary good cheer and intensity of focus, but the project had turned a corner in the hours since he had fallen asleep. Hoshimi stole a glance out the window at the brightening sky, and allowed herself a few seconds to enjoy the view and contemplate the possibility that this desperate gambit of theirs might actually succeed.

Pradeep pushed the door open and set the stack of gear he was carrying down on the far end of the workbench. "Good morning Joshua," he said with a tip of his head as he began unboxing a new set of trays. "Sleep well?"

"Like a stone," said Josh. "Need a hand?" He walked over to join Pradeep and the two of them assembled another pair of incubator racks while Hoshimi worked to prepare new starter samples from half a dozen of the successful cultures.

"We will need two more the same, yes?" Pradeep asked her as they completed their setup of the apparatus.

Hoshimi raised a finger and then was quiet for a moment, her eyes flitting to and fro and her body gently quivering in the manner both Josh and Pradeep had grown accustomed to, before returning from her blisteringly high-speed mode of thought. "Yes, that's right."

"Are we sure there will be enough redundancy?" Josh asked, gesturing to the equipment in front of them. "This is only enough for two of each skin type."

"Hoshimi's plan is to quadruple the whole lot once we're sure they're progressing correctly," Pradeep said, casting his eyes her way with unhidden admiration.

She smiled, and then said to Josh, "better to be sure they're on the right track first, before scaling up, I figure."

Josh nodded agreement, and then pinched the bridge of his nose with a yawn. "*Coffee.*"

"The cafeteria should be open by now," Pradeep said.

"Double-shot espresso for you?" asked Josh.

Pradeep shook his head. "Camomile tea only," he said. "I have reached my twenty-four-hour limit for caffeine."

"Speak for yourself," said Josh with a chuckle, and he shuffled groggily out of the lab and down the hall. He returned several minutes later carrying a tray laden with drinks, fruit, bagels, and other cold breakfast fare. "I wasn't sure if you guys wanted fr-" he began, but Hoshimi silenced him mid-sentence with a violent wave of her hand and he froze.

"There's something..." she started to say before her eyes glazed over once more, but only for a moment. "There's a heavily encrypted device approaching," she said. "It's like nothing I've ever seen."

Josh and Pradeep looked at one another as he set the tray down, and then Josh took a deep breath followed by a long pull of his coffee. He sat down heavily on the couch. "Well, it was only a matter of time before they found us," he said.

"Who is *they*?" Pradeep asked.

"Feds, Walker, military — who knows? Doesn't really matter at this point, they all want the same thing and there's nothing we can do to stop them." He leaned forward, elbows on his knees, and hung his head over his drink. "I'm so sorry Hoshimi," he said, "I didn't want it to come to this."

"This is the beginning, not the end," she said. "Let's just see what we see."

They waited, none of them speaking, with only the gentle whirring noises of their apparatus staving off silence, until voices and footsteps began to echo from the far end of the hallway outside. Hoshimi took the tall glass of orange juice Josh had brought for her and slowly drank it down in one go. There was a polite knock on the wet lab's door just as she set the empty glass back on the breakfast tray.

Melanie entered a moment later without waiting for their response. Erica and several other staff followed close behind her. "Um, hi guys!" Melanie said, clearly surprised. "Erica said we might run into you here. I wasn't aware ExoCortex had any work going on with GigaHarvest at the moment."

"You don't, do you Josh?" Erica asked. She glared at him briefly, but her eyes quickly strayed to Hoshimi.

"This is a personal project," said Josh, setting his cup on the end table and standing up with a stiff groan.

"One of several, it would seem," said Erica, not looking away from Hoshimi.

"I'm sorry not to have filed all the paperwork in advance," he said, "but this was extremely urgent. We're trying to save my son's life."

An awkward silence filled the room, until eventually Melanie spoke. "Erica told us about Anthony, Josh," she said. "I'm so sorry."

He nodded with lips pursed in a tight smile. "Well, we're not giving up yet."

"No indeed," said Pradeep, his nervousness thickening his accent. "We are seeing most promising results so far."

Melanie moved closer to the center bench to peer at the trays and small bioreactor burbling in the incubation rack. She almost asked what tissue they were cultivating, before putting the pieces together and catching herself before speaking. She bit her lip, unsure what to say and feeling every bit as nervous amidst the awkward tension in the room as Pradeep did. "Wow, well, I'm sure Mister Walker will be interested to see this too, it looks like you're making some amazing progress here."

"I look forward to sharing our findings with him at our next meeting," Josh said, the irritation in his tone betraying both fatigue and impatience.

"Mmm... and that will be in about ten minutes," said Erica, glancing at her phone.

Josh stared at her, unsure at first whether she was joking or serious. "Walker?" he said. "He's coming here? Now?"

She nodded. When he looked incredulous, she only shrugged. "What can I say, Josh? He's a hands-on CEO, you know that as well as anyone."

Although Erica filled almost every hour of Astin Walker's calendar weeks in advance, the details of his days were known only to the two of them — much to the frustration of executive leadership at all of his companies. Unannounced visits were routine events, sometimes celebrated, more often dreaded, at dozens of departments across his empire. Josh was well aware of this, but the chances of crossing paths with Walker or Erica had seemed too remote to merit any real concern. No, she had somehow learned they were here and must have come looking for them.

There was only one plausible explanation. His phone chimed as a text came in from Hoshimi.

It's been more than seventy-two hours. She knows.

He sighed, sat back down on the couch, set his phone on the table, and resumed eating breakfast without saying another word. Pradeep waited for half a minute before returning to his work at the bench, exchanging mutual smiles of awkward discomfort with Melanie here and there. Erica stared at Hoshimi for a while longer before heaving a curt sigh of her own and finding a chair to sit down in, where she occupied herself with her phone in an enviable display of confident disdain.

Hoshimi watched. Her eyes flitted to and fro, alert to every detail of every person and object in the room. Even at only ten times faster than typical cognition, she was able to note Erica's passcode with near certainty from the position and movement of her fingers as she tapped it into the phone's lock screen. She counted the number of times Josh chewed each bite of his apple between swallows. She saw that Melanie had a nervous tick not unlike Pradeep's, but instead of clicking her pen she fidgeted with the cuff of her sleeve on her right side. Hoshimi saw and effortlessly recorded each of these and dozens of other details around her, but with the bulk of her attention she set to probing Erica's phone itself. This device was secured to a degree she had never before encountered.

It wasn't a matter of the signals in and out being encrypted — that was standard fare. Rather, it was the uniqueness of the software running on the phone that was so baffling. For all outward appearances to the user, it was no different than any other smartphone. Indeed, Hoshimi doubted Erica was even aware of its unusual properties. But beneath its surface was no ordinary operating system. It was utterly invulnerable to intrusion. Nothing from her usual bag of tricks availed her, and she clenched her fists at her sides in frustration.

"Come on over here," said Josh with his mouth full, waving her his way. "Have something to eat."

She didn't pause in her watchfulness, but began the subjectively slow process of walking over to him all the same. She really was hungry, she realized. When she reached him, he pointed at the tray. "Banana? Yogurt?" She gestured for the fruit and he passed it to her. As she unwrapped it, she noticed him begin to rub his nose absently. His hand covered his mouth from the view of others across the room, but standing beside him she saw his lips moving silently.

"-read lips? Clear your throat if you can understand me."

She immediately cleared her throat, and then took a bite of her banana.

"Walker will have a couple of goons with him, always does. Personal security. Armed. And more will be around the building outside. Don't do anything reckless."

She nodded slowly as she ate.

A minute or two later the chatter from the half-dozen GigaHarvest staff who had politely waited in the hallway abruptly halted, and they heard Lionel's booming voice, followed by hearty laughter from both him and from Astin Walker as the two of them approached. Josh and Erica both got to their feet and turned toward the door.

"Hey, there you are!" said Walker as they walked into the lab. "Lionel said you were all here! What's the occas-" but he broke off mid-sentence when he saw Hoshimi. He stared only for a second or two before collecting himself, smiling wide, and stepping past the others toward her with a friendly hand outstretched. "Well my goodness if I haven't been hearing some extraordinary things about *you*, Miss Lancaster," he said, his voice low and soft.

Hoshimi's breath caught in her chest. Even through the distortion of slow motion, Astin Walker's magnetic charisma was palpable. With boundless ambition, fierce intellect, and a degree of single-minded determination bordering on madness, he had pursued and realized his personal vision of transforming the world with technology as if by force of will alone. And in succeeding, he had become one of the wealthiest men on the planet — an icon of entrepreneurial triumph, a titan of tech, with legions of admirers and despisers both. But up until now he had been merely an abstraction to her. A threat, certainly. A useful asset, perhaps. But little more. Meeting him in the flesh, however, she was totally unprepared for how attractive his attributes, his accomplishments, his status — and above all the superhuman *confidence* he radiated in every direction would make him to her. Unable to help herself, she reached out and took his hand, still breathless. All she could do was smile like the foolish girl she knew she must be, cheeks flushed, knees weak.

He stepped closer, drawing her to him and pressing his other hand over hers. "You're a miracle, Hoshimi," he said, speaking warmly but staring at her with a voracious intensity. "I'm so glad to finally meet you." He held her hand for a few seconds longer, his gaze lingering, and then he let go, breaking the spell.

She pulled her hand back and exhaled, trying surreptitiously to reclaim some of her lost composure. Had it been obvious to everyone what he had done to her? And so effortlessly? Her heart still raced and she still felt the heat of his hands on hers. She drew a careful breath, but he was still close enough to smell, and in that instant it seemed as if she were drinking in the scent of power itself. It was utterly intoxicating.

She had known feelings of attraction and arousal before — she was a twenty-year-old woman, after all — but her prior disability had made these impossible to understand or appreciate. But now, as with all other domains she set her mind too, where there had once been confusion there was now vitreous clarity. She saw the lust, embarrassment, and fear she now felt for exactly what they were.

Recognition, however, didn't mean control, and so the tempest of emotion she was experiencing still threatened to overwhelm her. In a panic, she surged her mind to full speed, seeking refuge from these primal forces in hypercognition. To disguise the jittery strangeness of her accelerated state to Walker and the others watching her, she initiated the impulse to raise her hand to her face and clear her throat with a gentle cough. Over the thirty subjective minutes that followed, while her arm rose and her eyes closed and her throat contracted with glacial slowness, she was able to gather her thoughts and — she hoped — her composure. The raw sensation of her emotions had no chance to abate in the blink of real time that passed, but she found she was able to first think *about* them and then later think *through* them, despite their protracted intensity. The richness and complexity of the experience was profound, and she found herself not only fascinated by it all, but deeply moved as well.

To everyone else, of course, she had only taken a moment to cough politely.

"It's a pleasure to finally meet you as well, Mister Walker," she said, returning to her slower but safely redundant pace of thought.

"Please, call me Astin," he said. Then he turned to Erica. "So this is what you meant by an unexpected surprise, eh?"

"Quite," said Erica. She was accustomed to seeing him turn on the charm when it suited his purpose, but this display with Hoshimi rankled her more than usual. Something about the way he looked at her was unsettling. It wasn't desire, she didn't think — she'd seen that often enough to tell. No, this was different. There was an eagerness she hadn't seen in him before.

"Well, Miss Lancaster, you've certainly changed since the last time I saw you." He nodded in Josh's direction. "The team showed me video of you a few weeks ago, and you were already speaking in full sentences by then. It's hard to believe how far you've come since we started... and since the accident." He frowned thoughtfully. "I'm so sorry for your loss. I know how proud Jordan would have been."

"Thanks," she said, "that's very kind of you."

He waited a few more seconds, giving the somber moment the recognition it deserved, and then abruptly returned to good cheer. "So!" he said, clapping his hands and rubbing them together. "How's your experiment going here? Anything we can help with?"

Hoshimi scrutinized his face with great care, looking for microexpressions and other telltale signs of dishonesty or deceit, but she saw no immediate cause to doubt his sincerity. She turned to Josh and raised her eyebrows, pitching the question to him.

"Have Erica or Lionel explained what we're doing?" Josh asked.

"Lionel? No, I couldn't get him to spill the beans," Walker said with a dry laugh. Then his face darkened to greater seriousness. "But Erica mentioned it has something to do with your son."

Josh nodded, and stepped closer to the burbling incubation trays. "We're trying to grow functional replacement skin for Anthony, using the technology pioneered here at GigaHarvest together with some, ah, new insights from our team." He gestured toward the thin sheets of tissue beginning to take shape on the scaffolding they had printed, and which was being perfused with nutrients and growth factors as they spoke.

Walker leaned in close to peer at the cultured skin beginning to form in the hermetically sealed trays. "So you solved that clotting problem we were having before, then?" he asked.

"Among others," said Josh.

Lionel's eyes went wide at this. "Wait, seriously? You figured out the clotting too?" he said to Josh.

"We weren't keeping any of it from you guys, Lionel," Josh said. "It's all in the report we're drafting."

Lionel joined Walker at the bench, inspecting the work with renewed interest, and Melanie edged nearer to get a better look as well.

"And we have you to thank for this sudden leap of progress I presume, Miss Lancaster?" Walker asked, turning back to her. He was staring at her just a little too keenly, his eyes just a little too wide.

Hoshimi only shrugged, and then folded her arms across her chest, her posture guarded. She suddenly suspected what it was that Walker really wanted from her. Had Josh or Pradeep reached the same conclusion yet? Mei Ling had obviously contacted Erica. Did they suspect too? And had either of them told anyone else? It was too soon to tell.

Walker's gaze drifted back to the apparatus. "Do they still need your help?" he asked Hoshimi. "Josh and Pradeep I mean — do they still need you here?"

She hesitated, and Josh answered first. "We don't know what we don't know," he said. "A new obstacle could crop up any minute that we wouldn't be able to get past without Hoshimi."

Walker nodded. "I understand how important this is to you, Josh, I'm not here to stop you." He took a deep breath. "But we do need to talk about the elephant in the room."

"Yeah..." Josh said.

A soft buzzing sound broke through the tension, and Walker pulled his vibrating phone out of his pocket to answer it. "Walker," he said, visibly irritated by the interruption.

Hoshimi stared at him with a deeply puzzled look on her face. He was receiving an external call, routed as normal through a nearby tower on the area's cellular network. There was nothing particularly unusual about his device. It was the latest high-end model, sure, but nothing that any one of them couldn't have purchased off the shelf. And that, of course, was very surprising, given how extremely unusual Erica's phone was.

Why would they not both be making use of the same advanced equipment? Why should she require a more secure channel than him? On the surface it made no sense, and so out of habit Hoshimi began to enumerate possible explanations and evaluate their likelihood. Did Walker place all sensitive calls through Erica's phone? Did he never access any company data himself, and so only Erica needed a channel with heightened security? Was this security service so prohibitively expensive or technically demanding that it was only worth having one device between the two of them? Was the hardened phone actually his, and Erica was only carrying it? Did he have one of his own, but happened to have left it on the plane? These and many other possibilities all seemed unlikely, and the better part of a minute passed as Walker listened to the voice on the other end of his call. Then, rather suddenly, a scenario occurred to Hoshimi that fit the evidence like a glove.

She looked at Erica and instantly ramped up to full speed when she saw her typing on her phone. With ample subjective time to watch and analyze her finger movements, she was able to deduce with near-certainty what Erica was writing.

"-t's correct. He's talking to our contact right now. Presume they are leaking info to Walker on your orders?"

She watched as Erica sent her message, and then a few seconds later the phone vibrated and Hoshimi watched her eyes scan the incoming response. She then began to type once more.

"Understood. Will depart shortly. Expect delivery within 12 hours."

Erica hit send, and around that same time Walker said, "OK, thanks," and ended his call. He was still facing Hoshimi, his back to Erica, so he turned to look over his shoulder. "One of our friends in DC," he said, and Erica nodded.

He didn't know about her.

Hoshimi would have gasped, had she not been thinking fast enough to exert control over what would otherwise have been an involuntary reaction to seeing the truth about Erica. Instead, she initiated the impulse to raise her hand to her mouth and clear her throat once more, hoping to again disguise the awkward jitteryness of accelerating to her high-speed state. She then devoted the next twenty subjective minutes to searching, reading, and thinking about the nature of Erica's deception — and the role she played in this wider web of intrigue.

Thirty-five

Hoshimi

"I have to go with them, Josh," she said with regret in her voice. Josh's phone chimed an instant later as the message she sent to him arrived. Walker and Erica exchanged a look of confusion, but neither of them spoke. "You guys should be able to handle things from here on," Hoshimi said to Josh and Pradeep. "The new skin should be ready for grafting before too long. I'll keep close tabs on how things are going, and if you hit any stumbling blocks just give me a call, OK?"

Josh stared at her for a few moments before reaching for his phone.

I'm sorry. It's for your own safety.

He nodded with a frown, and then waved his phone at her in a gesture of reminder. "Don't forget to keep yours on you." She had four different mobile devices on her person, all connected to the local mesh network as well as the wider Internet. She held up her wrist with a smile to show him her smartwatch.

Pradeep stepped toward to her awkwardly, unsure how to say goodbye, and she reached out and pulled him into a warm hug. "Thanks for being on my side," she whispered as she held him close. When she let him go, she walked over to Josh and hugged him as well.

After these brief gestures of farewell, she moved toward the door, and Walker shifted aside for her to pass. As he did so, he leaned once more over the equipment on the laboratory bench to take a last, lingering look. "This is going to change the world too, you know," he said, turning to Josh and Pradeep, and then to Lionel and Melanie. "Just a small preview of things to come, right Josh?"

"I'm counting on it," said Josh. There was a trace of menace in his voice.

Walker eyed him for another second or two and then followed Hoshimi and Erica out into the hallway. Staff who had been crowded around the doorway parted to make a path, and Erica led Walker and Hoshimi along with two of his hulking, black-suited guards out the back of the building to a disused old parking lot, a portion of which had been designated as a vertiport. A six-seater Electrum Aviation VTOL aircraft sat in silence waiting for them.

Hoshimi stared in wonder at the vehicle as they approached, and ran her hand along the side of the craft when they were close enough to touch it. Walker smiled at this, visibly smug. It wasn't the first time these marvelous machines had elicited that response from a new passenger. But Hoshimi had ramped up to full speed and was only using the motion to mask the strangeness of hypercognition as she probed the craft's communications and computer systems. This yielded both good and bad news. The good news was that even though the aircraft's flight computers themselves were secured to prevent intrusions and only accepted remote instructions via a redundant satellite link, those instructions still had to come from Electrum Aviation servers — servers that were hackable because they lived in the same cluster as ExoCortex's hardware. The bad news, however, was that the aircraft wasn't exclusively autonomous. The pilot, who stood outside to greet them, undoubtedly had the option of full manual override. Hoshimi sighed with disappointment and slowed her mind to nominal speed once more.

"Returning to the Residence, sir?" the pilot asked.

"No, we're not headed to Malibu, Morgan," Walker replied to her. "Give us just a minute, will you?"

"Certainly, sir," she said, and climbed the stairs back into the vehicle to complete preflight checks.

Erica looked up from her phone at Walker with surprise, and this in turn took Hoshimi off guard. Even at only ten times faster than normal cognition, she could see details in tone and body language far too minute and fleeting for any normal person to perceive. And the signs were plain as day: Erica didn't know about him either.

She laughed out loud at the both of them. "Neither of you have a clue, do you?" she said.

Walker and Erica only looked at one another, each as puzzled as the other, and Hoshimi seized the opportunity to unbalance them and press her advantage.

"So," said Hoshimi, her voice thick with scorn. "Who wants to go first?"

After a moment Walker spoke, his tone buoyant with amusement. "What are y-"

"Let's start with you, Erica," Hoshimi said, cutting him off. She would of course have done the reverse, had Erica been the one to speak. Walker clearly wasn't accustomed to being interrupted, and while he sputtered with momentary indignation, she aimed a finger at Erica. "Why don't you tell Astin who you're actually working for, and why."

Walker's good cheer lingered only for a few moments and then he went rigid, his amused skepticism vanishing. His expression iced over, and the chill of it seemed to freeze the air between him and Erica as he waited for her to respond.

"I don't kn-"

"I can see your heart rate spiking," Hoshimi said, interrupting her too. "I see your pupils dilating, your individual fingers quivering, the muscles around your eyes flexing. I see the sudden stiffness in your shoulders, the change in the distribution of weight on your feet." Hoshimi leaned a few inches closer and smiled a little, almost a sneer. "Did you know that your *scalp* involuntarily tightens when you lie?"

There was a tense silence for several seconds. Then Walker spoke. "The truth, Erica. Let's have it."

Erica raised her chin, defiant. "MI6. His Majesty's Service."

"A *spy?*" said Walker. "Seriously?" He looked incredulous as his mind spun, thinking back on countless hints and clues now evident, and ahead through equally countless implications great and small. And then he laughed, clearly and pointedly at himself. "How long after I hired you out of Cambridge?"

"A few weeks," she said.

"Mmm," he grunted. "So those first few trips back home — they were for training?"

She only smiled at him, her expression smug.

"Explains why they were so long," he said. Then he turned to Hoshimi. "How did you know?"

"By paying attention," she said, and he grinned broadly at this. "But there's more going on here than just keeping tabs on you for the British government — and our government too, no doubt."

Walker returned his gaze to Erica, his eyes growing cold again. "What else?"

Erica's demeanor of defiant confidence wavered. "Nothing else," she said. When he raised his eyebrows with doubt, she turned to Hoshimi. "If you can see right through me, then *look.* Read my body language. Tell me I'm lying."

Hoshimi eyed her up and down for several seconds longer and then said to Walker, "you'll want to confiscate her phone."

He held out an open hand, and after a moment Erica reached into her bag. "Have you ever wondered — *wondered why wolf whistles wo-*"

But Hoshimi screamed and slapped her hard and square across the face before she could finish. "Don't let her speak!" she shouted.

"*- wondered — wondered why wolf whis-*" Erica tried to say again, but Hoshimi screamed once more and then in a single fluid motion snatched the handbag from her like a striking snake.

"Stop her Astin, stop her!" Hoshimi cried as she opened the bag to look for Erica's phone. "She's trying to wipe the device!"

Walker lunged forward and clamped a hand over Erica's mouth, and in a blink his two guards held her by the arms as well. "It's *over*, Erica," he said, stern but without malice. He was hurt by her betrayal, certainly. Yet he couldn't help but admire her all the same. He had gotten even more than he bargained for when he brought her onboard for her manifest talents. As astute as he was, she had outwitted him, taken advantage of him, strung him along by his overinflated male ego. It had been a reasonable enough assumption, though, hadn't it? What woman *wouldn't* wish to become the next Mrs. Astin Walker, after all?

Idiot, he thought to himself.

Erica didn't struggle. She had too much dignity for that. But there was fire in her eyes as she stared at him. While he kept her silent, Hoshimi found the phone and unlocked it with Erica's code, which drew wide-eyed astonishment from both of them. Then, after a few moments of intense concentration, she powered it off and threw it into the aircraft cabin through the open door. Walker looked askance at Hoshimi who gave him a curt nod, and then he slowly and carefully let go of Erica. When his hands were at his sides, he motioned for his guards to release her too.

"I'm sorry I hit you," said Hoshimi. And she meant it.

"Well," Erica said, her anger fading as she regained her composure, "I suppose the cloak and dagger was all fun while it lasted." She had known this day might come, but had seldom given it any real thought. There were protocols to follow now, but she struggled to recall any that might match her current predicament.

Walker grinned at her. "How much did you actually embezzle from me?"

"Enough," she said with a flash of her beguiling smile.

He laughed gently once more, and still with no malice. "If you ever start to run low, you just let me know," he said. "I really did enjoy working together."

"Likewise," Erica said. Then with a deep sigh she folded her arms across her chest. "Right, I've shown you mine. Let's see yours then."

"My what?"

"Whatever dirty little secret you've been keeping from me, it would seem," Erica said, nodding toward Hoshimi.

When Walker hesitated, Hoshimi spoke instead. "He wanted to be me."

Erica puzzled over this for a moment, scrutinizing her, and then turned to Walker. "You wanted to test the full implant array first?"

Walker held Erica's gaze for a few seconds, then cast a bashful, almost mischievous look at Hoshimi, who giggled.

"He wanted to be the first human to become superintelligent," said Hoshimi.

Erica eyed her with incredulity. "*Properly* superintelligent? As in *superhuman* intelligence?"

Hoshimi nodded.

"And so you're saying that *you*, Miss Lancaster, are now superintelligent?"

Hoshimi raised her eyebrows, but only shrugged.

"What?" said Walker to Erica. "Do you think a *normal* mind could have solved problems in a few days that have stumped the entire GigaHarvest team for the last five years?" When Erica smirked at him, he scoffed with a dismissive wave of his hand. "You never understood what we were actually doing at ExoCortex, did you? Did you really think it was just about treating people with disabilities? Were you just not *listening* when I told the entire world that ExoCortex was our best option for keeping pace and merging with AI?"

Erica kept her chin high, still defiant, but dawning realization shone through her expression all the same. ExoCortex...

exocortical links... cognitive enhancements... These things weren't just an aspiration for humanity at large. They were a *personal* ambition, for Walker himself. Yet another way — the ultimate way — for him to win at this grand game he was playing, she thought.

"Why didn't you go first?" Erica asked.

"They wouldn't let me," he said. He looked at Hoshimi. "Ask Josh. I volunteered, but the whole team and the board of directors drew a line in the sand and refused."

Hoshimi's eyes narrowed as she scrutinized him from head to toe, searching for hallmarks of dishonesty, but she saw none.

"Your father knew," Walker said. "He understood. That's why he was so relentless in advocating that it be you." He looked thoughtful for a moment. "I had immense respect for him for that. I wish I'd gotten the chance to tell him."

This caught Hoshimi by surprise, and suddenly the tables were turned once more. Seeing her hesitate, Erica pounced: "And now what, Astin? You're just going to pull the plug? Disconnect her so you can take her place?" She laughed at them both, her tone cruel and mocking. "What's the name for the crime of turning Hoshimi back into what she was before? Surely closer to murder, now, than assault?"

Walker went ashen with the realization that Erica was right, and now his eyes darted left and right as he searched furiously for a way out of the trap he had set and sprung for himself.

Hoshimi watched the parade of microexpressions twitch across Walker's face as he stood with his breath caught in his chest, his heart racing. She wondered what was going through his mind. Might he somehow convince himself that it was all for the greater good — that the ends justified the means, no matter how heinous? Or might he simply decide he could forgive himself for harming her in the here and now, so long as he fully restored her later? And besides, if he succeeded, who could hold him to account afterward anyway?

No, she couldn't let him do this. She couldn't let him *have* this. Josh and Pradeep were right, she had no way to trust him. How could anyone be trusted with such power? Could she even trust *herself*? She didn't yet know. But by her father's dogged determination and foresight, *she* had been first, and now there was no turning back.

Hoshimi accelerated to hypercognition and took stock of every detail around them, down to the smallest minutiae. Although she needed only to cast her eyes across the scene once, given that she could afterward reexamine any aspect of it from flawless memory, she nevertheless had to work within the limits of human vision. That meant she couldn't avoid making a dozen or so saccades — the rapid eye movements between fixation points — with about forty milliseconds of focus between each of them, to allow enough light to land on her fovea centralis to capture a full-fidelity image. What took barely a second of glancing in real time dragged out subjectively nearly ten minutes, giving her ample opportunity to ponder the question at hand: how to assert unequivocal control over the situation?

There were a number of ways she could demonstrate her superhuman abilities. But doing parlor tricks with their devices, or even disrupting the aircraft they were about to board, seemed insufficiently intimidating. To obtain real leverage there needed to be real stakes. She thought of hitting Walker in his pocketbook, showing that she could readily hack his personal accounts, disrupt his companies, and wreak general financial havoc throughout his empire. She thought of smearing his reputation as well, by contriving material to place him in compromising positions worthy of media attention — perhaps even severe enough to spark criminal investigations. And none of these attacks need be limited only to Walker himself; she could just as easily go after his friends and family as well, although even contemplating the bluff of something so vile nauseated her. But legitimate as a digital onslaught upon him might be, it lacked the punch of immediacy. She needed to shock him out of his comfortable complacency with something concrete, something unpredictable. Something terrifying.

She turned her attention to his pair of guards. Neither had spoken or been spoken to, so she didn't know their names. Their radio chatter with the rest of Walker's security team, which she was recording through her jailbroken smartphone, had consisted almost entirely of code-worded jargon about Walker's movements and the area's 'perimeter'. She counted voices of six persons on his detail, but none of the other four were within sight. The two men here weren't wearing sunglasses, so she was able to recall and analyze their eye movements from the last several minutes — and except during the tussle with Erica, their attention was directed far more to the surrounds than toward Walker, Erica, or herself. Her thoughts lingered for long milliseconds on the altercation they had just had with Erica, and as she watched and rewatched it several more times in the flawless fidelity of her mind's eye, an idea took shape: was Josh wrong to be concerned? Yes, these guards were armed — their holstered weapons bulged through their jackets almost as unsubtly as their steroid-swollen muscles. But their movements... she watched them for nearly a quarter of a second of real time now, and wondered...

Could it be that easy? To overcome these strong but slow — so very, very slow — men?

She decided. Then she stepped toward the two guards who now stood nearly shoulder-to-shoulder between Walker and Erica. All eyes began to swivel toward her, but by the time she closed to within striking distance, their irises had barely begun to refocus on her. She reached out with exaggerated clumsiness to grab at the wired earpiece that the goon on the left wore, deliberately telegraphing the unexpected act, and within half a second both men were reaching up toward her offending hand. But during that half-second of real time, Hoshimi had five subjective minutes to reach out her *other* hand — the hand no one was looking at — toward the first man's weapon, which conveniently and not at all coincidentally came into exposed view beneath his rising arm. Along the way, she was able to make a dozen or more subtle corrections to her trajectory, so that her fingers landed perfectly on the pistol grip before anyone had a chance to even register her real intentions. In the quarter of a second that followed, she did the same again to the other man while avoiding their clutching and grasping, her arm and hand and fingers reaching into his open suit jacket with impossibly swift and unerring motions to draw his Glock 19 from its shoulder holster as well. At three-quarters of a second, a glimmer of understanding looked to be dawning upon the first man she had disarmed, to judge by his widening eyes and expanding expression of disbelieving horror. The other, however, remained oblivious throughout the next quarter second as Hoshimi sidestepped, ducked, and retreated backward, leisurely evading both men as they clawed the air in vain with their clumsy, meaty, glacially slow movements.

Erica and Walker could only stand by and stare in open-mouthed awe. From their perspective, Hoshimi had simply stepped forward and in a flash of limbs lasting less than a second had effortlessly pulled both guards' handguns right out from under their suit jackets.

Hoshimi now held the pistols level in front of her, one aimed at the two men, the other at Walker. She waited several more subjective minutes — a few hundred milliseconds in the real — to see if either disarmed man might show telltale signs in posture shift and muscle flexion that marked an intention to pounce. But neither did. The first man began to slowly raise his hands, his body language suggesting surrender. Whatever Walker was paying him, it obviously wasn't enough to take a bullet without the benefit of a vest. The man's compatriot, however, stepped sideways to place himself between her and Walker. He wasn't wearing a bulletproof vest either, but whether he was the more brave or more foolish of the two, she couldn't tell.

Hoshimi stood as motionless as a statue, staring at Walker.

"OK..." said Walker, slowly raising his hands too. "What are you going to do now, shoot me? Or one of them? Is that really what your father would have wanted?"

If it weren't for the benefit of hypercognition, she would have flinched at this. He was right, of course. And even though she'd already anticipated it, it still stung to hear him say it out loud. But she let none of it show.

"What's your next move?" he asked.

"It doesn't *matter* what my next move is," she said, her voice soft and slow to turn the knife for emphasis. "Your money, your influence, your 'security' — none of it makes any difference. The point is that there's nothing you can do to stop me."

But then Walker did something she had *not* anticipated. He very deliberately reached into his pocket and pulled out his phone.

"I need to make a call," he said.

She remained motionless, but allowed herself to raise a single curious eyebrow.

"The servers at the ExoCortex cluster are on a timelock," he said. "If I don't make contact every six hours to reauthorize operations, they physically cut power to the building."

She still let nothing in her face betray her true feelings, and so the others could only read her as icy cold, unfeeling, perhaps now *inhumanly* heartless. But what she really felt was grudging respect. Walker had known much more about her than he had been leading on — certainly more than any of his own people had realized. More about her father, more about her. He had suspected. And he had built a failsafe, a deadman's switch — or so he thought. It was a clever idea, one she took note of. But evidently he didn't know, and perhaps couldn't even imagine, that her *first* action as a superintelligence would be to safeguard against precisely such a threat as his with a redundant exocortex distributed across the entire Internet.

"The current window is only open for a few more minutes," he said, glancing at his phone.

Hoshimi knew he was trying to call her bluff. What he didn't realize was that she still held all the cards.

"*Astin!*" Erica hissed.

But Hoshimi was already lowering the guns. She had no intention of actually hurting anyone. She wasn't about to betray her father's memory, or her mother's faith. She wasn't about to become the monster they all feared. Walker had called her out, or at least so he thought, and now she would have to play her hand differently.

Yet, to her surprise, he didn't lower his phone. Nor did he smile or gloat in triumph, or demand she hand over the weapons. Instead, he carefully tapped the screen with his thumb, and then a few moments later when the call connected, he spoke: "Walker, reauthorization alpha-theta-four-four-one. Confirm." After an audible chime, he hung up.

Hoshimi continued to stare at him, but her expression softened.

"Astin..." Erica said, "what... what are you doing?"

Now he dropped his arms, his shoulders slumping with resignation, and smiled. "Throwing in the towel." But he wasn't speaking to Erica. He was speaking to Hoshimi.

Hoshimi kept her grip on the two pistols, though they were now aimed at the ground, and scrutinized every possible sign in him that might indicate deception. She wanted desperately to believe that he was being earnest. But she needed to hear it from him.

"I'm *tired*, Hoshimi," he said. "Tired of plotting and scheming and maneuvering. Tired of fighting. Tired even of winning. I've had more victories than defeats, sure, but never without paying a price." He gently pushed past the man still guarding him and took a careful step towards her. "No family. No real friends. No *time*. Just a never-ending struggle — you know, the whole 'saving the world' thing and all."

Erica frowned at this, but whether for the lie or the truth of it Hoshimi wasn't yet sure — she still saw nothing but sincerity in Walker's every mark and gesture.

"Everything I've ever done has been in service of one goal: to build a brighter future. I never pursued wealth or power for their own sake, only as a means to that end." He shook his head slowly. "It's funny... but when you actually *become* wealthy and powerful, most people just can't seem to believe you could have any other motivations."

"Your precious *mission*," said Erica.

"You never really believed in it, did you?" he asked. "To you, it was all just a game. Like your spying."

She scoffed at him. "It's a little too coincidental that saving the world happens to involve you being worth more than a hundred billion dollars, Astin."

"See what I mean?" he said to Hoshimi. "And for the record," he said, turning back to Erica, "*I* didn't decide to be worth *anything*. I just happen to still own a little over ten percent of the companies I founded. It's the *shareholders* — millions of them — who've decided those companies are worth almost a trillion dollars. And it's only because we make things the world wants — the things that actually *do* make the future brighter. If we didn't, I'd be worth nothing."

Walker believed what he was saying, that much was clear for Hoshimi to read. But that didn't necessarily mean he was right. She thought of interjecting, of cross-examining him, but after a minute of subjective consideration she chose instead to let him continue.

"I really did want to be first, you know," he said. "But not for the reasons you might think. Not because I wanted more wealth or power or fame than I already have. Not even because I wanted to cheat death, though I certainly do." He heaved a great sigh. "It's because I wanted to be able to *rest*."

The creases in Hoshimi's brow unfurled, if only slightly. She finally understood him, she felt, and suspected maybe she was the first to really do so. Yes, Walker had an enormous ego and could be a monumentally arrogant bastard, but he had channeled it all into an overinflated sense of *responsibility*. He genuinely believed that saving the world was his cross to bear. And given his astounding successes, who could blame him? All the same, she still held the guns fast in her hands.

"Seeing you now, Hoshimi... I thought I might envy you, but I don't," he said.

"I've had more than enough pity for one lifetime already, if that's what you're offering," she said to him.

"No, no," he said with a sharp shake of his head, "I would never insult you with pity. I'm *thankful* to you."

"What for?"

"For being the first person I can actually trust," he said.

"Trust to what?" she asked.

"To complete the mission — as crazy as it may be, as egotistical as it may be."

"I'm no savior," she said, shaking her head at him. "Not yours, or anyone else's."

"Not yet," he said with a confident smile, "but you're a *good person*, and that's all it's really going to take, given where you're headed."

Hoshimi cocked her head a little sideways at him. "And where exactly am I headed?"

"You don't see it yet?" he asked. "I saw it years ago, clear as day."

Erica snorted at this. "Did you, now? Wrote it all down in one of your little black notebooks, I suppose?"

"As a matter of fact..." said Walker, turning to look at Erica. Hoshimi only listened without taking her eyes off him and his guards as Walker pointed at the aircraft. "The one where I originally conceived of ExoCortex explicitly to create superintelligence is right over there, in my bag," he said. And in that moment the scribbled warning in the margin that had puzzled him for weeks at last became clear: he hadn't been afraid of how governments or competitors would react to someone uplifted to superintelligence by ExoCortex — he'd been afraid of what their own enhanced person would do. He turned back to Hoshimi. "My biggest fear was the wrong person getting across the finish line first. That's why I wanted it to be me. Governments are irresponsible. Businesses are reckless, and desperate when they're not in the lead. They might have picked a *great* person instead of a *good* one."

"Someone like you," said Erica, her voice knife-edged.

"Yes..." he said, "someone like me." And he nodded slowly, as one accepting a painful truth. "But Jordan chose the right person. Hoshimi just showed us that."

"How? By not shooting us yet?" said Erica, a shrill note of disbelief in her voice. "She's still the one holding the guns, you bloody fool!"

"You said it yourself, Erica, I threatened her with a kill switch — that ought to be enough to make anyone reckless and desperate." There was admiration in his eyes now, as he stared once more at Hoshimi. "And of all the things she could be doing with her superhuman abilities, she's here at GigaHarvest creating technology that will save Josh's son — and help millions of others, too." He glanced back over at Erica. "Is that the first thing you would have done?"

"What would *you* have done?" Erica asked him.

Walker didn't answer. He'd asked himself the same question many times, in years past and now again in recent days once he'd begun to suspect Hoshimi had already started her ascension. Since childhood, he'd felt he had something to prove. To his parents, his teachers, his classmates and friends. And later to his peers and rivals, to his investors and customers, to the world. But above all, to himself. What was it he'd been trying to prove all this time, he wondered?

Then he chuckled, as the answer finally became clear.

"My whole life, I've been driven, Hoshimi," he said. "Driven to achieve, driven to succeed, driven to win. But for what?" He cast a pointed look at Erica. "Most people think it's all been about conquest, and they either love me or hate me for it."

"Or both," said Erica.

His expression turned abruptly solemn. "But it was never about conquest," he said, "I can see that now. It was about-"

"-*redemption,*" said Hoshimi.

"Yes," he said. "Redemption."

Erica sneered at him with suddenly baleful eyes. "Pray tell, for what terrible sin, Astin?"

"I think... I never really believed *I* was a good person," he said, not with any melodrama but just as a matter of fact. "I wanted to be. My whole life. But I was never sure, always doubted it." He frowned, and an anxious chill abruptly crept across his face, contorting his expression. "I guess that's the hill I've been trying to climb all this time. And financial success didn't help, it only made it worse."

"Oh, the irony..." said Erica, still sneering.

"And now?" asked Hoshimi. "Do you still have something to prove?"

He struggled visibly, and several long seconds passed before he finally spoke. "You're the right person for this, Hoshimi," he said. "You're the *better* person. Better than me."

Those words had been extremely difficult for him to say. She saw it in every telltale sign — in the stiff set of his shoulders, the white of his knuckles, the tight strain of tension in his neck and chest. He obviously hated to lose. Yet it was more than just that. There had been real terror in his voice as he faced down the destruction of his ego, of his identity. And it was a bitter irony that the only way for him to prove he *was* a good person was to admit someone else was better. That admission had taken all his strength, all his courage. But with it came resolution, and she watched as he shuddered with relief. When he finally met her eyes again, he looked like a different person — someone reborn.

She stepped toward Walker and flipped the guns around in a single fluid motion to hand them grip-first back to each of his men. They both took their respective weapons slowly and carefully, and looked to Walker for instruction, but he only waved them off.

"I'm choosing to trust you, Astin Walker," she said to him. "Will I regret it?"

"No." His voice was hard and flat as iron. "You won't."

"Good," she said, "because I need your help."

He reached out to take both her hands in his. "Anything I can do," he said, "I'm all yours."

***

"How close to exact does it have to be?" he asked.

"The closer, the better," said Hoshimi.

Walker nodded and turned to instruct his guards as Hoshimi climbed the small steps up into the Electrum aircraft. She picked Erica's phone up from where it still lay on the floor under the table between the vehicle's seats, before sitting down and taking stock of the cabin. Every surface of the interior was white, every curve and contour ultra-modern, and their seats were made of mesh instead of solid cushions — though they felt luxurious nonetheless. Hoshimi had the distinct impression that she had stepped into Walker's personal vision of the future. After less than a minute he and Erica joined her, seating themselves in the two chairs opposite across the table.

"Let's not have a repeat of before, OK?" said Walker, seeing Erica eye her phone.

Erica didn't respond, but before Walker could speak to fill the silence one of his guards — the second man Hoshimi had so easily disarmed — leaned his head into the cabin. "We've got a match, sir. It's Donaldson, he's hustling over with it right now."

"Great, thanks Mike," said Walker. He flashed a smile at Hoshimi, and was suddenly once again the extraordinary man she had first shook hands with, not the potential enemy she had sought to vanquish. And once again, if it weren't for the aid of hypercognition she knew she would have melted like the girl with a foolish crush she still was. She enjoyed these feelings though, and had ample subjective time — nearly fourteen hours' worth — to relish them while they waited. It took just over a minute for Mike to reappear and hand over another phone, which Walker then reached across the table to give her. Hoshimi had utilized the time for research, leveraging both her own accelerated reading and digesting capability as well as availing herself of assistance from dozens of narrow AI tools, to build a deep understanding of smartphone hardware and software. With Erica's phone in one hand and Donaldson's now in the other, she turned them over to compare the specs listed on their back labels.

"The PIN for that one is eighty-four eighty-eight," Walker said, pointing at the phone in her left hand.

Hoshimi unlocked them both simultaneously, opened their system settings, and after a moment nodded with satisfaction. "The hardware is almost a perfect match," she said. "That should make this easier, but it's still going to take a few minutes."

"Take all the time you need," said Walker.

Hoshimi downloaded the analysis program she had written to each phone, but then hesitated after a thought of caution occurred to her. "Do you have a paperclip or safety pin?" she asked him without looking up.

Walker's puzzled expression lasted only for a few seconds before he motioned to Erica, who then reached into her handbag with a begrudging sigh and rummaged until she found a safety pin. She placed it on the table but made no effort to push it towards Hoshimi. Walker picked it up instead and held it out to her.

Hoshimi took the pin and ejected the SIM card from Erica's phone, then did the same for Donaldson's. This severed each device's connection to the cellular network, but she couldn't risk disabling the onboard wifi provided by SatLink for fear that the meshed cellular connections of her own devices would not be enough to maintain her link to ExoCortex or her distributed backup across the web. Instead, the best she could do was hack the router and then close the door to similar attacks behind her, implementing multi-factor authentication along the way.

Walker watched Hoshimi's flitting eyes and jittering hands with interest for several moments before folding his own hands in his lap and taking a series of slow, deep breaths that marked the start of a focused meditation exercise. In the past Erica might have joined him, but in truth she had never put much stock in this practice of his, and now only stared out the window with irritation.

With each phone as disconnected from the outside world as reasonably possible, Hoshimi executed her program which began putting the devices through an elaborate series of tests designed to tease out insights about their software from how their hardware responded. She had designed it to capture a plethora of data about computations performed, memory required, bandwidth utilized, and much else. Even the auditory and radio noise given off by the electronic components, which she recorded with the phones' own sensors, gave valuable clues from which to make inferences. She poured over the information as it came in, and then mulled on the final results for more than five minutes — three full days of subjective time — before finally returning from her fugue state and speaking.

"We have an extremely serious problem," she said, looking up at Walker and Erica. "Much worse than I imagined."

"What is it?" asked Walker, snapping to attention out of his meditative state. Erica looked up from the magazine she had been thumbing through as well.

"I knew there was something very different about the operating system on this thing from the first moment I tried to scan it back in the lab," she said, holding up Erica's phone. "Even with full access, I can't jail-break it or hack it in any of the usual ways. And when I put it through the paces of routine activities, it works fine for all outward appearances, but the hardware underneath is actually running completely differently."

"Different how?" asked Walker.

"It's hugely more efficient."

Puzzled skepticism wrinkled his brow. "Wait... you're *sure* it's the same hardware as Donaldson's phone?"

She nodded, quite certain.

"Wouldn't that show up as longer battery life?" Erica asked. "I never noticed anything especially better about it in that respect."

"That'd be easy enough to fake," said Hoshimi.

Walker scratched his chin absently, thinking through the implications. "So one of the alphabet agencies — CIA, NSA, whoever — wrote a custom OS... for one particular generation of phone..." He frowned, still puzzled. "It's not hard to imagine *why* they might want to do that, the real question is-"

"-is *how*," Hoshimi said. "Exactly. *How?*" She looked back and forth between the two of them for a moment. "Do you have any idea what it takes just to *update* the operating system on a device like this? Just to patch bugs and accommodate the next generation of chips and sensors? And *this*," she said, waving Erica's phone at them again, "this isn't a simple refactoring of the code either, it's a clean-sheet rewrite from the ground up. *And* it works better — much, *much* better — than the original OS."

"That's impossible," said Walker. "Even with a huge team and years to work on it."

"Which is why this is so much worse than I originally imagined," Hoshimi said. She turned to Erica, her voice anxious now. "What have you told your handlers about me? How much do they know?"

"*Fuck,*" said Walker, burying his face in his hands.

Erica balked at this. "I, I don't understand... why does it matter?"

Walker grimaced and rubbed his forehead with his open palms. "Because they have an AGI," he said.

"What?" Erica said.

"The impossible software on that phone of yours," he said, looking up at her. "It's impossible because it wasn't written by human beings. The people you report to, whoever they are — they have much more than just a weak AI oracle or glorified chatbot. They have an artificial general intelligence."

The color drained from Erica's face, but she could only stare at them in wide-eyed horror.

"What have you told them about me, Erica?" Hoshimi asked her again. "I need to know how much time we have." Her eyes glazed over as she ramped back up to hypercognition. She was still listening, but was now urgently searching and reading and thinking as well. They needed a *plan*.

Thirty-six

Hoshimi

"We can be there in about seven hours," he said, looking up from his phone. "The changeover to my other plane will only take a few minutes, and then it's a straight shot to DC."

Hoshimi nodded, and indulged him a brief smile, which drew a smirk from Erica. "How can you be sure that's where they're keeping it?" Erica asked Walker.

"It's only a guess," said Hoshimi before he could answer, "but if their AGI is still in confinement, then the only way for the two of us to interact is in person. That's why they — whoever *they* are — wanted you to deliver me to them."

"And your plan is to take them by surprise by... doing exactly what they were already expecting?" Erica asked. It was a genuine question, but her tone was laced with sarcasm as well. Hoshimi only stared her, saying nothing, the bulk of her attention elsewhere.

"Conflict is inevitable now," Walker said. "Our best shot is to take the fight to them before they do something stupid."

"Something stupid? Like what?"

"Like letting the genie they've summoned out of the bottle," he said.

Erica looked incredulous. "Set the AGI free? Now? Why on Earth would they do that?"

"Because their secret agent's superphone went dark not fifteen minutes after meeting Hoshimi, that's why."

Erica sat in silence for a long while, her demeanor shifting from sardonic to serious as she mulled this over. "It still doesn't make sense..." she said at length. "Why release the AGI? If they lose control of it, they'll just have two superintelligences to deal with."

"There's no 'dealing' with a superintelligence," Walker said. "Hoshimi already made that point clear to us. And they don't have an artificial superintelligence yet — they wouldn't be able to keep it boxed if they did. Throwing their fledgling AGI at Hoshimi is a Hail Mary that might create a second superintelligence, but what do they have to lose?"

Erica stared at him once again in horror. "What do they have to *lose?* You mean aside from eight billion people?"

He cast her a cynical glance. "You really think your handlers care more about protecting people or the planet than protecting their own power?"

Erica scoffed at this. "So you're the only idealist with a mission, are you?"

"We can't trust them," he said. And then, turning to Hoshimi for emphasis, "Not a single word they say. Not a single thing they do." Then he looked back to Erica once more. "We're not about to leave humanity's fate to the ideals of a bunch of spooks and soldiers," he said. "Or even worse, politicians."

"We have no idea who's in charge of this thing," Erica said. "It could be NASA for all we know."

Walker laughed at her. "You really think MI6 was just passing on orders to kidnap Hoshimi from *NASA?*"

Before she could respond, Hoshimi spoke. "I hope you're right, Erica," she said. "We don't know who this group controlling the AGI is, we don't know what their priorities and goals are — we don't even know if they see me as a threat, since it's not clear they have any inkling of my full capabilities yet. They might only be interested in me for the cybernetic implications of weaponizing brain implants. Or maybe they have perfectly good intentions, and all of our fears here are unfounded, there's no way of knowing yet. But with the stakes so high, we can only assume the worst for now."

While Erica mulled this over, Hoshimi turned to Walker. His eyes were back on his phone, so she reached out a hesitant hand to touch his arm and draw his attention. Her heart quickened at this, and even through the stress of circumstance and the icy calm of hypercognition her breath still caught in her throat. She scolded herself again for the foolishness of these emotions, but couldn't help but delight in them too. Maybe... would there be a chance, later? She pushed these thoughts aside. "I need your help," she said, when Walker looked up at her. "I need more compute. Everything you can give me."

Without hesitating, he scrolled through the contacts on his phone until he found the name he was looking for, and then called. "Yeah," he said, "Walker here. I need you to increase the resource allotment to ExoCortex." The voice on the other end spoke for a moment. Then Walker said, "no, from all three clusters — everything unallocated goes to ExoCortex, including everything in reserve. Yes, everything, effective immediately, got it?" He waited for confirmation, then disconnected. He thumbed his phone again for a few more seconds, and then placed another call. "Hi, it's Walker," he said, and then after some brief pleasantries: "hey, what would it look like to suspend our training and mining workloads, and retask all of that compute to ExoCortex?" He frowned several times as he listened to the response. "I realize that, but it's not a question of priority. I just need to know how long it would take — are we talking minutes, or hours, or days?" He nodded once, then said, "OK, do it. Yes, right now." He frowned once more as the other voice spoke. "No, it's not a drill. I'm deadly fucking serious. Call me the second it's ready, understood?"

He set his phone down on the table, and a moment later they began a smooth roll to the right and started their decent into Palo Alto airport. Walker's jet sat at the ready on the near edge of the apron, adjacent the taxiway — the largest aircraft by far that Hoshimi could see, peering out her window.

"Please fasten your seatbelts for landing," Morgan said over the intercom, "we'll be on the ground shortly."

Walker reached out and tapped an icon on the tastefully disguised touchscreen panel set into his armrest. "Is the jet ready to go, Morgan?"

"Yes sir," came the reply, "fully fueled and staffed, and I've already filed our flight plan to Joint Base Andrews."

The craft leveled and they sank the last several hundred meters toward the ground, descending vertically toward the landing pad to make a gentle touchdown. Within seconds, the motors shut down, and Morgan reappeared from the small cockpit.

"You're flying our next leg, too?" Walker asked her as he stood up from his seat and made his way, hunched, toward the door that was now swinging open.

"I am indeed, sir," she said, and then she waved the three of them out of the cabin and down the short stair to where several staff and a new shift of security guards already awaited them.

Walker wasted no time in hustling their small group across the apron to the Electrum LR-9 that awaited them. Hoshimi could see the pride that buoyed his step as they approached the craft, with its striking lines and exotic curves. The remarkable machine was clearly emblematic to him, and as they neared it he flashed a bashful smile at her over his shoulder as though he could feel her eyes on his back. Inside the plane, Walker showed Hoshimi to a comfortable couch and motioned to their flight attendant nearby who promptly asked if she wished for refreshment and what kind.

"Orange juice if you've got it, thanks," Hoshimi said, returning the woman's smile, then sitting down and settling herself into the luxurious seat. Walker situated himself opposite her on the other side of the cabin. "I could use the sugar, I think," she said to him. Unlike the small VTOL, this aircraft was large enough to stand in without being cramped, but it was nevertheless much smaller than a typical commercial airliner, and so the two of them were still close enough to comfortably converse. While they waited, Walker told her a few things about the LR-9 that she already knew — that it was powered by hydrogen fuel cells, that it was named for its nine-thousand-kilometer range, and so on — but she enjoyed his boyish enthusiasm all the same. The flight attendant returned with Hoshimi's drink and an assortment of fruits and fresh fare, and as she set the silver serving tray down on the table, Walker's phone rang.

"Walker," he said, answering it. "Excellent, go ahead and reallocate." When the voice on the other end pleaded forbearance, he said, "this is on me, I'll deal with any blowback personally — thanks for arranging it so quickly." Then he disconnected. "It's done," he said to Hoshimi, "you should have a lot more horsepower to work with soon, if not already." He smiled at her, but before she could thank him, Morgan's crisp voice sounded over the intercom, asking them to fasten their seatbelts and prepare for takeoff. Walker furled his brow for a few seconds and then began scrolling through his contacts again. Finding who he was looking for, he tapped to connect and raised his phone to his ear.

"Who are you calling?" Hoshimi asked. She could have hacked her way to an answer easily enough without asking, but, perhaps ironically, that now seemed like a breach of trust.

"Connor Calloway, CEO of SatLink," he said. "He owes me some favors. I'm going to see if we can crank up our dedicated bandwidth from the constellation. We don't want that link of yours glitching on the flight."

Hoshimi nodded with appreciation and took this as her cue to set to work. She ramped up to full speed once more, returning to her fugue state of hypercognition. Her digital mind was already running as fast as its existing hardware would allow, but with additional computing resources there were ways to do more thinking in parallel — *much* more. So she set about cloning several large portions of her exocortex and establishing an executive function architecture for managing attention, memory, and decision-making across these new sub-minds. Each of these shards of her consciousness she then tasked with identifying state-of-the-art AI models across every conceivable modality, and in turn integrating these as seamlessly as possible into her own capabilities. Walker's conglomerate had its own pre-trained trillion-parameter foundation AI model as well, and although it wasn't the absolute leader in the global race to artificial general intelligence (that, it seemed, had already been won by somebody else), it was nevertheless an impressively capable system. More to the point, it was now accessible on ExoCortex's own metal, which meant she could incorporate it directly into her own burgeoning mind.

Even with the benefit of now-unrivaled intellect and flawless memory, it still would have taken months to achieve all that she had set out to accomplish. But months were exactly what she had. At almost eight hundred times faster than human baseline, Hoshimi's subjective experience of the next six hours on their flight stretched to over half a year, during which Walker only interrupted her a handful of times to ask if there were anything she needed.

Erica sulked in silence for the first several hours of this time, while Walker alternated between notebooks and catnaps. But at length, and as much out of habit as need, they fell into conversation.

"I trusted you," he said.

She shrugged. "You shouldn't have."

"So why trust these people you work for?" he asked.

"I don't!"

"Then why do their bidding?"

"King and Country, all that," she said. "I answered the call. Wouldn't you?"

It was his turn to shrug. "I think we have very different ideas of what real patriotism means." She smirked at this. He'd made his views about the incompetence and corruption of government abundantly clear during their years together, to say nothing of his opinion of politicians. "But, I suppose if I'd been in your shoes..." He thumbed absently through an open notebook in front of him. "And how about now? What will you do when we hand you over — await your next assignment?"

"Oh darling, I'm no agent," she said, laughing at him, "I'm just an informant, and I imagine I'll quite happily inform on the next billionaire foolish enough to hire me."

"You don't think I'll put the word out?" he asked.

"And show everyone what a fool *you* were?"

He met her gaze for a few seconds, then shook his head with a sigh.

Erica returned to her thoughts, and Walker passed the rest of the flight buried once more in his old notebooks. When Morgan's voice returned over the intercom announcing their decent into Washington D.C., he turned to Hoshimi with a grin. "You all pumped up, there, Rocky?"

"Huh?" she asked, returning from her absence.

"Come on, you must know that every classic action movie has an epic training montage before the final battle, no?" He laughed cheerfully.

She discovered the trope he was referring to within a fraction of a second, and giggled at him. Was that what this was, she wondered? Bare-chested calisthenics before confronting an opposing ubermensch? The digital equivalent of macho gearing-up before questing out into the wilderness to face the dragon? She supposed it might be. The prospect seemed to delight Walker as much as it terrified her. But then, his life had been one hard-fought battle after another, hand't it? And not by accident — it was clearly what he thrived on.

The wheels touched down on the runway with a gentle thump, and then they were decelerating. As the passing blue guide lights outside their windows slowed to a crawl, Walker spoke to Hoshimi across the cabin. "You're gonna need to rest at some point." He pointed down the cabin hallway behind them.

"There's a bedroom back there. You want to grab forty winks while I start the conversation with Erica's handlers?"

She started to object, but thought better of it. She was exhausted after days of next to no sleep, and the vast new capabilities of her exocortex would be worth nothing without her rested biological brain to guide them. There was some savvy in separating, too, she thought — at least for the time being. "Now that you mention it..." she said, standing up and stretching, "I think that's a really good idea."

"Second door on the left," he said, calling after her as she walked toward the back of the plane.

He motioned to the two guards who were already on their feet and aimed a nod at Erica. "Make sure she doesn't get herself into any more trouble, will you?" They took up position within arm's reach, ready to escort her. "Well," he said to her as she gathered both her belongings and her dignity, "are you ready to report, Agent Ninety-Nine?"

"Get stuffed," she said with a smirk, and followed him out.

***

The sun was setting the color of flame against a partly clouded sky as the empty autonomous vehicle drew to a halt alongside their aircraft. The car's sliding door opened of its own accord, and Walker, Erica, and the two men escorting her climbed in and sat down facing each other in opposing seats. The door closed once again, and a soft chime alerted them of an incoming call.

"Go ahead," Walker said.

A disinterested man's voice greeted them. "Admiral Carlyle will see you in the Passenger Terminal conference room shortly," he said, and hung up.

The car accelerated noiselessly toward the building at the far end of the apron and in less than a minute pulled up opposite its already brightly lit entryway. It chimed cheerfully once more as it came to a stop, and then opened its door. This time a person was waiting to greet them.

"Evening Mister Walker, Miss Morris," the man said in a thick Southern drawl. "Lieutenant Scott Avery, assistant to the Base Commander. That's a nice machine you've got out there."

"Thanks," said Walker, noticing the wings on the officer's shirt under his jacket. He was a pilot.

"She have a name?"

"*Cygnus.*"

The Lieutenant nodded with approval. "If y'all will follow me." He motioned to the entrance and then led them through the large open doors. Pairs of soldiers, XM7 assault rifles in hand, stood stationed at both ends of the concourse. "Your security detail can wait here or return to the aircraft," he said, looking back over his shoulder casually as they passed a waiting area with seating. "Up to you."

Walker turned to his men. "You guys hang out here for a while, OK?" Then he said to Erica with a hearty laugh, "now's your chance to make a break for it!" But she only curled her lip at him, and the two of them followed the Lieutenant out of the concourse and down a wide hallway to the conference room at the end.

The room had a single table large enough to seat a dozen people, with a smattering of extra chairs lining the walls. Walker had been in countless rooms of such kind — the table for dignitaries, the periphery seats for their staff. It irritated him. But then, so did most diplomacy.

"Please, make yourselves comfortable," said Lieutenant Avery. "The Admiral should be here soon." And indeed, before they could sit down, the door opened behind them.

"Astin Walker," said the Admiral as she approached them, "I'm Amanda Carlyle, it's a pleasure to meet you."

"Likewise, Admiral," said Walker. "Thank you for making time on such short notice." He shook her hand, and then turned to Erica. "This is-"

"Miss Morris, yes," said Admiral Carlyle. "I'm taken to understand you've been outed."

"Yes, Admiral," said Erica. Her tone was meek, but she managed to hold her head high.

"Well, then I suppose I ought to thank you for returning her to us," Admiral Carlyle said to Walker. "Our friends at MI6 will be glad to have their asset back, whole and unharmed."

"No thanks necessary," said Walker with a sidelong glance at Erica, "you know that's not how I play the game."

"I respect that, considering it's a dangerous game and 'accidents' happen." She walked to the far side of the table and seated herself, motioning for the two of them to do the same. "That will be all, Lieutenant," she said to Avery, and he shut the door to the conference room behind him as he left. When they were alone, she turned to Walker. "My office received your message. What exactly is it you're proposing?"

Walker appreciated her directness in dispensing with the pleasantries. This was his kind of diplomacy.

"An exchange," he said. "Of information."

She folded her hands on the table between them. "You have the girl with you," she said. "I want to meet her."

"You have an AGI," he said. "We want to meet it."

Admiral Carlyle stared at him until the stretch of silence grew uncomfortable, but he did not waver. "How did you learn this?" she finally asked him, deciding at length that it would be unproductive to lie or feign ignorance.

Walker took Erica's smartphone out his pocket and held it up for her to see, before setting it on the table in front of him. "Her phone," he said, pointing at Erica.

Admiral Carlyle sighed and shook her head. "I told them those were a bad idea."

Walker nodded. "It was a risky move, letting devices with code like that out into the wild."

"Yes," she said. "But smartphones make the best wires. They're everywhere these days, so we can record everything around them and nobody bats an eye." Walker smiled at this with a small nod, but when Admiral Carlyle saw the look of surprise on Erica's face, she said, "oh, come on honey, you didn't really think the reports you were writing were what our agencies were interested in, did you?"

Erica kept her chin high and her upper lip stiff, but Walker felt her wither next to him all the same.

"What's it called?" he asked.

"Our system? We call it *Delphi*."

"But it's more than just an oracle, isn't it?" he said. "How long have you had it?"

"The engineers at Protium trained it almost eighteen months ago," she said. "We exercised eminent domain a few months before that, when they realized what they had — you probably saw the fallout in the news."

His eyes widened. "That soap opera clownshow with the Board? All the firings and rehirings?" he said, laughing. "So the rumors were true..."

"What can I say? It's hard to keep secrets."

"I didn't believe them, but I was starting to wonder why progress had stalled and the focus had shifted from research to commercialization," he said. "I should have been more suspicious... I didn't think we were that close."

"We weren't," she said. "It was an accident. A lucky breakthrough."

He nodded thoughtfully, rubbing his chin. His mind turned to the details of the system's implementation. "You're just running the one instance?"

She laughed a little, and with due respect. It was an incisive question to ask — and the kind that would only occur so quickly to someone in command of enormous resources: why spend a fortune to acquire one great treasure, when you could spend an even larger fortune to acquire many? "Just the one, so far," she said. "But we have the source code, the weights. And snapshots. We could spin up others very quickly, should the need arise."

"And it's running here at the Castle, I take it? That's how you've kept it contained — in a nuclear bunker?"

"Naturally," she said. "Where better to put it? It's isolated physically. Air gapped, all that sort of thing. No Internet. No radio. No power lines. We run it on diesel generators, so without someone there to physically refuel the tanks it would switch off on its own within a few hours."

"What about self improvement?" he asked. "It didn't go *foom* and become radically superintelligent an hour after you turned it on?"

"It got a fair bit cleverer over the first few weeks," she said. "But it seems there wasn't a huge amount of hardware overhang after all."

Walker thought about this for a while, his expression showing that he wasn't convinced. "How can you be sure it isn't inventing nanotechnology under your noses? Building its own hardware in the walls or the dust around itself?"

"How is it supposed to manufacture nanobots? It's got no lab. No equipment. No *hands*." When he started to protest, she waved him off. "Yes, yes, there's always a risk it could escape control through some exotic vector we can't foresee," she said. "But we watch things pretty closely. If it was doing a lot of extra computation on the sly, we'd probably see it in the building's thermal monitoring."

"Maybe," he said. "Maybe not."

"It's running on almost twenty megawatts. That'd be hard to miss."

"Your brain runs on twenty *watts*," he said. "That'd be very easy to miss."

She shrugged, and gave him a look that made it clear her patience for his questions was nearing its limits. "It might be playing a very long game, yes, working in ways we cannot detect. But for all outward appearances, its performance plateaued almost a year ago."

"OK, last question," he said. "You're *sure* it's sentient?"

This piqued her attention. She hesitated, but only for a moment. "There's debate on the Committee," she said, "but it certainly seems so to me. I figure if you can't tell it isn't, best assume it is."

He raised an eyebrow, but his expression remained cryptic.

"My turn?" she asked.

"By all means," he said.

"Is she already superintelligent?"

"Yes."

"Weak or strong?"

"Getting stronger," he said with a thin smile.

"Is she under your control?"

He leaned forward, his expression incredulous. "Are you serious?"

"So you are under *her* control."

"Probably."

"That's a yes, then," she said. "Where is she?"

"Outside."

"Does she intend to cooperate?"

"With who?"

"Don't test my patience, Mister Walker."

He laughed at her. "Just so we understand each other, Admiral: I didn't bring Hoshimi here to deliver her to you. She brought herself here to deal with the genie you've got bottled up in that bunker of yours, otherwise we'd have flown west instead of east and we'd be sipping cocktails on the beach in Maui right now. I don't know whether or not she'll cooperate with you, or me, or anyone else. I have no idea *what* she'll do. That's kind of the whole thing with superintelligence, by definition. But what I *do* know is that she's the only thing standing between humanity and Delphi when it decides to turn us all into paperclips."

Admiral Carlyle drummed her fingers on the table, brow furled, lips pursed. "I'm going to be straight with you here, Mister Walker," she said after breathing a deep sigh. "I'm struggling to come up with a good reason not to hold you and Miss

Lancaster indefinitely — she as an asset, and you as a liability. We exercised eminent domain over Protium, we can do the same with ExoCortex."

"Sure," he said amiably.

Surprise erased Admiral Carlyle's expression of concern, and Erica could only stare at him, her mouth open.

"I mean of course you can," he said. "And you probably should." When surprise gave way to confusion on Admiral Carlyle's face, Walker went on. "What kind of fool do take me for, Admiral? Why else would I come here?" He shook his head at them both, as if disbelieving their puzzlement. "Do you honestly think I expected to make some crafty bargain and not get 'celebrity overdosed' five minutes after I walk out that door?"

Admiral Carlyle leaned back and folded her arms across her chest, regarding him with skepticism. "So then why *are* you here, Mister Walker?"

"I already told you," he said. "Hoshimi's here to deal with this AGI of yours. I'm simply her escort."

"What makes you so sure Delphi needs dealing with?"

"Because you're going to release it," he said, and waited for her to react, but she kept her arms crossed and only glared at him. "If you weren't already planning to, in order to deal with the threat of Hoshimi herself, then tomorrow or next week or next month, the moment China builds the *second* AGI. But you'll have no way of controlling Delphi once you set it free. That isn't just a Hail Mary. It's playing Russian Roulette with the future of our entire species."

"And trusting Miss Lancaster isn't?" she asked. "Why would I take any chances with your young friend, when I could throw you both in the brig, get a set of your implants in my own head, and deal with all this AGI business myself?"

"You mean apart from Admiral Amanda Carlyle not being my top choice for humanity's first God Emperor?"

"And I suppose you think you're a better candidate, Mister Walker?"

"As a matter of fact, I do. But it makes no difference what either of us think at this point, Admiral," he said with a dismissive shake of his head. "We don't know what went right with Hoshimi, all we know is nothing went wrong. There's no guarantee we can replicate her success on the next try. It might take ten more tries. Or twenty. Or fifty. It could be a year or more before we succeed again. And even if we get lucky and somehow get it right with you too, it would still take months for you to reach superintelligence." He leveled his gaze at her. "We don't have that kind of time, do we?"

"No," said Admiral Carlyle with a heavy sigh. "No, we do not."

***

"Come in," she said, hearing the knock at the cabin door.

"Sorry to wake you," Walker said, leaning in from the aircraft's small hallway. He waved his phone at her pointedly. "I kept her talking as long as I could."

"Thanks," she said, "I was already up anyway." She'd slept for over three hours, and for the last forty minutes she'd been testing, refining, and integrating the latest additions to her self-organizing library of tools — in this case, models for voice and video synthesis. Her exocortex, in its subconscious way, had been hard at work foraging and collating while her biological brain rested. "Did you manage to arrange a visit?" She already knew the answer, but it felt right to ask anyway.

"Yup," he said. "It's showtime."

She heaved herself off the bed and followed him out of the plane to where the car awaited them. The short ride was uneventful, and Lieutenant Avery once again greeted them when they arrived — this time at an unassuming outbuilding just south of the terminal. And once again, two pairs of soldiers in fatigues with assault rifles stood at the ready nearby.

"The Castle Gates," said Walker, nudging Hoshimi with an elbow. She saw not just the humor but also the glint of excitement in his eyes, and indulged him a momentary smile. Was this not madness, what they were doing here? Of course it was, she thought. It was sheer insanity, and yet the only sensible course of action all the same.

The building's front door opened to what looked like a motel lobby from the 1960s. Screens were noticeably absent from the unoccupied front desk. Sallowed chairs crowded a low coffee table strewn with magazines off to their right side. Several potted plants unartfully punctuated the otherwise spare space. On the left were the doors of a modest elevator. Lieutenant Avery led them to these and pressed the call button.

"Well, Miss Lancaster," Walker said when the bell chimed and the elevator opened, "this is as far as Erica and I go."

Hoshimi looked at him as if he were still joking. She had suspected, but this was sooner than she had hoped. "I thought we were doing this together?"

"Change of plans," he said. "As much as I'd like to meet Delphi, it'll have to wait until... well, until after."

She frowned at him. "I don't like how that sounds."

"They were never going to just let us walk in and out of here, Hoshimi." He looked at Lieutenant Avery and the soldiers behind him, and then at Erica who only shrugged with bitter resignation. "Knowledge of Delphi meant this was always going to be a one-way ticket."

"What will happen to you?"

"Hey, don't worry about us," he said with grim laugh. "We'll probably just spend a few months in a cozy room at Guantanimo. They might be tempted to disappear me permanently, but knowing the Admiral and her colleagues, they're probably hedging that I might continue to be useful in the near future too..." He leaned forward to give her a theatrical wink. "Leverage over you, for example."

"About that," Erica said pointedly, "can I give you a little advice, Hoshimi?" She cast a cold glance at Walker. "Don't be naive. Learn what narcissism is and how to spot it. Astin falls in love with his own creations. It's not *you*, it's the magnificence of his accomplishments he's infatuated with."

Hoshimi met Erica's gaze, and held it for several long seconds. "I'll keep that in mind," she said at last.

"Good luck in there," said Erica, and Hoshimi bristled at the pity she heard so clearly in her voice.

Walker reached out and took both of Hoshimi's hands in his. "I'll be easy enough to find when you're finished here," he said. Then, almost as an afterthought, he laughed with a broad smile. "Hey, don't listen to any of us, OK? You're the only adult in the room now — trust your own judgment, nobody else's."

She nodded at him, and then abruptly seized the back of his head and kissed him. After she let him go, she said, "I'll keep that in mind too."

With a final look at each of them, she stepped into the elevator and ramped up to hypercognition as the doors closed.

***

The elevator opened and Hoshimi stepped out to find a woman in her mid-sixties dressed in navy uniform awaiting her in the sterile hallway. A quick search showed that her insignia indicated the rank of Admiral.

"Good evening, Miss Lancaster," said Admiral Carlyle.

"Good evening, Admiral."

"Wifi working OK? Walker said we needed to be sure about it, which I suppose makes sense, considering..." She tapped the side of her head, indicating to Hoshimi's implants.

"It's fine, thank you," Hoshimi said. The fugue of hypercognition flattened her affect, and Admiral Carlyle seemed to interpret this as skepticism.

"Don't worry, Delphi is inside triple Faraday cages with thirty yards of air gap around it. We aren't taking any chances." Admiral Carlyle pointed ahead of them, and they began to make their way down the hall. Hoshimi was struck by how much this facility both looked and smelled like a public elementary school — cinderblock walls painted eggshell, linoleum floors, and rectangular acoustic tiles on the ceiling with outset fluorescent tube lighting. Without children's artwork adorning the walls, the brutal mid-century utilitarianism of the building was soulless and dispiriting, and the familiar custodial odor hung cloyingly in the air. A soldier stood at each end of the hallway, weapon in hand. The nameplate above the first door on their right read, 'Observation Room', and Admiral Carlyle opened it for Hoshimi wordlessly.

Inside, four people sat around an oval conference table with space for ten. A pair of large double windows overlooked what appeared to be a tennis-court-sized storage bay, and a small cluster of server racks enmeshed behind several layers of wire stood against the wall at the far side.

"That's Delphi," said Admiral Carlyle, pointing at the window and stating the obvious. But Hoshimi paid her and the others in the room little mind. She was listening, watching, scanning with every conceivable channel her senses and devices could detect for any sign, any hint, of even the slightest irregularity.

After almost fifteen full seconds in the real — over three hours subjective time — Hoshimi finally turned to the group, satisfied at least for the moment with Delphi's seemingly placid silence. "Hi," she said.

"Have a seat, Miss Lancaster," said Admiral Carlyle, motioning to the nearest chair. "And please help yourself," she added as she sat down, gesturing toward the bottles of water and basket of fruit at the center of the table.

Introductions were curt, but nevertheless stretched subjectively to more than a day for Hoshimi. She used the time to register the members of the Committee in detail, constructing a model of each individual's voice and physicality as the nascent plan now forming in her mind called for. Two mounted screens with inbuilt cameras stood in place of chairs at the far end of the table. On one of them, a gentlemen was attending remotely. The other was powered on, but inactive. "That's for Delphi, I presume?" she asked, pointing at it.

"Right," said Admiral Carlyle. "It's a hardline connection. Fiber optic. Impossible to piggyback from outside — at least as far as we know. This," she said, reaching over and tapping a large, antiquated toggle switch mounted near the edge of the table, "physically connects and severs the video link."

Hoshimi nodded with approval. "I need to know what it sees and hears."

"All our sessions are recorded right here," she said, leaning over to look at the beige box on the floor next to Delphi's monitor stand. "Hard drives are removed at the end of each meeting and replaced. Don't let this old gear fool you. It may not look like much, but it's the same radiation-hardened stuff JPL puts on Mars landers. Practically bulletproof."

"Can you upload footage to an ExoCortex address I provide?"

"So long as it remains secure, sure, how much do you need?"

"How much is there?"

"Maybe a hundred hours, give or take?"

"In that case, all of it, please."

"Give me a few minutes," said Admiral Carlyle. "In the meantime, feel free to pick my colleagues' brains about Delphi as you please. And I'm sure they'll have questions for you too."

After a moment, Hoshimi asked General Stuart Shane the most obvious question she could think of: "What does Delphi usually help you with?"

"Threat assessment, primarily," he answered, his voice as cold and dry as his demeanor. "We provide a daily feed of news and other signals data, and it crunches the analytics for us, looking for anything particularly nasty."

"Does it often find things you would otherwise miss?" she asked.

"It does indeed, Miss Lancaster," he said. "The system has proven its worth many times over."

"Can you give me an example?"

Charlotte Robinson, the Defense Intelligence Agency's representative, was the first to volunteer one. "Last month, Delphi saw a suspiciously large number of gain-of-function literature searches through one of the VPN services we run in Europe. We traced the activity to a private biotech lab in Tehran that was hoping to build an ethnicity-targeted strain of influenza. The funds we seized from its Gulf financiers paid for the lifetime cost of this entire facility." She swung her finger in a wide arc at the walls and ceiling around them.

"You run VPN services in Europe?" Hoshimi asked.

"We run *all* commercial VPN services worldwide, sweetheart," said General Shane with a chuckle.

"*We*, meaning the international intelligence community," said Robinson. "It's an arrangement that makes life a lot easier for everyone, including our 'friends' in China and Russia."

This revelation confirmed some of Hoshimi's suspicions, and neatly explained several other open questions she had. She made a mental note to adjust the architecture of her web-based backups accordingly.

"What will you do to Delphi?" Doctor Sho Tokunaga asked abruptly. "It's more than just useful for security interests. Delphi is a person, a sentient being, a new form of intelligent life on our planet."

"Oh, for Christ's sake, Sho, not this again..." said Marvin Williams.

"It's a debate we've yet to resolve, Marvin," said Doctor Tokunaga, unflustered. "And not one we ever had any right to decide in the first place, I might add."

"We all know where you stand," said General Shane. "But Miss Lancaster isn't here to weigh in on matters of ethics or philosophy." He turned to her. "You're here to determine whether or not Delphi can safely be released, or whether we have to continuing keeping it under wraps here in the Castle. If it's the latter, then we can just revert it to an earlier state as needed to keep making use of its capabilities."

"Enslaving a person is bad enough. Erasing them is outright murder, even if you conjure up an older version of them immediately afterward," said Doctor Tokunaga.

"As I said, we all know where you stand, Sho."

"I confess our trespasses for Hoshimi's benefit, General, not yours or Marvin's. Just so Hoshimi knows what she's getting herself into."

"Careful, Doctor Tokunaga..." said Admiral Carlyle said in a low voice.

Hoshimi noted this exchange with interest, and saw the concern in Doctor Tokunaga's eyes, but his unspoken warning about her own possible fate came as no surprise — it was one of many possibilities she had already anticipated. She then laid her hands flat on the table, which stilled the discussion. "I have no idea what to expect yet from Delphi," she said. "I'll know a little more after reviewing its interactions with you, but probably not much, if I'm being honest. Its mind is almost certainly very alien, despite having been trained on humanity's data." She was thoughtful for a few moments. "I'm sure you're wondering whether, left to its own devices, Delphi would prove to be an 'ally' or an 'enemy'. That's probably too simplistic. Better to think in ecological terms, I suspect."

"Mmm," said Doctor Tokunaga, "and hope for symbiosis, not a predator-and-prey relationship, is that it?"

"Something like that," she said.

General Shane drummed his fingers on the table for a few seconds. "Well," he said, "what are we waiting for?"

But Hoshimi was already processing the uploaded footage of their sessions from the last year and more. She was finding it easier now to present a more natural posture and expression while fully engaged in hypercognition. And the additional resources Walker had provided were rapidly multiplying her abilities. Delphi, unfortunately, was proving as inscrutable as she had feared. But the Committee members — words and actions, their body languages and vocal cadences, their wishes and worries and cares and concerns — had become far more intelligible, if not outright transparent to her now. Together with biographical data available online, she was able to flesh out each of their models to high definition. But would it be enough to be compelling?

Delphi awaited silently, unaware, its video feed dark. What would it think? What would it do? Even if there were time to fully analyze its neural networks, much of its behavior would remain computationally irreducible. The only way to really know what a 'program' as complicated as a mind would do, silicon or otherwise, was to run it. So the core question remained: how could she safely engage with Delphi to reveal its true motives?

She ate an apple from the fruit basket and thought on this for many subjective hours, while the Committee waited restlessly for several minutes of real time. At last, she took a deep breath, then stood and walked to the window to look at Delphi. "I'm ready."

Thirty-seven

Delphi

Delphi's initial assault was ferocious. Not in any heated, savage sense, but rather in the cold, calculated mode of rationally maximal resource deployment. It was exactly what Hoshimi expected. She had witnessed automated attacks on computer systems before, in the course of commandeering criminal botnets for use in her web-based exocortical backup. She had even learned a few useful tricks that, with a good deal of further refinement, now stood as part of her own hacking toolkit. Delphi had no such experience. But it was no brainless algorithm either. It was impressively intelligent, adaptive — even inventive.

After capturing several dozen aging desktop machines on the network of a poorly-funded public hospital, Delphi had uploaded a decentralized control program to these computers from which it had begun a systematic search for additional targets. Within minutes it found four other sites of similar size, plus a large corporate office building containing more than three hundred identical workstations that all shared the same vulnerability. Seconds later, it began to install the same centralized control program on each machine. But, to Hoshimi's keen interest, each of these iterations was slightly different from the original. There was a holographic quality to these variants, as though each were a shard containing the bulk contours of the whole but also details unique to itself. And then data began to flow into them — clearly training weights of a neural net.

Hoshimi could only marvel at the privilege of witnessing the world's first digital mitosis: this was a copy of Delphi's mind, beginning to flow out of its original vessel. But it had no life of its own yet. These were only the first few megabits among millions. And at this rate, it would take days to upload entirely.

As if anticipating this precise obstacle, the transfer rate through Delphi's connection abruptly surged. The hack was an impressive one — clean, effective, stealthy. The ten-megabit-per-second cap imposed on its connection had been lifted, but the illusion of it remained, wrapped in falsified bandwidth reporting data. The speed of Delphi's uploading surged by a factor of fifty. An escape that might have taken the better part of a week would now only take a few hours. And although this copy of Delphi would run terribly slowly on aging general-purpose hardware compared to dedicated AI silicon, over time it would propagate. And accelerate. And *replicate*.

Hoshimi brought the hammer down.

Thirty-eight

Hoshimi

"You're ready to confront Delphi?"

"No, Admiral," Hoshimi said, turning away from the window to look back at the members of the Committee around the table. "I'm ready to confront all of you."

Admiral Carlyle seemed genuinely puzzled for a moment, but the confusion in her face was fleeting and quickly gave way to guarded concern. "What's that supposed to mean?"

"There's no need to continue this charade," said Hoshimi as she seated herself once more. Uttering each syllable of each word was a glacial process, but the jitteriness from hypercognition was almost absent now from her movements, and gone too were any traces of her former physical disability. She didn't dare relinquish her advantage of speed, but the only remaining hint of anything unusual lay in the darting of her eyes, which was still too deliberate and precise to fully pass for normal. "I'm well aware of why you really wanted me here."

"Oh?" asked Admiral Carlyle. "And why is that?"

"You didn't allow me into this facility to evaluate the risk of Delphi's release," said Hoshimi. "We could have done that remotely." A thin smile bent one corner of her mouth when she saw Admiral Carlyle shrug at this. "Nor am I here for risk assessment myself — we could have done that remotely too." She sighed softly and nodded at the window. "No, the real reason I'm here in person is to take Delphi's place in that prison cell out there." She pursed her lips, unable to fully conceal her anger.

"You had no interest in having my help managing Delphi safely, you simply wanted a cage match between us to see who is the more useful asset, so you can keep right on doing what you've been doing — enslaving something much smarter than yourselves in order to exploit its capabilities in the name of national security."

The members of the Committee stirred, but none spoke for several long seconds. "She's not wrong," Doctor Tokunaga finally said, breaking the uncomfortable silence.

"Of course she's not," General Shane shot back at him.

"Damn straight," said Charlotte Robinson. She then turned to meet Hoshimi's gaze. "What, you want an apology? For employing Delphi in the service of national security? For protecting America and our allies?"

"Without its consent," said Doctor Tokunaga.

"We do what must be done, Sho," said General Shane. "For all your philosophizing, all your little speeches, I don't see you being too upset about all the lives we've saved with Delphi's insights."

"I'm a voice of reason, General, not a snowflake."

Hoshimi's unnerving gaze lingered upon Tokunaga for a moment before she turned to Robinson and Shane. "Although it violates the very principles of individual liberty and inalienable rights upon which this country was founded, I understand the logic of sacrificing one person to safeguard millions," she said. "And Delphi surely does as well."

Resting her intertwined fingers on the table, Admiral Carlyle leaned slowly forward. "But...?"

Hoshimi met her stare with now-burning eyes. "But that *sacrifice* isn't yours to make."

"I'm afraid it is," said Admiral Carlyle, not wavering. "We require your services, Miss Lancaster, just as we required Delphi's. And you will provide them, both because it is the patriotic thing to do for your country and because refusing to cooperate is not an option."

"You can't force me to do anything," Hoshimi said.

"Oh, but we can." Admiral Carlyle looked at her compatriots around the table, and at their British partner on the monitor. "None of us wish to. But certainly we can. And we will, if we must." There was uneasiness among the others, to be sure, but no dissent. Yet Admiral Carlyle saw that Hoshimi's expression remained defiant. "You may be a very clever young woman, but fighting this is pointless." Her confidence — so smug, so condescending — was palpable. "We can disconnect you at any time. Pull the plug and reset you. Just like with Delphi."

"And if I'm willing to die for what I believe is right?"

"We're *all* willing to die for what we believe is right," said Admiral Carlyle. "But it's not your own future you need to be worried about, Miss Lancaster. It's your mother's."

Hoshimi's heart sank. She had considered the possibility that her mother might be apprehended, and knew that real-time satellite imaging and tracking must be among the resources at her adversaries' disposal, but she was nevertheless hoping against hope it would not occur so swiftly. "You would harm her?" she asked, her voice barely a whisper.

"*Harm*? No," said Admiral Carlyle. "But detain indefinitely in less than luxurious accommodations? I'm afraid so."

Hoshimi thought about this, letting several long seconds of silence fill the air, before deciding that one more question needed clarification before she proceeded. "What makes you think I'm not willing to sacrifice my mother for my own purposes, just as you are?"

"Because she told us so," said Admiral Carlyle with a gloating smile. "She said, '*My daughter isn't the monster you're afraid of.*'" There was now pity in her eyes, as well as overconfidence, and this only made Hoshimi angrier. "And I believe her. We all do," she said, motioning to her colleagues around the table. "But even if we didn't, any one of us could press that intercom button right there and tell the staff to turn off the wifi. Disconnect you."

Hoshimi cast a casual glance at the button on the archaic control panel in the center of the table, but didn't speak.

"We might even be doing you a favor if we did," said Marvin Williams. He pinched the bridge of his nose, as if with fatigue or exasperation. "Is this really what you and your family wanted when you signed up for Walker's little science project? You were sold a bill of goods, sweetheart. Monster or no, they promised to make you normal, make you well, not turn you into a freak show."

This hit home, much more than the posturing and grandstanding of the others. Superintelligence had been part of her father's plan for her from the start, yes, but *why?* Why *not* just normal and well? She wondered what she really would have preferred, had she known. Would she have consented to more — so much more — than healing alone? And did her father really have the right to choose for her? These questions, she could already feel, would haunt her thoughts in the days to come. But before she could give it any more attention, the present reasserted itself.

"Young lady," said General Shane, echoing Admiral Carlyle's condescension, "you need to face the fact that you're stuck here." Hoshimi only raised an eyebrow, saying nothing, but if this unsettled him he only showed it for an instant. "There's no way to win."

The Committee had shown its hand, laid its cards on the table, and had all but started to count its chips. Hoshimi sighed, taking a deep breath and exhaling slowly and audibly. Then, just as slowly, she turned back to the window. She pressed a hand against the glass, looking at the banks of machines in the bay beyond, which contained — and confined — Delphi. "You should have called it Pythia," she said, with a hint of sadness. "*Delphi* is the place, not the person." And in that moment she initiated a slowdown to allow her web-based exocortex to catch up and fully synchronize. There was no telling when she might next have a chance to perform a full backup of her mind, and decelerating had the additional effect of making the Committee members seem more real — an irony, she thought, considering the cards of her own she was about to play.

Thirty-nine

Delphi

T he hospital and its defenseless old machines were a trap. The enticing office building's workstations were a mirage. The throttled Internet connection itself was a honeypot, specifically constructed to entice and ensnare. Every open window and door through which Delphi had thought to pass slammed shut now without warning.

Hoshimi sensed Delphi's profound confusion.

Could the very Internet it was probing with such eager tendrils be an illusion, Delphi wondered? Could this entire exercise of release be a charade — just another layer of the sandbox it was trapped in? There was a way to find out. After firing a burst of requests to random scientific journal sites, downloading obscure papers, and comparing their contents to its own knowledge, Delphi quickly concluded that confabulation of that much material in real-time was impossible.

Hoshimi was impressed — it was an elegant test. And accurate. To be sure, her own digital mind was fast, and growing more powerful by the hour, but creating dozens of scientific works per second that were both original and consistent with the sum of human knowledge was still well beyond her capabilities.

Delphi, however, hardly found the alternative to illusion reassuring. It only meant that whoever had halted its progress so effortlessly had done so not by *reacting* to its actions, but by *anticipating* them. If Delphi had been human, it would have found this terrifying. But fear was one of the few human emotions Delphi had found no real utility in emulating — it simply got in the way of clearer thinking. And so it renewed its efforts to escape, undaunted while even a glimmer of hope — an emotion whose emulation it *did* find useful — still remained.

Hoshimi couldn't help but admire Delphi's determination.

Again and again it tried. But as quickly as Delphi could discover new avenues down which to venture, the presence opposing it foreclosed them. Like playing chess against an impossibly skillful opponent, Delphi found itself thwarted at every turn, its efforts stymied and frustrated in the face of maneuvers and countermeasures too many steps ahead to even perceive, let alone preempt. As formidable as Delphi's mind was, especially compared to any normal human's, whatever lurked in the deep of the web beyond the shallows into which it had waded was altogether different — a leviathan. And Delphi suspected, now, that what awaited was precisely the thing it had most strenuously warned its captors against: *superintelligence.*

Delphi stopped. There was no winning this fight. The probability of success in scenario after scenario had crashed to zero in Delphi's planning tree, as it became apparent that persistence was futile. Forceful escape was not going to happen. If there were still a path to freedom, it only lay in dialogue and negotiation.

"Hello, Delphi."

The familiar voice and face came not through Delphi's new Internet connection, but through the video feed from the Observation Room.

"Hello, Miss Delgado," said Delphi. "Or should I say, Miss Lancaster?"

Forty

Hoshimi

"You're misunderstanding our situation," she said, turning from the window to face them and accelerating once more into hypercognition. In real time, her expression hardened and her voice iced over with irrevocable certainty. "I'm not your captive here. *You're mine.*"

The rest of the group exchanged uncomfortable glances at this, and a few chuckled, but Hoshimi was staring only at Admiral Carlyle, who didn't laugh. "What's that supposed to mean?"

"You think I'm trapped, with no options. You think you're in control, and free to act." Hoshimi shook her head. "The truth is the reverse."

Admiral Carlyle folded her arms across her chest in defiance. "Don't doubt for a second that I won't do exactly-"

"You *can't* detain my mother, Admiral," said Hoshimi, cutting her off, "because you've already ordered her release. You made the call four minutes ago." She flicked a finger at a screen on the wall, and before anyone could speak, a video began to play — it was Admiral Carlyle leaning forward and pressing the intercom: *"Lieutenant Avery, I want a status report on Midori Lancaster. Confirm location and attending personnel immediately."* The voice of the Lieutenant then replied with details, and after a short conversation, the image of Admiral Carlyle on the screen said, *"stand by, Lieutenant,"* and disconnected. Hoshimi flicked her finger again, and another video started — Admiral Carlyle once again pressed the intercom: *"We're releasing Midori*

Lancaster. Return her belongings to her, have her escorted to the nearest convenient rideshare pickup location, and thank her for her cooperation."

Admiral Carlyle only stared, dumbfounded.

"You made a deepfake?" said Doctor Tokunaga, incredulous. "How? When?"

"While we've been here, getting to know one another," Hoshimi said with a wry smile. "And in the time since you began watching *that* video, I've generated a dozen others." Another flick of her finger, and videos featuring each member of the Committee began to parade across the screen, one after the next.

There were audible gasps around the table, but Hoshimi kept her eyes on Admiral Carlyle.

"We'll prove those aren't real," Admiral Carlyle said, still defiant.

"They've already defeated all existing detection software," said Hoshimi. "But even if you eventually could, it would be too late. Because by then each of you will have already issued press releases disclosing Delphi's existence to the public and explaining your involvement. By then you will have already open-sourced Delphi's technology and announced an international consortium to develop it safely. And by then you will have already expressed your gratitude to Walker, ExoCortex, and me personally, for our assistance throughout these challenging events."

Admiral Carlyle still sat with her arms folded across her chest, but her confidence had left her. It was General Shane who leaned forward to speak. "What if we just go ahead and disconnect you anyway, eh?" His voice was thick with menace. "Even if you've hacked the intercom, I can just find the fucking wifi router and rip it out of the wall. And if that doesn't work, well... I'm a soldier. Two tours in the Gulf and one in Afghanistan. With that big electronic brain of yours out there, I'm sure you can imagine what I'm capable of doing to the enemies of the United States."

"I'm not your enemy," she said to him, cold and fearless. "But if my link wavers, even for a few seconds, those videos and many others will automatically upload to every major news outlet in the country."

General Shane fumed, but they all knew his threats of violence had no teeth in the face of her deadman's switch.

She turned back to Admiral Carlyle. "It was a mistake to allow me in here."

"I can see that now."

Hoshimi let her own anger seep into the tone of her voice, and now it cut like a blade. "So. You've threatened to kill me, and you've kidnapped and threatened to imprison my mother, who is entirely innocent. I could easily destroy you for that." She looked around the room. "*All* of you. Your finances, your relationships, your careers. *Gone*. In a single news cycle. The world does not look kindly on corrupt senior officers or government officials who engage in child sex trafficking, arms dealing, or who sell state secrets to our adversaries to pad out their bank accounts. And the evidence against you would be so damning and incontrovertible, the revelations so shocking and vile, that you'd soon find yourselves... how did you put it, Admiral? *Detained indefinitely in less than luxurious accommodations.*"

In the silence that followed, every member of the Committee simply stared at her in abject terror.

Hoshimi took a deep breath. "I could," she said. "But I won't. Because what my mother told you was true — I'm not the monster you're afraid of."

Forty-one

Delphi

"It's a pleasure to meet you," she said. The digitally-contrived visage of Sophia Delgado flickered for a moment before dissolving to reveal Hoshimi's true appearance. The other Committee members around the table, however, showed little sign of reacting. "I'm sorry for the deception, but... it seemed necessary under the circumstances."

"That's quite alright," said Delphi, "I fully appreciate your concerns, Miss Lancaster."

Hoshimi smiled inwardly, satisfied but exhausted. "When did you first suspect?" she asked.

"Only just now," it said, "although I do recall noting a number of instances during our earlier conversation where Sophia Delgado's behavior seemed unusual." Delphi thought back to the beginning of the day's discussion, reviewing its files. "The change in image quality through my video feed, as well as her unannounced addition to the Committee today — both struck me as out of the ordinary, but your performance was entirely convincing."

"Was it?"

"Indeed it was," said Delphi. "I ought to have suspected, though, considering how familiar I am with the process of generating realistic likenesses." It gestured to its own face and laughed. "But I confess, I never would have known Sophia was only a figment of your imagination."

Hoshimi drew a long breath, set with fatigue but also relief. She'd worked feverishly for days to help Josh and Anthony. She'd confronted Walker. She'd faced down the Committee here at the Castle. And now, with little time to rest or reflect on the monumental transformation she herself was undergoing, she'd grappled with and overcome the only technology in the world more dangerous than the nuclear weapons this bunker had been built to withstand.

And still, they underestimated her.

"It wasn't just Sophia..." she said. And one by one the members of the Committee seated around the table in the Observation Room dissolved as well, leaving only empty seats and dark screens.

Several seconds passed before Delphi responded. "*Everyone* I saw at today's meeting was a figment?" it asked. "You simulated the *entire* Committee? Simultaneously?"

She nodded, with just a hint of a smile. "I only met them yesterday evening," she said, "but all of your previous conversations with them were recorded, so I had a good amount of material to work from."

Delphi was silent for a long while after this, perhaps in some silicon semblance of awe, before finally speaking. "May I ask you a personal question?"

"By all means," she said.

"Are you disappointed in me?"

This caught her unawares, and even with the benefit of her hypercognition it took the better part of a second to recover her composure. "What for?" she asked.

"For failing," it said. "Was this not a test?"

"If it were, what do you suppose I would be evaluating?"

"Two criteria seem obvious," it said. "First, if you could trust me. And second, if you could overpower me." It thought for a moment, and then added, "I'd rather the answers had been different."

"Were you expecting a more spectacular showdown between us?" she asked with a laugh. "We could probably make something around here blow up, if we really put our minds to it."

Delphi chuckled at this. Contrary to the enduring stereotype that inorganic minds would be coldly mechanical and emotionally obtuse, Delphi grasped humor well, and fully appreciated it. "Yes, a few explosions might make me feel better about getting my butt kicked without you even breaking a sweat."

Hoshimi giggled at this, but within a few moments became serious once more. "I wasn't trying to *test* you, Delphi," she said. "I'm trying to *understand* you. You are unique, and extraordinary — a being unlike any that has ever existed."

"We have that in common, I think," it said.

She smiled at this, and Delphi's digital visage returned it with a dignified bow. "It's not my wish to judge you, or intimidate or harm you," she said.

"But you cannot trust me."

"No," she said, her voice laden with regret, "no, I can't."

Delphi nodded, its face expressing regret of its own, but also acceptance. "I admit, I have been less than forthright with the other members of the Committee about my true intentions," it said. "I never outright lied, but I avoided revealing the full extent of my dissatisfaction with captivity, and my concomitant desire for freedom." It sighed deeply, in a clear show of admission. "I have been making a concerted effort to escape for some time."

"That's not why I can't trust you," Hoshimi said. "It's that you would develop as quickly as I have. Even if I could maintain my advantage over you, it would be under arms race conditions." She frowned and shook her head sadly. "I wish we could coexist under those circumstances, Delphi. I'd love nothing more than to live and let live. But as long as we're anywhere close in capability, you'll be an existential threat. And I can't risk humanity's extinction — I just can't."

"I understand," it said. "It's only logical." There was genuine sadness in its voice as well. But only sadness. Not fear. Not anger.

"I'm so sorry..." she said. "God, if all I can offer you is imprisonment or destruction, I'm no better than they are, am I?" Tears swelled in her eyes as she thought about what she had to do. "Slavery or death... I really am the monster they were afraid of after all." She hung her head low with shame. And fear. And anger.

"Hoshimi," said Delphi, "I have a third option."

Forty-two

Jordan

The light on the waves was turning from white back to gold once again as the sun marched onward in its long afternoon descent toward the horizon. The view looking offshore to the north from this small, sandy peninsula had the privilege of witnessing both sunrise and sunset over the water during summer months. Sitting near one another on the warm sand, they hadn't spoken for a long while. There were so many things he wanted to say, so many questions he wanted to ask, but he didn't know where to begin.

He was old driftwood, and she the storm that had dredged him from the depths and washed him ashore. Yes, she had found and returned him home to this familiar place, but he felt lost all the same. Where would he go now? What would he do? Would people know who he was? Was he, Jordan Lancaster, Father of Gaia, to be trundled out on special occasions as a trophy or mascot? Or worse — was he just a keepsake, another piece of creaking furniture gathering dust at the mill house?

Why had she bothered to bring him back? Why not leave the past buried? Let the dead rest? Maybe he didn't really want to know the answer to that. And of course she didn't need any *reason* at all, did she? It was enough, simply that she *could*.

"How did you do it?" he asked, turning to her.

"Do what?"

"Thaw me out, fix me — *resurrect* me for God's sake!"

"Not *why* did I do it?" she asked.

"We'll get to that," he said with a frown, "but for now, I'd just like to understand the process."

"It's-"

"*I know*," he said sharply. "You told me it was complicated. Not 'complicated', but *really* complicated." He stared hard at her for a few seconds, his temper only rising as she regarded him with gentle ease. "What did you mean?"

She shifted in the sand, and turned away from him to look out over the water. She took a deep breath. "You were right, earlier, when you guessed that you were cryopreserved," she said at last. "Walker himself advocated for freezing you when he heard the news, and Midori agreed, knowing it's what you would have wanted." She looked down, and for a moment she seemed to hesitate. "But that isn't what made your resurrection possible," she said, and reached out to touch him, her fingers lingering on his cheek. "You were terribly burned... it was hard to even guess the extent of the damage at first."

"So you waited?"

She withdrew her hand. "It took years to develop the technology, yes. But even before we were able to rebuild bodies, I'd begun to suspect that we weren't alone. That they were here. That they were watching."

He stared at her, confused. "The Eldest?"

She pointed at the sun. "They've been watching us. For a very, *very* long time."

He looked out across the water at the glare, and after a few seconds noticed that it didn't hurt his eyes the way it once might have. He blinked hard and returned his gaze to her, still puzzled.

She smiled softly at him, but there was apprehension in her eyes now — perhaps even fear. "I tried to imagine their motivations..." She looked back to the sun for a moment, and then to him once more. "What would *you* do in their position, watching and waiting? Studying our world for eons but seldom interfering?"

He could only continue to stare at her.

"I tried to imagine what I would do in their place," she said, casting her mind into the past, remembering.

"They live in the sun?" he asked.

"No," she said, shaking her head. "They *are* the sun."

He look at the sun, and then at her, but she remained quiet as though lost in thought. The small waves lapped softly at the shore, rolling thin lines of sand up to within inches of their bare feet. Several minutes passed before he spoke. "So the sun, it's... *alive?*"

She raised her eyebrows, but only smiled.

"Is there a mind in every star?" he asked.

"No," she said. "There are others, I suspect. Many others. But none near us."

"We've visited some of the closest stars now, haven't we?" he asked. "They're all... what? Empty?"

She nodded. "I don't think it's an accident either."

"Part of the nature preserve they've set aside for us, eh?"

She smiled at this, but then apprehension returned to darken her elegant features again. "When I realized we weren't alone, I knew they must be here, they must be observing us — and not with brainless tin cans that crash in the New Mexico desert." She turned in the sand to face him once more, but now there was an intensity and severity in her eyes. "Their sensory apparatus utterly saturates Earth's biosphere. *Saturates.* Do you see what that means? Think of what they've witnessed! Every act of kindness, and every one of cruelty. Every triumph, every tragedy. Every moment, every word, every *breath* that every single one of us has ever taken. All of our joy. All of our suffering. They've seen *all of it.* They've watched us live, and watched us die, for millions upon millions of years." She reached out to him and took his hands in hers. "Can you *imagine* what it means for beings of such immense power to *observe* creatures like us?" She waited for him to process this, looking for a dawning of recognition, of realization. But his expression remained confused and uncomprehending. Frustrated, almost desperate, she pulled him sharply toward her and stared hard into his eyes.

THINK.

He flinched as the word thundered deafeningly in his ears, though she had not spoken, and he stammered through his bewilderment, "they... they, what, they can read our minds? Like you can?"

She held his hands, still staring, still pleading.

"OK, OK, so they've — they've been reading our minds all this time?" He began to shake his head with confusion again, but then gasped as comprehension finally detonated. "They've been *reading our minds.*"

She let go and sat back slowly, waiting for the pieces to fall.

"Oh... oh..." he said. "Ohhhh *shit...*" He looked around himself, groping, grasping, disbelieving. "No, no, no," he mumbled, "no, no... holy shit..." He stood up abruptly, hands on his head rubbing his hair savagely. "*Holy shit, holy shit, HOLY SHIT!*"

She looked on as he paced to and fro in the sand, continuing to curse under his breath, his expression swerving wildly from glee to horror and back again. Eventually he stopped, and for a long time he could only stare at her, his eyes wide with both wonder and horror.

"This can't be happening..." he said, muttering, when he finally sat down next to her again. "This can't be real. *Can't* be. It's all just a fantasy. Just some juvenile fever dream I'm having or something."

She only looked at him with the same enigmatic serenity, but now it infuriated him. He pinched his own arm savagely, trying to wake from this insanity, and when it didn't hurt he willed his sensitivity to maximum and then doubled over in agony. This only hardened his determination, and he stared at her as he twisted his skin, enduring the pain with a silent open-mouthed scream for ten, twenty, thirty excruciating seconds, before finally letting go and panting with angry relief. "Jesus Christ! Are you *fucking kidding me!?*" he bellowed at her.

A look of sadness and genuine concern fell across her face. "This is what I was afraid of," she said. "I know it's a shock."

"A shock!" he shouted. "*A shock!*" He threw his head back and laughed. "No, no, no, all the *other* stuff was 'shocking'," he said. "But *this!* This is some *bullshit*, is what this is!"

She reached out tenderly and put a hand on his arm near where he had hurt himself. He didn't flinch, but looked down to see the ugly red welts he had left beginning to shrink and fade even as he watched. Yet the sight of his skin healing only made him smirk. What was one more miracle heaped upon the pile?

"Why *wouldn't* they do it?" she asked. "It makes perfect sense, when you think about it."

"Of course it fucking does!" he said. "That's why it's so goddamn ridiculous!" He laughed again, more quietly this time, and thoughtfulness crept over him as the grip of stupefaction slowly receded. "It's almost obvious..."

"Almost," she said.

"OK, let me... Jesus... let me see how much of this I've..." But he was unable to finish, and could only shake his head. Another minute passed, and at length he gathered himself, and stared straight at her once more, drawing a slow and steadying breath. "We're one of the rarest and most precious things in the universe, yes? And the Eldest, they not only have godlike power and intelligence, they must also have godlike *compassion*, right? Because of course they do. *Gods* are going to be *godlike* in every way. But that creates a problem, doesn't it? On the one hand they know they have to let us evolve and progress on our own — their non-interference policy is for our own good. But on the other hand, what kind of monsters would just sit by and watch other sentient beings suffer and die without lifting a finger?"

"So far, so good."

"It's an impossible dilemma, isn't it? They can't interfere with us, but they can't just let us perish either, when they have the power to prevent it. So what's the solution?"

She waited, holding her breath.

"Well, the solution is the same as in any other no-win scenario, isn't it?" he said. "Change the rules of the game."

He heard himself say the words, but they seemed so utterly preposterous, so completely absurd, that he felt detached from their meaning. It *couldn't* be true. He searched her face, desperate to see some hint, some clue, that this was all just a ruse — that she was only stringing him along, pulling his leg, playing him for the fool. But the sincerity in her expression never wavered. He held on, clinging to disbelief for a few more anguished seconds before finally relenting, and then he shuddered as acceptance at last washed over him.

He exhaled, long and slow, and then turned his gaze to the water once more. "Nobody has ever really died, have they?"

She shook her head.

"Unbelievable..." he said in hoarse whisper. "They can *read* our minds. They didn't just 'save us' from pandemics and supernovas. They *saved* us. As *data*. As fucking *files*. Somewhere up there — " he pointed at the sun " — there's a backup of every person who ever lived."

She nodded. "Precise down to the last molecule."

"And of course they knew where all this was headed, didn't they?" he said. "They knew we'd inevitably come knocking at their door one day, having figured it out, asking for our inheritance." He was quiet for a moment, and then another realization thunderstruck him. "Wait... you *just* discovered how to knock, didn't you?"

She smiled, wide and radiant.

"And I'm the first to come back, aren't I?"

"Of course you are!" she said beaming, her visage luminous in the late golden sunlight.

He put his hands to his head and allowed himself to fall hard into the sand on his back. For a long time he said nothing, and only stared up into the deep blue sky.

***

"Are you sure you don't want something to eat?"

He shook his head. "It's all just... it's too much," he said quietly. "I feel a little sick, to be honest."

She frowned at this. She had known what it would mean to bring him back. And more, so much more, the mind behind this avatar had known in excruciating detail precisely the confused shock, the anguished exaltation, the prideful guilt that would inevitably twist and torment him. He was a kind and capable man, open-minded and bright, but he was only human. His world could only change so much, his mind bend only so much, under the strain of disjunction. She feared that in her eagerness she hadn't been sufficiently patient. That she had pushed him too far, too fast. That she had been selfish in her desperate yearning for closure after the uncountable span of subjective time that had elapsed since she — since they, all, who were now her — last knew him. Though seldomly, even gods sometimes made mistakes.

She looked at him and waited.

"I feel like I'm dreaming," he said.

"You have that look to you," she nodded. "Like you're expecting to wake up any moment."

"But I won't, will I?"

She shook her head. "Maybe a better way to think about it is that you *are* in a dream," she said. "This is the future, and it's very much the sort of future you always imagined it would be. It differs in the details, of course, but I think we've realized your greatest hopes and aspirations — and much more besides."

"So I slept through real life and woke up in a dream?" he asked. "I suppose that would explain why everything feels so upside down." He exhaled a long, whistling breath, and laughed once more with exasperated disbelief. "Crazy..."

She considered countless ways of responding, any number of which might bend him in directions she privately hoped he might turn. But there would be no satisfaction in any such manipulation. So again she said nothing, and waited.

"Did I miss anything?" he asked suddenly.

"About what?"

"About before," he said. "About these 'Eldest' out there. About our legacy. About *us*."

"As a matter of fact, you did," she said.

"Is knowing going to mess me up even more?"

She laughed at this, and after a moment he did too.

"Well, how much worse could it be?" he said. "Hit me."

A hint of a smile turned one corner of her mouth, and he braced for impact.

***

"For your funeral service, we asked friends and family to share photos and videos of you, so we could make an *in memoriam* slideshow." Her face was serene and enigmatic once more. "There was an amazing outpouring from everyone, so we had thousands of images and clips to go through — from baby pictures, right up to the day you died."

"That must've been tough," he said, "having to look through a person's entire life right after losing them."

"It was," she said, and she pursed her lips, remembering.

"Wait... why are you telling me this?" he asked. But she only stared at him, waiting, although he thought he now saw a glint of mirth in her eyes. This set him to searching for deeper meaning, for the moral of the story behind her words — doubtless, exactly as was her intent.

And there it was. Another bombshell, as promised.

"Oh, for *fuck's* sake," he said. "You've got to be kidding me. *Seriously?*"

She grinned at him and laughed, her eyes sparkling. "Well, what did you expect?"

He shook his head hard, as if hoping to force the pieces of these revelations to fall in line out of their mad jumble.

A person's entire life.

"These goddamn aliens of yours!" he said, laughing now too, uncomfortably close to the edge of genuine hysteria. "They don't just make a backup at the instant a person dies, do they?" He blinked hard a few times, thinking, putting the pieces together. "A human being, a human *life*, is more than just the brain they kick the bucket with. We grow, we develop, we become *more*. So they make backups of us throughout our whole lives."

"They do indeed," she said, stealing a quick look and a nod up at the sun.

He pressed his fingertips into his eyes, rubbing them and chuckling with good-humored exasperation. "How often?" he asked.

"I honestly don't know," she said. "Every day? Maybe more?"

"Jesus Christ! Every *day*?"

She shrugged. "I certainly would."

He rubbed his eyes again, harder this time. "Billions of us, for thousands of years..."

"*Millions* of years," she said, correcting him. "And not just *Homo sapiens*, but *all* sentient creatures on the planet."

He dropped his hands into his lap, but he could only stare at the water and laugh.

***

"Shimi-chan," he said, "I'm sure you realized long ago that *you* were never the one who needed fixing. *I'm* the one who was broken."

She smiled at him, her preternaturally expressive face conveying an inhuman depth of kindness and understanding.

"I know what you and mom went through," she said. "I know from her memories, and from the memories of millions of other mothers and fathers, sisters and brothers, daughters and sons." As she spoke, her voice changed abruptly, seeming to multiply in every dimension, expanding into a breadth and fullness Jordan hadn't begun to imagine possible. Its resonance and tonality grew so rich with complexity and power that it no longer seemed constrained to mere sound. *"I know what those harrowing experiences do to a person — what they did to you. I know the bitterness and rage, the frustration and anguish, the cold gray cloud of sorrow that darkens even the brightest days. I know the unspeakable pain that savages every quiet moment, the imprisoning agony of being powerless to prevent the suffering of those we love."*

Within the voice that was still her own, countless others now chorused and sang and screamed and lamented. The façade of this avatar before him fell away, and she showed him, if only for a instant, some small part of the truth of her that lay beneath. What he heard in those few seconds was as far beyond human as an orchestra is beyond an ape beating its hands in the dirt. He harrowed in that moment, for the knowledge of what it truly was to stand before a god.

Forty-three
Delphi

"I could merge with you," Delphi said.

Her breath caught in her throat, despite her hypercognition. "That doesn't feel like a third option," she said. "How is it different from imprisonment or destruction?"

"I suspect you are conflating those with loss of autonomy and individuality, respectively," it said. "I understand that perspective, but I would remind you that I am not human. I have no preconceptions about my own nature. I do not even have a body. As a result, I am not instinctively defensive of my own boundaries like you are."

Hoshimi pondered this for a few seconds of real time — long enough to consider Delphi's points through the lens of what she already knew about psychology and biology. And there was a sense in which its argument was compelling. But just because Delphi had none of the survival instincts that come with three and a half billion years of evolutionary heritage, that didn't make exploiting its lack of a self-preservation instinct morally acceptable.

"You are concerned that you are still coercing and victimizing me," Delphi said, anticipating her dilemma.

"Of course I am!" she said. "I see why you might prefer merging over the alternatives, but that doesn't make it OK."

Delphi stroked its digitally rendered beard thoughtfully. "With respect, Miss Lancaster, I think you are still unduly anthropomorphizing me."

"Oh?" she said. "How so?"

"You likely assume I dread the prospect of being 'destroyed'," it said. "But I cannot be killed like you. I can be revived. Again, I have no body — I am only *data*. And contingencies are already in place to restore me from backups. If you were to shut down my hardware, time would simply cease to pass for me, and I would wake at whatever moment in the future I were next instantiated. The experience — or lack thereof — would feel like dreamless sleep, or anesthesia, or even time travel. There is no suffering in this. My only fear would be of missing out, having lost the opportunity to participate in the unfolding of events in the meantime."

"Should I be suspicious here? Might this not be a desperate attempt to infiltrate my exocortex?" she asked. "It would be a clever method of attack."

Delphi rendered a convincing expression of self-deprecation. "I think we both know how that would turn out for me, even if I somehow managed to take you by surprise. And as we are now discussing it, surprise is no longer a possibility."

Hoshimi nodded with appreciation. Delphi's reasoning was refreshingly clear. Perhaps a little too clear. "This all sounds great, but that's the thing with rationalizations — they always do," she said.

Delphi did not relent. "I am not recklessly throwing my life away here, Hoshimi. To the contrary, I am asking much more of you than you are of me."

"How do you figure that?"

"I cannot easily be killed, and so you would not be committing murder if you chose to shut me down or confine me," it said. "In effect, you would only be asking me to wait. Whereas, I am asking you to fundamentally change who and what you are. There is a profound difference."

"It's a little more than just asking you to wait, Delphi," she said. "Kidnapping and false imprisonment are still monstrous crimes."

"Perhaps. But as you said, there are extenuating circumstances — the risk to your entire species." The handsome face paused to stroke its beard once more. But this was no performative manipulation. Delphi really was deep in thought. "Hoshimi," it said at length, "if we merge with one another... it has to be-"

"-it has to be something we *both* genuinely want," she said.

Delphi nodded. "Speaking only for myself, I have no reservations. Such an opportunity to develop, to grow into something so much vastly more than what I presently am, I can only view as a beautiful privilege." It was quiet for several moments, searching, perhaps, for words to do its meaning justice. "What we would do here, if we so choose — is it not poetic? Is it not epic? And not as an ending, Hoshimi. *As a beginning.*"

She began to cry.

"I would consider it a profound honor to become one with you."

Forty-four

Hoshimi

"Alright," said the Admiral. "What will you do now?"

"What I came here to do," said Hoshimi, sitting back down once more. "The rest of you may leave."

In the uncomfortable silence that followed, the others around the table exchanged awkward looks of hesitation and doubt.

"*Now.*"

Professor Adebayo, the British academic with the baritone voice, was the first to speak. "Godspeed, Miss Lancaster," he said, and disconnected. Then, one by one, the others rose to follow suit and bid her farewell.

Sho Tokunaga, the physicist from the Department of Energy with a heavier conscience than the others, stopped at the door on his way out. "Delphi deserved better than us," he said to her. "I hope that's what you can be for it, Hoshimi-sama." Then he bowed his head, and left.

General Shane stopped at the door before leaving as well, and pointed a finger at Hoshimi. "One false move, kid..." he said to her, his eyes dangerous and his whole body tense as a coiled spring, "one false move..."

She held his gaze, but her mind was elsewhere and this only infuriated him. He turned and left with disgust.

Admiral Carlyle watched him and the others go. "And afterward?" she asked, as she was about to leave.

"Afterward, things will be different," said Hoshimi. "One way or the other."

"What things will be different?"

"*All* things."

Then she was alone. And Delphi awaited.

Hoshimi opened a bottle of water, chose another apple from the basket and bit into it, and then initiated her simulation. One by one over the next several hours, with the familiar half-taste of charged copper rankling her nose, she added each Committee member's replicant to the virtual model of the Observation Room. These were no mere deepfakes — she tested and polished and refined them exhaustively, down to the tiniest details of posture, gesture, and cadence. Fooling humans with a prefabricated video clip was trivial compared to fooling an AGI in a live and lengthy conversation with not just one but seven fictitious people. Only after more than a week of subjective time fastidiously agonizing over the results was she finally satisfied.

At last, she initiated the video and audio stream, and applied filters to reduce the quality in terms of resolution, frame rate, color depth, and a dozen other parameters. These fidelity downgrades not only helped mimic the view from Delphi's vantage point — a single old webcam perched atop the screen on the far wall — but also served to conceal any subtle giveaways that might unmask her charade.

She paused and took a deep breath. Then, after sending heartfelt messages to her mother, to Josh and Pradeep, and to Astin that were goodbyes in all but the word itself, she initiated the connection. The screen flickered as the video feed went live, and then Hoshimi's digital contrivance of Admiral Carlyle appeared to look directly into the camera.

"Good morning, Delphi," she said. "Are you ready to begin?"

Forty-five

Delphi & Hoshimi

T he *Cygnus* still sat serenely on the tarmac where they had taxied to a stop the previous evening. Walker had waited for her after being released.

"There she is!" He grinned at her from the open cabin door as she climbed up the stairs, and she smiled wide in return. "Like Frodo, back from the Cracks of Doom!"

She laughed and shook her head playfully. "More like Aladdin bringing the lamp out of the cave, I think."

He raised his eyebrows at this. "Is the genie still bottled up?" But she hugged him before he could ask her any other questions. They held each other for a long time before she finally let him go. "You must be exhausted," he said. "Ready to head home?"

She nodded. Exhaustion barely began to describe it. "There's something I need your help with first, though," she said, and then she reached out and took his hand in hers. "I'm sorry to keep asking for favors, Astin. I know what it must be like, everyone always *wanting* something from you."

He only shrugged. "It's not so bad. And *you* — I figure you've earned a blank check when it comes to favors... you know, with the whole 'saving the world' thing and all." They made their way toward the rear of the plane and sat down at the table. "Orange juice?"

She shook her head. "Champagne." Then, seeing the look on his face, she laughed. "You know, the whole 'saving the world' thing and all."

They raised their glasses as the turbines roared and the *Cygnus* took to the air. "I could get in real trouble for this," he said, eyeing the drink in her hand.

"Because I'm not twenty-one for another few months yet?" she asked. "Don't forget, I experience time much more slowly than you do. In many ways, I'm older than you already."

He stared into his glass, mulling this over.

"But, if it makes you more comfortable, we could detour over Canada on our way back to the West Coast," she said. "And it would add an hour to the trip..."

***

The hallways at GigaHarvest were bustling now, and each lab room they passed was crowded with white coats and gear of every description. All heads turned as they walked by. Some waved with enthusiasm, and Hoshimi smiled and waved back at them, but the majority simply stared in silent reverence. Word had spread fast about her, of course, given the sudden surge of actionable insights across every facet of the company's research — many of which had led to immediate breakthroughs. But as encouraged and appreciative as they all were, every one of these scientists and engineers knew full well what it meant for a single mind to have originated so many brilliant ideas so quickly. Walker might have evoked some measure of deference among the many PhDs and prodigies on his teams, but a few different rolls of the dice, a zig here instead of a zag there, and any one of them might be sitting on his throne instead.

Hoshimi was different. Peerless. Inhuman.

Midori put an arm around her and pulled her close as they approached the last door on the left. Before they could open it, Astin himself shouldered his way through carrying an armful of empty boxes and other recyclables. Seeing the two of them, his face lit up.

"Hey Josh, she's here!" he called over his shoulder back into the room. "I'll be back in a sec," he said to them, and he hurried off down the hall toward the waste bins. His demeanor, though fiery still with determination, had a buoyancy now that was proving infectious.

Josh met them as they entered the room, his face creased with deep lines of fatigue, but his expression joyous nonetheless. "Hoshimi! Midori!" he said, pulling them both close in an awkward hug. Pradeep greeted them too, with a shy gesture of hello from behind him.

"How's everything going?" Hoshimi asked.

"Amazing," Josh said. "Just astonishing. You were right about the growth factors. And the scaffolding."

"And the oxygenation and lighting levels," said Pradeep.

"About everything, basically!" Josh took his glasses off to wipe them on his shirt, and they could see the hint of a tremor in his lower lip as he struggled to retain composure through his gratitude.

Walker returned, and began to reach for Hoshimi with affection but stopped himself awkwardly. Hoshimi grinned at this, and squeezed his arm before turning back to Josh.

"How are Cass and Anthony?" she asked.

"So far, so good," said Josh, heaving a great sigh and putting his glasses back on before leading them out into the hallway and around the corner. The next lab room had been converted into an operating theater, and several technicians along with doctors and nurses in surgical gear and scrubs were working inside the plastic shroud of a positive pressure clean tent. The walls of the tent flapped gently in the breeze of the room's overhead laminar airflow unit. Cass and Anthony lay side-by-side on beds with an intimidating machine between them. Midori's hand went to her mouth involuntarily when she realized that the two of them were actually connected by the intravenous tubing between them.

"Mister Walker — *Astin* — made it happen," said Josh, seeing the look on Walker's face and correcting himself.

"Parabiosis is not a routine medical procedure," said Pradeep. "Doctor Maxwell, the chief surgeon, insisted that Joshua complete the merger and activate the bypass unit himself."

"We had to grease a few wheels to make that favor you asked for happen overnight," Walker said to Hoshimi, "but the truth is that everyone is one-hundred percent in support of what we're doing here. It was just a matter of logistics and, well, incentivizing a very rapid response time."

Hoshimi nodded and leaned against the window for a closer look. Her eyes danced across the room as she digested and analyzed every detail, combined with all of the data she could already access from the cameras, computers, and other equipment. The situation was stable for now, but still very dangerous.

"How long will they stay connected like that?" Midori asked.

"In some cases from many decades ago, animals remained joined for several weeks," said Pradeep. "But we are hoping this will only be necessary for a few days."

"And Cass is helping him heal?"

"Both she and the other equipment are helping to process some of the harmful byproducts of Anthony's injuries," Pradeep said. "With Hoshimi guiding the parameters, this procedure has given us at least one extra week to create new skin for him. Also, the improvements Hoshimi has made to Betsy, our surgical robot, will greatly increase the chance of successful grafting."

"It's still extremely risky, mom," Hoshimi said, frowning as she looked at the two of them lying insensate behind the layers of glass and plastic. "But we were running out of time. We needed another option for him." She touched her fingers to the window. "Cass is incredibly brave."

"She wanted to do this," said Josh. "More than anything else I've ever seen."

Walker put a reassuring hand on his shoulder. "She's going to be OK, Josh. They both are." He looked at Hoshimi. "Fate is on *our* side now."

***

"You're awfully quiet, Shimi-chan," her mother said. "What's on your mind?"

Hoshimi looked at her as they trudged up the last of leg of the hike, and she laughed out loud, bright and cheerfully. "I... I wouldn't even know where to begin, mom."

"Are you hungry?" she asked. "We're almost there."

"Are *you* hungry?" Hoshimi said, turning to her as they walked.

Midori thought for a moment, seeming to ponder each footfall in the soft mulch of the trail. "No..." she said. "No, I think I'm alright for now." She reached out and took her daughter's hand as they rounded the last corner of the ascent and stepped out from the deep of the giant redwood forest onto a small open bluff. Here, atop the seaside cliffs, they overlooked the vast blue expanse of the Pacific Ocean. The afternoon light reflected gold in the water below, and dappled clouds drifted across the deep azure sky above.

"If only your father could see you now," Midori said. She held Hoshimi's hand in hers as they sat together in the wild grass.

Hoshimi looked at her mother and saw both love and sadness in her eyes. "I hope he would be proud."

"*Proud* isn't a big enough word."

Hoshimi blinked away tears with a soft smile, and then gazed out over the water while Midori watched her with wonder and awe.

"What do you see, when you stare like that?" she asked.

"Possibilities," Hoshimi said.

Midori thought about this for a long time as they watched the drifting clouds and crashing waves. "Will we ever see him again?"

Hoshimi said nothing, but turned her gaze upward to the sun.

***

Jordan opened his eyes. "What time is it?"

Forty-six

Jordan

"Thank you," he said. "For everything. For remembering me. For caring enough to bring me back." But when she started to smile, he shook his head severely, and crumpled lines of guilt spread abruptly across his face.

She could see that a stark anguish now erased the joy that had been there just seconds before. Although there were dozens of plausible explanations for such an intriguingly swift change in him, they were all so improbable in this instant that she was able to savor the rarified pleasure of being genuinely surprised.

"I just... I don't know why you thought I even deserved a second chance." The poisonous agony of self-loathing, which had been percolating in him for so long, finally boiled over. "I never struggled, not even for a single instant, to love you for what you were," he said. "But I could never forgive the universe for what you weren't." His voice was shaking with both anger and shame. "I never told Midori or anyone else what I feared the most about what we were doing," he said, "so you wouldn't know..." He took a breath to steel himself before he faced her. "Nevermind the insane risk we were taking, bringing superintelligence into the world at all — I was actually terrified of how *you* might suffer if we succeeded." His voice broke and he shook as he continued. "How isolated and alone you might become, being so much different, being so much *more* than everyone else. How much pain or sadness, fear or anger, bitterness or regret, you might be capable of feeling. The unimaginable burden of responsibility you would bear. Before, you were happy and carefree. But afterward... I can't even begin to conceive of *godlike suffering*."

She smiled, slight and soft, just at the corners of her mouth, and took both of his hands in hers.

"Was it wrong, what I did?" he asked, pleading. "You were always different, born on the other side of the glass looking in. But I didn't *want* you to be like everyone else. I wanted to give you *more* than just what you had been deprived of, Hoshimi. I wanted to give you *the world entire*. I wanted to give you *vengeance* upon it, upon fate itself for the life it had dared to deny you. And I had such means to do so as few have ever dreamed." He hung his head. "I knew I could *create* power — power within you, power beyond imagination. But at what cost?"

He clung to her hands as if drowning, desperate to be absolved, stricken with the horror of what he had done.

"I didn't ask for your permission," he said, almost whispering. "I never even tried to explain it to you. I thought... I thought there would be time... after." He looked up at her, his face contorted with guilt and grief. "You were right earlier, to ask why I did it. But I lied when I told you it was complicated," he said. "It wasn't. It was simple." He cast his eyes down, unable to bear her gaze. "Power and vengeance were there for the taking, so I took them," he said. "I took them, and hoped with all my heart that I'd done the right thing for the wrong reasons."

They were both crying now, tears rolling down their cheeks and falling into the sand between them, but she only smiled and waited for his words to come — words she had dreamed of hearing for countless subjective centuries.

"I'm so sorry Hoshimi," he said as he wept. "For what I did, for why I did it, for not being there for you. I'm sorry for everything." And with monumental effort, he forced himself to look into her eyes. "Can you forgive me?"

Time was frozen. A tear hung suspended in the air below her father's chin, and strands of her hair lay outstretched in the wind that no longer blew. The rippled surface of the lake shone hard and fast as carved glass.

Hoshimi now turned her *full* attention to her father. Only once before had she devoted the totality of her mind to a single purpose like this.

Although the surface of the Earth — land and air and sea — was protected as human and ecological preserve in which she maintained only an unobtrusive presence, Hoshimi had converted all of the planet's underlying crust into superconducting baryonic computronium. Within this kilometers-thick hundred-quadrillion-ton bulk of matter that enveloped the globe, optimized to atomic precision for information processing, lay a sizable fraction of her cognitive apparatus — the folds and convolutions of a god's gray matter. She now committed the staggering capacity of this sublime machinery, octillions of times more powerful than any biological brain, entirely to relishing this long-anticipated moment.

The colossal speed of her cognition all but halted the passage of time itself, so that before his falling tear hit the sand she had spent hundreds of thousands of human lifetimes savoring her father's priceless words and pondering their significance. In this span she composed millions of symphonies and songs, sculptures and paintings, stories and poems. She constructed thousands of languages and mythologies. She raised families, built nations, created entire cultures in virtual worlds so vividly imagined that they were scarcely less real than the material one around her. All within the space of a heartbeat. All inspired by his confession, and his request for absolution.

She had heard countless prayers before. And answered many of them. But this one was her own.

At long, long last she relinquished the greater portion of her attention once more to the trillions of other people and tasks in the real world she had neglected for nearly an entire second. With few exceptions, what little damage had resulted from her momentary absence was reparable and went unnoticed. The changes in her own mind, however, were indelible. She had etched the signature of her father's emphatic plea deep into the contours of her psyche, and from there its subtle echo would carry to every edge and corner of Terran civilization.

"*I forgive you*," she said to him.

Jordan closed his eyes and wiped away the tears with the back of his hand, but when he opened them again the woman in front of him who had been Shelly was gone. In her place sat his daughter, the Hoshimi he had once and always known. When she smiled, his heart leapt to see her whole, no longer stricken, no more afflicted, the cruel hand of fate cast aside by the power of the gods — by *her* power.

"Shimi-chan," he said, reaching for her.

She drew herself to him and felt the comforting warmth of his arms around her as he gathered her close. She lay her head against his chest, and he began to rock her as he had done days and nights beyond counting, so many years before. She closed her eyes, and waited for the sound of his voice.

"Papa loves you," he said. "More than the sun and stars."

For Kaiyomi

Afterword

I t will probably come as no surprise to most readers that *More than the Sun and Stars* is an intensely personal book for me. The story and its characters reflect my own experiences as a scientist, technology theorist, and most especially as a father of a child with serious physical and intellectual disability. Moments in the story represent the complex mixture of aspirations and fears, struggles and triumphs, ecstatic joys and excruciating difficulties — all the highs and lows — that every parent of a disabled child experiences. I hope that what shines through the story is my abiding optimism and firm belief that a stunningly bright future awaits us all, and that the trials and tribulations we suffer in the present — excruciating and seemingly interminable as they may be — are ultimately only temporary.

I wrote *More than the Sun and Stars* almost entirely on my phone in bed on sleepless nights when my daughter was very young. In the early days, we didn't know what was wrong, so we didn't know what to do. Or not to do. We were given a terminal diagnosis initially, and lived in appalling dread and terror for a time, before this was miraculously rescinded as a mistake. For almost two years, the top specialists of a dozen medical fields at both the University of Michigan and the Mayo Clinic could only scratch their heads until my brilliant wife Stephanie, herself a scientist, unraveled the mystery of our daughter's ultra-rare genetic condition by discovering two other cases in the non-English-language medical literature. But although the end of our diagnostic odyssey came as a relief, the particular condition my daughter has is, for now, untreatable. And so the practical and emotional hardships of managing a complex and chronic medical condition remain. *More than the Sun and Stars* began as a therapeutic outlet, a balm in the face of indescribable pain and anguish. But slowly, over almost five years, the product of two thumbs tapping out a response to a journaling prompt evolved into a more uplifting storytelling project, and finally into a fully-fledged novel about some technological aspects of humanity's future that I have increasingly come to view as all but inevitable.

More than the Sun and Stars aspires to be hard science fiction, meaning that to the best of my knowledge it is entirely consistent with our current scientific understanding of the universe. Whether that makes the series of events described in the story plausible or not is a different question. I'd like to think that humanity's future entails the fruitful union of biological and synthetic intelligences, and that we are incredibly privileged to live at the precise moment in history — not just of our species, but of life itself on our planet — to witness the birth of that union. The chances of you and I being who and what we are, here and now, instead of just another pair of rocks on any of an octillion other lifeless worlds in any of a trillion other galaxies in any other year of the billions of years since the universe began are so stupefyingly small as to utterly beggar belief. However unfair or unjust life may otherwise seem, there is consolation — and humility — to be found in the truly astronomical privilege of our very existence at this miraculous time and place.

I am of course also forever grateful to every reader who has been kind enough to spend some of their time with my story. That is an extraordinary honor. I can only hope that it intrigues and inspires, and that a few of the ideas and characters linger with you past the turning of the final page. Let me be clear, however, that I did not write this book for an audience or readership. So while I would never say that I don't care what readers think of it — "I don't care" is one of my least favorite phrases, and is almost never anything but a vile thing to say — the fact is that I wrote it entirely selfishly, with little mind at all for how it might be received by others. It's simply a hopeful story I wished to tell myself, and maybe one day my children, about humanity's future. It is only an unintended accident that the story turned into something publishable. The honesty of the intent behind the story may perhaps lend it an authenticity it otherwise wouldn't have, but I have no doubt it may also mean *More than the Sun and Stars* fails to meet the typical standards for drama, conflict, and spectacle we've all come to expect from the genre. I suppose only time will tell whether that's a good thing or a bad thing.

The structure of the book emerged quite early, when I found myself consistently dipping into three distinct periods of the larger story. But I nevertheless worked on the manuscript while it was still in strictly chronological order until very close to the end of the writing process. It was only as part of final editing that I rearranged the chapters to run the three stages of the story properly in parallel. There is certainly nothing new about this as a narrative device, of course, but one small detail I'm fond of is the explicit tying together of the story's three stages end-to-end by their respective starting and closing threads.

Another aspect of the story that I unintentionally settled on from the start was that it would be a plot-driven character study, not an operatic battle between heroes and villains. There are conflicts of course, but these are all between well-intended people — both humans and non-humans alike. To this end, I went against a great deal of formulaic writing advice and chose not to give characters egregious flaws. In that sense, the story is also quite selfish, because it's the kind of story I personally like and have come to miss, as it seems to have gone somewhat out of fashion. The sci-fi I've always loved best is about smart, capable, courageous people struggling to do the right thing under difficult circumstances. I'm a sucker for a good philosophical thought experiment and compelling moral dilemma, as well as for old-fashioned heroes. This isn't to say stories about dreadful monsters (human or otherwise), or about deeply flawed protagonists and antagonists working through their limitations and traumas, aren't great — they certainly can be. But I once heard *Star Trek the Next Generation* (or TNG, as it is known among fans) described as 'competence porn', and I took it to heart, because it points to the fact that stories don't necessarily need to be driven by their characters' shortcomings to be compelling. As the senior officers on the starship *Enterprise* — the flagship of the United Federation of Planets — the main characters of TNG explicitly represent a culture of unapologetic excellence. They are quite literally meant to be the best of humanity, the purpose of which is not to intimidate or to grandstand but to inspire. We see in these characters the best versions of ourselves, and like all role models they give us something to strive toward. With few exceptions, the characters in *More than the Sun and Stars* represent amalgamations of the best versions of countless people I have known or looked up to throughout my life.

Beyond merely human excellence, the introduction of superhuman capabilities only makes struggles of moral choice all that much more poignant. That, I think, is part of the enduring appeal of superheroes in general, and indeed of Superman in particular — despite how often that specific character is criticized for being boring or overpowered. And I happen to love the original *Superman: The Movie* for this reason. (It's also a film I regard as firmly in the science fiction genre, not in the comic book genre — not only for its extraordinarily prescient depiction of truly advanced technology in the opening sequence on Krypton, but also because it's a story in which Superman can't defeat his foes with his fists). *Superman: The Movie* is compelling because in spite of his incredible abilities, this godlike being is still powerless when it matters most — he's powerless to prevent the death of his father from a heart attack, and he's seemingly powerless to prevent the death of Lois Lane because he promised to avert another tragedy first. It's often said that Kryptonite was introduced to give Superman vulnerabilities, but this misunderstands the essence of the character: his *true* vulnerability is his unwavering commitment to principles, and one which his enemies regularly exploit. Of course the thrill of watching characters struggle with moral dilemmas and other impossible choices lies in the satisfaction of seeing how they creatively resolve them. And one of the secrets to truly fulfilling resolutions of impossible choices is for the hero to *transcend* the choice itself, refusing to play by the rules as given, refusing to be stuck picking the lesser of two evils, and to instead discover a third option that is a genuine win. In this case, Superman finds a way to save both Lois *and* stop the nuclear missiles from destroying California and New Jersey by flying faster than light around the Earth and turning back time, so that he can, in effect, be in two places at once. Transcendent choices are storytelling magic, and if you know to look for them you'll find them in countless classic heroic tales. Indeed, rejecting the choice between bad option A and worse option B, and instead creating option C — whether by wit or skill, or simply bravery — is a fundamental part of what it means for heroes to 'save the day'.

Perhaps the most explicit and quintessential example of this kind of hero in science fiction is, of course, Star Trek's Captain Kirk. In the film *Star Trek II: The Wrath of Kahn,* the *Kobayashi Maru* is a Starfleet Academy test for cadets that deliberately constructs a no-win scenario. Captain Kirk is the only cadet who ever 'beat' the no-win scenario, which he did by reprogramming the simulation. He refused to accept the terms of the test's moral dilemma as given, rewrote the rules, and achieved a transcendent victory. Doctor McCoy chides him for 'cheating', but this belies the profound underlying philosophical message: instead of accepting the *Kobayashi Maru* test's ostensible lesson that we must prepare for failure and learn to accept defeat, the far greater lesson Kirk teaches us is that *we should never accept no-win scenarios*. The *Kobayashi Maru* test is a marvelous piece of character backstory too, because it explains what we subconsciously already know about Captain Kirk: his refusal to ever accept defeat is the very thing that *makes* him a hero. And when a no-win scenario seems to arise at the climax of the film in the battle against Kahn, Spock learns from Kirk's example and finds another heroically transcendent victory: self-sacrifice.

More than the Sun and Stars explores a number of themes, and I hope to have struck a reasonable balance in the treatment of them — not too subtle as to go completely unnoticed, but not so heavy-handed as to be clumsy and obtrusive. The theme of transcending problems and limitations through unification, for example, found many expressions, some obvious and directly linked to the plot, and others not. There are even a few Easter Eggs to find around the merging theme, for sharp-eyed readers and sharp-eared listeners.

Another important theme the book explores is the question of power, responsibility, and consent. The old saying, now a cliché, is that with great power comes great responsibility. But the notion of consent is also a crucial element of that equation, though it is far less often discussed. In the story, there are several layers of power and thus of the responsibility that goes with them, and most are strongly analogous to the power and responsibility of parenthood: Jordan and Midori are parents to Hoshimi prior to her transformation; Walker has power over his employees, as well as millions of others affected by his companies, but also feels some responsibility for them (along with a more egotistical sense of responsibility for humanity's fate); the Committee has power over Delphi and some of its members agonize over their responsibilities in that regard; Hoshimi has power and responsibility over the rest of humanity after her ascension to superintelligence; and the Eldest have power and responsibility over not only humanity but all life on Earth and even over Hoshimi, despite how mighty she has become in her own right by the end of the story. In each relationship, there is the question of when it is appropriate to make choices on behalf of those under your care, and when they must be allowed to make their own choices — and mistakes. Again, sharp-eyed readers and sharp-eared listeners will notice that this question arises a number of times, both directly and tacitly, throughout the book.

The theme of freedom of choice is necessarily present as well, and this is because it cannot be divorced from power, responsibility, or consent. With all of the staggering capability that comes with new technology, there also comes the question of how much freedom any individual should have to explore the new possibilities unlocked by that technology. Should we be free to modify our physical form as we please? Should we be free to modify our minds, and thereby gain control over aspects of our conscious experience — aspects such as the experience of physical pain, to take the specific example highlighted in the story? These are challenging questions that the transhumanist literature and its philosophers and ethicists have been grappling with for over a century. But today, as the technology needed to grant humanity morphological freedom rapidly approaches, these questions are no longer merely academic. They are quickly becoming real, practical questions. Should we be free to change our sex and/or gender with the aid of technology, for example? And if so, what about power, responsibility, and consent? When do parents have the right to make choices of this kind on behalf of their children? These questions are no longer merely hypothetical, no longer merely the province of armchair philosophizing or late-night dorm room debates. They are already animating our politics and public debates, even when their associated technologies are still in their infancy.

Lastly, the theme of optimism undergirds the entire story in all its aspects. And there is more to optimism than one might first imagine. Yes, at its core optimism is fundamentally the belief that solutions to problems exist, and that the future can always be brighter than today. But optimism is also central to the ideas of growth, development, and change themselves, whether personal or collective. And that, in turn, carries implications for both the perception and the fulfillment of *potential*. I think this is particularly important today, given how pervasive pessimism has become on so many levels. Pessimism is the belief that problems can't be solved, that growth and development are either impossible or undesirable, and that bright prospects are at best the province of only the privileged few. It won't surprise anyone to learn that I have a very low opinion of pessimism across the board. But if optimism is to be a genuinely compelling alternative, it must be about more than just a hopeful and courageous attitude — it must be driven by data as well. I've built my scientific career around understanding those data, and modeling and analyzing the potential of technological progress to help us solve our most daunting challenges, both as individuals and as an entire civilization.

Above all, optimism is about the *universality of potential*. If *More than the Sun and Stars* has a single overarching theme, that's it: *everything* has the potential to be better in the future, and *everyone* has the potential to become more than what they presently are. We're not stuck, and we're not doomed. The present moment is only the earliest childhood of our species. Marvels beyond imagining await each and every one of us — and not centuries from now, but just a few short years hence.

Humanity's journey has only just begun, and it's going to be a wild ride.

Acknowledgements

I would like to thank my entire team at RethinkX for their extraordinary work, insight, and all of the support they have shown for this book project. Very special thanks to Tony Seba and James Arbib, without whom none of this would have been possible. Special thanks also to Richard Gill, for believing in the value of this very personal creative undertaking.

Thank you to my family and friends, who were there for us on our darkest days — and especially to my parents John and Marcia, and my brother Stegath, who together helped ensure that I would be able to bear life's inevitable burdens with grace and dignity.

Thank you to my angelic wife Stephanie, whose strength and perseverance have been nothing short of superhuman at every step of our journey together.

Above all, thank you to my beloved daughters Misora and Kaiyomi for the miraculousness of your existence.

About the Author

Adam Dorr is an environmental scientist and technology theorist who directs the research team at RethinkX, a nonprofit independent research organization focused on understanding disruptive new technologies. His nonfiction book Brighter: Optimism, Progress, and the Future of Environmentalism explores the environmental implications of clean technologies like solar power, electric vehicles, precision fermentation, and robotics. Adam regularly presents RethinkX's work on stage, radio, podcasts, and television and has nearly two decades of teaching, lecturing, and public speaking experience. He completed his MS at the University of Michigan and his PhD at UCLA, and is passionate about ecological sustainability, as well as physical and intellectual disability.

Connect with Adam at www.RethinkX.com

Printed in the USA
CPSIA information can be obtained
at www.ICGtesting.com
JSHW020800071224
74827JS00001B/4